THE DESTROYER!

Oh, God, she thought. I'm dangerous. Even to the man I love . . .

"I want to tell you something," she said, "but something inside won't let me." A wave of nausea rushed through her.

"I might . . ."—the nausea was getting worse—"I . . . I might hurt you."

"Mary!"

And then, with every ounce of willpower she had, Mary grabbed her husband and said: "I lied, Tom. Goddammit!" she screamed, "I lied. I'm defective and I lied!"

The whole world seemed to be sick, painful, confused. Mary was only vaguely aware that she was flailing at Tom, slipping down his legs to the floor, babbling in a little girl's voice:

"Oh, please, Sister. Please don't. I'll be good. Please. Please. Please."

MARY, MARY

B.W. Battin

PUBLISHED BY POCKET BOOKS NEW YORK

Distributed in Canada by PaperJacks Ltd., a Licensee
of the trademarks of Simon & Schuster, Inc.

Another *Original* publication of POCKET BOOKS

POCKET BOOKS, a division of Simon & Schuster, Inc.
1230 Avenue of the Americas, New York, N.Y. 10020
In Canada distributed by PaperJacks Ltd.,
330 Steelcase Road, Markham, Ontario

ISBN: 0-671-47787-0

First Pocket Books printing January, 1985

10 9 8 7 6 5 4 3 2 1

POCKET and colophon are registered trademarks
of Simon & Schuster, Inc.

Printed in Canada

To Sandy

Prologue

AFRAID TO MOVE, AFRAID THAT EVEN SHIFTING HER
weight might be taken as a sign of irreverence, the little
girl stood in the cold night air with the other children,
watching in silence.

Speaking in a language the little girl did not understand, Sister stood before the altar, her slender black-
robed form illuminated by the candlelight and the glow
from the crackling fire. She picked up a large silver cup,
drank from it, then handed it to her assistant, who also
raised it to his lips. Unlike Sister, who had no other
name, her assistant was named Seymour, and the
children addressed him as Brother Seymour.

The little girl knew that she and the three children
who stood with her were special. Sister had told them
so, had explained that the four of them had been
chosen from all the children in the orphanage to do
something very important. To the little girl's right was a
blond boy named John/Jack. On her left stood a
red-haired, freckle-faced girl named Margaret/Peggy

and a dark-haired boy named Carl/Charley. The little girl was uncertain what the important thing was that they were supposed to do. And, although she realized she should feel proud to be chosen for something special, she couldn't help feeling frightened.

But then, almost everything about Sister made her afraid. The little girl recalled the last time she'd been in the punishment place and she shivered.

Picking up a sword from the altar, Sister made a quarter turn, pointed with it and spoke a strange word, then repeated the act three more times, making a complete circle. Then, despite the chilly night air, Sister allowed her robe to fall from her body and she stood naked before them. A frigid breeze stirred her long dark hair and the candles flickered.

"Tonight is Walpurgis Night," she said, looking at the children. The little girl felt as though Sister's eyes had found hers—hers alone—and had locked onto them.

"For the four of you, this is a very special day. You are preparing so that, on this date many years from now, you will be able to take the most important step of your lives." As she spoke, Sister's eyes seemed to glow the color of the flames. "Hail the master!" she shouted.

"Hail the master," the children echoed.

Brother Seymour struck a gong.

Then, behind the little girl, the door to the orphanage opened, and there was a rustling of cloth as the children in the building joined the ceremony. Although the little girl was unable to see them, she knew they had quietly assembled behind her. She could feel their presence.

"Hail the master!" Sister shouted.

"Hail the master," a chorus of young voices responded.

Again, Brother Seymour struck the gong.

Shifting her eyes to the right, the little girl could dimly make out the woods that surrounded the orphanage. Most of the snow was gone now, but none of the trees had leaves yet. Suddenly, it occurred to her that no one stood between her and the trees, that she could run, escape. Instantly, a pain shot through her stomach, and the little girl gasped, trying as hard as she could not to cry out.

Sister always knew when you had bad thoughts.

The little girl's eyes found the slender naked form at the altar, and she thought: I won't have bad thoughts again, Sister. I promise, I promise.

One

MARY TAYLOR WAS STACKING BOXES OF PATCHING PLASTER on the shelf when a customer came down the aisle, a lost look on his face.

"May I help you with something?" Mary asked.

"Uh, I need a pipe fitting," the man said. He was a burly fellow in his thirties with a thick black beard.

"What kind of fitting?"

He looked at her skeptically, obviously uncertain about a woman helping him with anything as manly as plumbing. Finally, he said: "A union, three-quarter-inch."

"Follow me," Mary said, heading for the other side of the store.

Zel Home and Builders Supply's modern store in suburban Boston sold almost everything anyone would ever need for construction or home improvement. The building was enormous, with aisle after aisle of tools and nails and fasteners, whole sections devoted to

4

displays of bathtubs and sinks, kitchen cabinets and counters, doors and windows. Out back was the yard, in which you found huge stacks of lumber, cement, plasterboard, and other materials.

Mary led the man to an aisle with numerous metal bins of various sizes. She reached into one of them and grabbed a three-quarter-inch pipe union, which she handed to her bearded customer.

He eyed it doubtfully, frowning. "It looks bigger than the old one. You sure this is a three-quarter-inch?"

Mary nodded. "Did you measure the pipe?"

"Sure, I measured it."

"How?" Mary asked.

Giving her a peculiar look, he dropped the union back into the bin. "With a ruler."

"I mean, did you measure the inside diameter or the outside?"

He hesitated, looking very uncomfortable, then said, "The outside. I just laid a ruler across the pipe, and it measured a little over three-quarters of an inch."

"That's your problem. Pipe size goes by the inside diameter. If you got a little over three-quarters of an inch by measuring the outside, then your pipe's half-inch." She reached into a bin and took out a smaller union.

"Yeah," he said, studying it, "that looks about right." Again he gave her an odd look, then he turned and walked away.

Behind her, Mary heard a soft chuckle. She turned; the sound had been made by Lynn O'Donnell.

"You ruined that poor fellow's day," Lynn said, grinning. "No woman's supposed to know what a pipe union is."

Mary shrugged. "What brings you back to this part of the store?" Lynn worked the checkout aisle and rarely left her cash register.

"Coffee break."

"You already had one."

"But Adkins was out during that one, so as far as he knows this is the first one of the afternoon." She winked. Lynn was short and a little on the chubby side, with curly blond hair. Mary was just the opposite: tall and thin with straight brown hair. At twenty-three, Mary was two years younger than Lynn.

The two women were good friends. In fact, had it not been for Lynn, Mary would probably still be single. It was one of those things that never should have worked out. Lynn had asked Mary over for dinner, and Lynn's husband Bob had invited one of his friends. For Mary and Tom, it was practically love at first sight—they were married four months later. The O'Donnells, of course, now considered themselves unequaled as matchmakers.

"Oh, oh," Lynn whispered. "Old jerko's giving us the hairy eyeball."

Following Lynn's gaze, Mary saw Walter P. Adkins, the assistant manager. He was two aisles away from them, walking toward the front of the store. A slight man, he wore plastic-rimmed glasses and combed his thinning hair up from the sides in an unsuccessful attempt to hide his baldness. He was giving the two women a stern look—what Lynn had referred to as the hairy eyeball.

Lynn smiled politely. Mary, who lacked her friend's bravado, hurried back to the boxes she'd been stacking.

Mary had been working at Zel Home and Builders Supply about a year. It was a job in which she derived absolutely no benefit from her college education, but

6

then there weren't that many job openings for English majors. And in many ways, she found the work exciting. The company had trained her, teaching her about plumbing, tools, construction materials, and a whole wealth of other information about which she'd known absolutely nothing. To Mary, it was every bit as fascinating as studying Jane Austen or William Shakespeare. She simply loved learning, whatever the subject.

An orphan, she had been raised in the small town of Evans Ridge, Maine, by foster parents, although she really didn't think of them as such. They were her mother and father, her family, the people who loved her and cared for her and helped her to get through college. That was what made a family, not biology. That her name had been Kensington and theirs Caldwell was unimportant. No family, she was sure, had ever been more warm or loving or wonderful than hers.

They had understood when, after graduating from college, Mary had decided to come to Boston. There was, after all, nothing to keep young adults in Evans Ridge; most of them left, seeking their opportunities—both economic and romantic—elsewhere. The Caldwells had driven her down, helped her find an apartment. She'd cried herself to sleep her first night alone in the city.

At times she wondered about her biological parents. Was she the daughter of a pregnant teenager, a rich man and his mistress, a pair of mass murderers from whom she was taken by the court? Mary knew absolutely nothing about her ancestry. She could be a descendant of Irish immigrants, Spanish conquerors, the czars of Russia. . . . Even her name held no clues, as it had been given to her at the orphanage and wasn't really hers at all.

7

Her stomach tightened, and she immediately pushed all thoughts of the orphanage from her mind. The time she'd spent there was a blank, a part of her life about which she could remember almost nothing, and yet she was afraid of that place, afraid to even think about it. Shakily, she finished putting the boxes of patching plaster on the shelf, then took the empty carton to the trash bin behind the building.

Lynn, who worked the day shift, left at five. Mary stayed until nine, when the store closed. After the last customer had been rounded up and ushered out, Walter Adkins did the same with the employees, and then locked the door behind him, leaving the place in the hands of the janitors.

It was a nice spring evening—the temperature, though cool, no longer had the chilly bite of winter. As she walked through the unlit parking lot, Mary glanced back at the building. It was a simple structure with a flat roof and brick walls. To her left, she heard footsteps on the asphalt and peered into the darkness, trying to see who was there.

"Good night, Mary."

"Oh, it's you, Mr. Adkins. I was wondering who was there. Have a nice evening."

Finally, she reached her car, a green Plymouth Horizon. Once she had slipped behind the wheel and locked the door, she felt somewhat relieved. Employees had to leave their cars at the far end of the lot so customers could have the choice spaces, and the nightly walk through the shadowy parking area was always a bit unnerving. Come on, she told herself sternly, you're not a little girl anymore, and there's absolutely nothing in the dark to be afraid of. Yeah, she added nervously, except muggers and rapists and murderers.

Mary started the engine, and a moment later, she was on her way home.

As usual, the porch light was on, a reminder from Tom that she was loved, missed. His Toyota station wagon was at the curb, so she pulled into the driveway —two strips of concrete with grass between them—and followed it to the separate garage. She left the car in the driveway and, checking to make sure the doors were locked, dropped the keys into her purse and then headed for the front door.

The house was a small wooden home in a neighborhood of small wooden homes. Its principal distinguishing feature was its yellow color; most of the houses on the tree-lined block were white. Before she reached the front door, it opened and Tom stepped out. She took the two porch steps in a one leap-stride, collapsing into his arms.

"Gee," he said, hugging her, "you must have had a bad day."

"No more than usual. I just like flinging myself at you."

"Come on," he said, leading her inside. "Your dinner awaits."

"You really don't have to cook for me, you know."

"I've got to cook for myself. All I do is keep yours warm. I'd wait and eat with you if I didn't get so hungry."

Tossing her purse on the couch, she reached around his neck, pulled his head to her, and kissed him. "You're wonderful."

He returned the kiss. "So are you. Now, how does meat loaf sound?"

"Terrific. I'm ravenous." Releasing Tom, she collapsed on the couch. Across the room a sitcom played on the TV set.

Tom headed for the kitchen. An inch under six feet, dark-haired, and athletic-looking, he was what one of Mary's high school girl friends would have referred to as a hunk. They'd been married for six months.

Like Mary, Tom was not from Massachusetts. He was, to use his words, a service brat. The son of an air force officer, he had lived all over the country. Before his father was transferred to Hanscom Air Force Base near Boston, Tom's home had been in San Antonio, Texas, and in California before that, and South Dakota before that. When his family had moved from Boston, Tom, then a freshman at Boston University, had remained behind. He'd been in Boston ever since. His parents, whom Mary had never met, were living in Germany, but would be returning to Boston for a visit during the coming summer.

Nine years older than she, Tom had been divorced when Mary met him. In what he referred to as a friendly parting, his first wife, insisting that all she wanted was her freedom, had vanished from his life, leaving him everything except her clothes. Mary occasionally found reminders of her predecessor: hairpins that had once secured Anne's blond curls, a large cloth-covered button from a feminine garment, a misplaced birth control pill.

As Tom told it, Anne had wanted more social life, more travel, and more things than he had been able or inclined to give her. Then when she found someone who appeared willing and capable of providing her with what she wanted, she had asked Tom for a divorce. Realizing the marriage was not only over but never should have been in the first place, Tom readily agreed.

In his words: She wanted a jet-setter, and I'm only the assistant manager of a sporting goods store.

"Five more minutes," he called from the kitchen. "As soon as the broccoli's ready."

"Need some help?"

"Not unless you think it takes two people to lift broccoli out of the water and put it on a plate."

"I guess you can handle it."

The living room, decorated by Tom's first wife, contained the same ornate, fragile-looking furniture as the rest of the house. Pseudo-Chippendale, Mary called it. It was the sort of stuff you came up with when you had high aspirations and a limited budget. Had Mary been the decorator, she would have chosen pieces of a different, more solid-looking style, doing without until she had enough money to get what she wanted. She'd already resolved to begin phasing out the existing furniture as soon as it began to show signs of wear—if she could convince Tom to spend the money. To him, decor was a matter of complete indifference.

"Here you go," Tom said, setting a TV tray in front of her. On it was a plate with a large chunk of meat loaf, macaroni and cheese, and broccoli, everything steaming. He hurried back to the kitchen, returning a moment later with silverware and a glass of milk.

After taking a bite of the meat loaf, Mary said, "Delicious."

It was, too. Whether preparing a simple meal like this or something elaborate, Tom was an excellent cook, far better than Mary knew she would ever be. But then Tom truly enjoyed cooking, and to Mary it was a chore, like mopping the floor. Because of their schedules—Tom's workday started at nine, Mary's at one in the afternoon—he cooked most of the dinners, she most of the breakfasts.

Sitting down at the other end of the couch, Tom resumed watching TV. Mary studied his handsome profile while she chewed a mouthful of broccoli, thinking what an idiot Anne had been to give him up—and how glad she was that Anne had been an idiot.

Two

SETTING TWO PLATES OF SCRAMBLED EGGS WITH BACON and toast on the small wooden breakfast table, Mary sat down facing Tom. As he usually did, Tom had risen early, donned his jogging suit, and gone out to run. Dressed and showered now, he was ready to face the day. Jogging was not an activity they shared. As far as Mary was concerned, running wasn't something you did unnecessarily; you saved it for things like being chased by muggers.

She took a bite of toast, then washed it down with coffee. Through the window by the breakfast table, Mary had a view of the backyard, which looked bright and cheery in the early-morning sunshine. The grass was greening nicely; soon the trees and shrubs would be budding. Spring was her favorite time of year.

"You know what you did last night?" Tom asked.

"What?"

"You denied being you."

She swallowed the scrambled eggs in her mouth. "I did what?"

"You denied being you."

"What are you talking about?" she asked, feeling vaguely uneasy.

"Last night, we'd just gone to bed, and I thought you were still awake so I said your name. For a moment you didn't answer me, then you said, 'I'm not Mary. Don't call me that.'"

"I–I don't remember saying it." Nor did she understand why she found the incident disturbing.

Apparently noticing her concern, Tom said, "It's nothing to worry about. You were just talking in your sleep."

Mary nodded.

"I think it's pretty obvious what you meant. Mary Kensington was the name given to you at the orphanage. You really might have another name, one given to you by your parents."

"You're probably right," she said, hoping he'd drop the subject. She didn't want to talk about anything connected with the orphanage, with the time she couldn't remember.

"Oh, Jesus," Tom said, glancing up at the clock on the wall. "I'm going to be late if I don't get my ass in gear." He quickly finished off his eggs and toast, then stood up, gulping down the last of his coffee.

Less than a minute later, Mary stood in the doorway, kissing him good-bye. Returning to the kitchen, she finished her breakfast, and then washed the dishes.

About eleven, Mary closed the paperback romance she'd been reading, laid it beside her on the couch, and stretched. She usually spent her mornings with a book, although not always with a pulpy love story. She also liked spy thrillers, as well as the good solid literature former English majors were supposed to read—particularly Jane Austen and Oscar Wilde.

She stood, stretching again, and decided to get ready for work. In the bathroom, she peeled off her clothes, pausing to examine her nude body in the full-length mirror on the back of the door. Though a little too thin, she was reasonably attractive. Her legs were long, her waist narrow, her breasts small but perky.

As she'd done so many times before, she stared at her face, hoping it would reveal something about her lineage. As always, the image told her very little. It was an ordinary Caucasian face, a face that could easily be English, Irish, Italian, German, Scandinavian, Slavic. . . .

Why do I keep doing this? she wondered. There's no way I can ever know anything about my ancestry. I'm Mary Taylor, wife of Tom Taylor, and what I see is what I am. There's nothing more. With that, she turned on the shower and stepped under the spray.

A few minutes later, her wet hair wrapped in a towel, she stood before the dresser in her bedroom, choosing clean underwear from the top drawer. Suddenly she froze. There, in the back of the drawer, behind the bras, was something small and black, something she was sure hadn't been there earlier this morning. Oh, God, she thought. Don't let it be happening again.

Hoping it was something innocent that had gotten there by mistake, Mary picked up the black object. Immediately, she discovered it wasn't one item but two, a top and a bottom. She was holding a black bikini. Her hands were shaking, and she flung the bathing suit away from her as if it were contaminated.

Modesty would prevent her from wearing such a thing; she simply wasn't the type to display her body. Afraid of what she'd find, she looked in the wastebasket beside the dresser. The only thing in it was a small bag, which she picked up. Inside was a sales slip for one bikini bathing suit.

Five minutes ago, she'd have stated under oath that she'd been reading all morning, that she hadn't left the house. But she *had* left it; she'd gone out and bought a bathing suit she'd never wear, and in her hand was a store receipt for it, bearing the day's date. She crumpled the sales slip and the bag and dropped them back into the wastebasket.

Suddenly feeling weak, Mary backed away from the dresser. When her legs touched the bed, she sat down on it, putting her head in her hands. This was the first time it had happened since she married Tom. She'd foolishly allowed herself to think that being married had somehow cured it. Oh, please, she thought. Let it stop. Please let it stop. A tear trickled down her cheek.

Blank spells, she called them, and she'd had them for as long as she could remember. Sometimes, as had happened today, she'd find things she couldn't recall buying. On other occasions, someone would refer to a conversation or an event she'd been involved in but which she was completely unable to recollect. Or it could simply be a matter of trying to recall what had happened earlier in the day and finding she had no idea.

It was frightening to have chunks of one's life vanish. These were periods during which she'd done *something*. But what? Had she lost her virginity? Robbed a bank? Fomented a revolution? Once, when she was thirteen, she'd lost two whole weeks. Another time,

16

she'd found the notes for a college class she was unable to remember attending that day. They were written in her notebook, apparently with her pen, but in someone else's handwriting. Later, talking with a friend who was taking the same class, Mary learned she *had* been present for that day's lecture. The strange handwriting, however, remained a disturbing enigma.

Mary had never told anyone about this, not even her foster parents or Tom. Although the fear was inexplicable, the thought of anyone learning about her blank spells terrified her.

Many times, she'd desperately wanted to tell the Caldwells, to ask for their help, but the words had always died in her throat, as if something inside, some internal censor, had forbidden her to speak. Mrs. Caldwell would be cleaning or washing dishes, and Mary would stand there, desperately wanting to force the words from her lips, yet knowing she was totally incapable of the act. On occasion, her foster mother would turn and, seeing the child's tears, come to her and ask what was wrong. Unable to tell her, Mary would cry harder.

That she hadn't told Tom was a constant source of guilt. She felt as if she were a disreputable salesperson passing off shoddy merchandise as first-rate—the slick talker who failed to mention that the car had a serious transmission problem. She'd tried to tell him. But, as always, the words had refused to come, and she'd knowingly allowed the man she loved to marry a woman with—she shivered—with a defect. The words "mental problem" hung on the periphery of her consciousness, words that were too threatening to be dealt with, and she pushed them away.

Then, giving in to the tears that wanted so desperate-

ly to come, she pulled the towel from her head and lay
back on the bed, her nude body shaking as she sobbed.
When the tears finally stopped, she took a few moments to pull herself together, then continued getting
ready for work.

Twenty minutes later, after having used a blow dryer
and styling wand on her hair, she stood in front of the
bathroom mirror, putting the finishing touches on her
face. The phone rang, and she hurried into the living
room to answer it.

"Hi, hon." It was Tom. "How's your morning
going?"

She hesitated, then, with as much nonchalance as she
could muster, said, "Oh, I did some reading."

Maybe it wasn't a lie, but it certainly was a deception
because it omitted so much. It wasn't her nature to be
dishonest, and she bit her lip, hoping Tom hadn't
noticed her hesitation and that he wouldn't ask anything that might force her to tell him an out-and-out lie.

"After this morning," Tom said cheerfully, "I can
tell you unequivocally that summer is just about here. I
sold six-hundred-dollars worth of camping equipment
and a pair of water skis."

"I'm glad to hear business is so good," she said,
relieved. She was glad now that he had called; just
hearing his voice made her feel warm, loved.

They talked idly for a few minutes, about the weath-
er, about Lynn and Bob, about everything and anything. Finally, Tom ended the conversation, saying he
had to get back to work, and Mary hung up, feeling
much better than she had before his call.

Things would be fine, she decided. Today's blank
spell had been the first in more than a year. It might be
another year before it happened again. Perhaps it
would never happen again.

She returned to the bathroom and finished applying her makeup.

In his small cluttered living room in Lewiston, Maine, John Edwards sat in a threadbare easy chair, halfheartedly watching a game show on TV. The set, an old black-and-white console, allowed the image on the screen to roll every few seconds, but Edwards had grown so accustomed to it he wasn't sure he could watch a TV with a stable picture. In his early twenties, he was dressed in jeans and a T-shirt. On his left arm was a tattoo of a lizard.

Big fuckin' deal, he thought. That's what his whole life was. A big fuckin' deal. The picture rolled, and he threw it a finger.

Edwards was upset because of what had happened the night before with his girl friend, Doris. He'd slugged her, twice. Not that he felt that badly about it—after all, it didn't hurt to let your old lady know who was boss every now and then. What bothered him, though, was that he couldn't remember doing it. And he'd bruised her—bad. He'd done more than just slap her around a little bit.

Six weeks ago, he'd lost his job as a construction laborer the same way. They said he'd knocked the foreman down, that he'd kicked him again and again, until some of the guys pulled him off. But for John Edwards, the incident was a blank; it had never happened.

It was the same way with the trouble he had gotten into as a kid—slashing tires, breaking street lights, and the rest of it. He could never recall having done any of it. Of course, he couldn't tell anyone that. They either wouldn't have believed him, or—and this was the part that had really scared him—they'd have sent him away and locked him up with the real crazies. It was the kind of thing you kept to yourself if you were smart. And to this day, that's just what he had done.

A knock on the door brought him out of his thoughts. "Shit," he muttered, getting out of the chair. It was probably some asshole selling encyclopedias or one of those crazy women who want to read to you from the Bible.

Opening the door, he found a tall, thin man who eyed him nervously.

"Mr. John Edwards?"

"Yeah. What do you want?" Pushing some strands of blond hair out of his eyes, Edwards glared at the man.

The man simply stared at him, saying nothing, and Edwards noticed the tormented look on the man's face. Whatever this guy's problems were, Edwards wanted no part of them.

"Look, man," he said, "I don't have all day to just stand here while we look at each other."

"I know what you really are," the man said. "I know about Walpurgis Night. And I know about Jack."

If Edwards hadn't been in such a lousy mood, he'd have laughed. Jack? Walrus night? Christ! "Hey, you see that green house down the block there?" he asked, pointing. "Well, there's a little old lady there who's as crazy as you are. She'd love to play 'Twilight Zone' with you, but I'm afraid I just don't have time right—"

The man's arm shot forward, and suddenly a pain ripped through John Edwards's chest.

And then the arm shot forward again. More pain. Edwards stumbled backward, his entire system in a state of shock, the room swirling. And then he was falling. Though vaguely aware that he had hit the floor, he still seemed to be dropping, tumbling continuously downward. He saw the man standing over him, a

pointed object in his hand, and then he saw only
blackness, and there was a strange buzzing in his ears
that slowly grew fainter and fainter until it stopped.

That evening, Detective Lieutenant Daniel K. Larson sat on the arm of the worn, overstuffed chair,
waiting for the medical examiner to finish checking
John Edwards's body. A heavyset man in his fifties,
Larson had been a police officer in Lewiston for
thirty-two years. He was the kind of cop who went
about his job slowly but doggedly, checking out even
the most dubious of leads, hating it whenever he had to
give up and let a case go into the records unsolved.

So far, all he knew about Edwards's murder was that
the victim's twenty-year-old live-in girl friend had arrived home from work about five-thirty and discovered
the body. At least that was her story. Larson had seen
the black eye and bruise on Doris Mitchell's face and
was fairly certain he knew who had put them there.
Until he had more to go on, Doris was definitely a
suspect. She'd broken down during questioning, so
he'd had a uniformed officer drive her to her mother's
place. Later on, he'd talk with her some more.

Obviously, neither she nor the dead man had been
inclined to clean up the place. Beer cans littered the
floor in the living room and bedroom. The kitchen floor
was grimy, the sink full of dishes, and something in the
refrigerator smelled. Throughout the house were filthy
ashtrays that apparently had been emptied but never
washed.

The medical examiner, who'd been squatting beside
the body, straightened, turning to face Larson. Frank
Jenkins was tall, about forty, and had a full head of
thick blond hair.

"Well?" Larson asked.

"Stabbed twice in the chest with something small and sharp—an ice pick, maybe."

"Care to take a guess at the time of death?"

Jenkins frowned. "Ummm, I'd say noon, one o'clock, somewhere around there. That's all I can tell you till we cut him open."

"Okay, Frank. Thanks."

Picking up his bag, the medical examiner left. Larson heard him speak to someone outside; then Detective Jim Grant entered.

"What'd you find out?" Larson asked.

Grant took out a small notebook and flipped it open. He was tall, thirty-five, dark curly hair. "Couple neighbors said there was a car with a guy sitting in it parked down the street all morning. One of them"—his eyes dropped to his notes—"a Mrs. Ross across the street, says the guy went to Edwards's door about midmorning, talked to him a moment, then went back to the car. I got a description of the guy. Nobody got his license number."

"Figures. What'd the guy look like?"

"The two descriptions are just about identical." He flipped over a page in his notebook. "Six feet tall, slender, brown hair, balding, about fifty-five years old." He turned another page. "Uh, the car was either a Chevy or a Ford, depending on which neighbor you want to believe. Both of them agreed it was old, beat up, and dark blue." He closed the notebook.

Larson grunted. "How many houses with nobody home?"

"Two."

"Keep checking until you find someone in. Maybe we'll get lucky."

Grant nodded.

"The ME says the time of death was around noon.

The girl friend says she was at work all day. Let's see if just maybe she forgot to tell us about an unusually long lunch break."

"You figure the victim put those bruises on her?"

Larson sighed. "You know how it works. Violence is just like charity; it begins at home."

His eyes dropping to Edwards's body, Grant said, "Meat wagon's outside."

"Send them in."

Three

M ARY KISSED TOM GOOD-BYE, THEN WATCHED THROUGH the window as his compact station wagon pulled away from the house. A light mist hung in the early morning air. It would burn off in an hour or two.

It was Thursday, her day off, two days after the bikini incident. Before long, Lynn would be here to pick her up so the two of them could go shopping. Because Zel Home and Builders Supply was open seven days a week, most of its employees worked at least one day on the weekend. Mary and Lynn had arranged to get the same schedule: Thursdays and Sundays off.

After finishing her coffee and washing the dishes, Mary headed for the bathroom to check her hair and makeup. Both were fine, but she had a spot on her shirt, so she hurried into the bedroom to change. Checking the contents of her dresser while she unbuttoned her blouse, Mary spotted her blue-and-white University of Maine sweat shirt. She was in jeans; the sweat shirt would be perfect. She snatched it from the drawer, revealing what was underneath. There, exactly where she'd put it two days ago to get it out of her sight, was the black bikini.

Suddenly, its presence in the house was intolerable; as long as it was here, she'd be constantly rediscovering it like this, a grim reminder that she wasn't . . . wasn't well. Dropping the sweat shirt, she grabbed the bathing suit and rushed from the room. In the kitchen, she yanked the lid from the plastic garbage can, flung the bikini in with the egg shells and coffee grounds and potato peelings, then slammed the cover back in place as if she were afraid the bathing suit would try to escape.

She stood there with her blouse unbuttoned, staring at the plastic container. It wasn't good enough. The next time she put anything into the garbage, the bathing suit would still be there, on top, waiting for her. Or worse, Tom would find it, ask her about it, force her to tell a lie.

No, that wouldn't work at all. The thing had to be gotten out of the house now, today. From a drawer beneath the stove, she grabbed a small paper bag, then retrieved the bathing suit from the garbage. Brushing off a few loose coffee grounds, she dropped the bikini into the sack. In the living room, she grabbed her purse from the couch and stuffed the brown paper bag in on top of her comb and keys and checkbook. While shopping, she would throw it away, and that would be that.

Relieved, she returned to the bedroom and put on her sweat shirt.

Then it happened again.

For a moment, she wasn't sure what was happening; so many sensations bombarded her simultaneously that

25

she couldn't sort them out. People were screaming. She was in the water. Hands were reaching toward her. No, not toward her. They were pulling someone else out of the water. A woman. She was yelling something.

"No," Mary heard herself saying. "I didn't try to drown you. I don't know what you're talking about."

The woman was pointing at her, accusing her, screaming. A crowd had formed.

"No, no, no," Mary said. "You're wrong. I wouldn't." Slowly becoming aware of her surroundings, she realized she was in a large indoor swimming pool, clinging to its edge while her legs lazily treaded water. She had never been here before.

Suddenly, the hands were reaching toward her again and, this time they did grab her. She was pulled from the water.

"Let's hear your version of this." He was a muscular blond in his early twenties, wearing swimming trunks.

She wanted to scream that she had no idea where she was or how she had gotten there or why that woman had accused her of anything, but instead she simply stared at the man.

He waved his hand in front of her eyes. "Hey, are you okay?"

"Don't do that," Mary said, pushing his hand away from her face.

"You want to tell me what happened?" Beyond him, the woman stood, still surrounded by the people who'd pulled her from the water. She was middle-aged, dumpy, and wore a white bathing cap. She waved her arms as Mary spoke.

"I don't know what happened," Mary said.

"She says you tried to drown her."

Mary shivered. "I didn't," she declared weakly.

"She says you did."

"I–I've never seen her before. Why would I try to drown her?"

"Why were you wrestling with her in the water?"

Mary shook her head. "I don't know. Maybe I just bumped into her, and we got tangled up or something. I wasn't trying to hurt her."

The man left her and joined the group surrounding Mary's accuser, which had moved farther away, out of earshot. Mary stood there, wondering what they were saying about her. Every so often, one or more of the participants in the discussion would glance her way. She felt alone and vulnerable.

Finally, the blond man left the conference and returned to Mary. "She's not going to press charges," he said. "The whole thing's blown over, okay?"

Mary nodded. "That's it? I can go?"

"Yeah, and to tell you the truth, I wish you would." He stood aside, clearly waiting for her to walk past him to the exit.

She found the women's locker room, and it wasn't until she saw herself in the steamy mirrors above the sinks that she realized she was wearing the black bikini. Resisting the urge to find something and cover herself, she tried to think. Her clothes . . . Where were her clothes? Bewildered, she looked for someone to help her and spotted a teenage girl sitting on a wooden bench, pulling off her shoes.

"Have you seen my clothes?" Mary asked, stepping up to her.

"I beg your pardon?" The girl eyed her warily. She was about fifteen, a little on the plump side, and had light-brown hair. There was a wire basket on the floor by her feet.

"My clothes . . . Have you seen my clothes?" Oh, God, Mary thought, I'm not making any sense. I've got to pull myself together.

The girl pointed to Mary's bikini bottom. "Didn't you check them?"

Mary's eyes dropped to where the girl was pointing. Pinned to the black cloth was a metal disk with a number on it. For a moment, she was confused, then she realized what the object was.

Hurrying past the showers, she turned a corner and found a counter with a thin blond woman behind it. Mary unpinned the metal disk and handed it to her.

"Number nineteen," the woman said and disappeared through a doorway behind her. A moment later, she was back, carrying a wire basket, which she laid on the counter. In it were Mary's things—her University of Maine sweat shirt, her purse, her jeans, her shoes.

"Thanks," Mary said, taking the basket.

"Hey, what was all the commotion out there anyway?"

"I don't know," Mary replied. "I must have missed it." Clutching the basket, she hurried away from the counter. This had to be the only women's locker room; her accuser would probably be here any moment now. Mary never wanted to see that woman again. She never wanted to see this place again.

She passed the teenager, who was carrying her basket up to check it in. The girl was wearing a one-piece red bathing suit. They avoided each other's eyes.

With the girl gone, Mary had the dressing area to herself. She frantically pulled off the bikini. Having no towel, she hurriedly pulled her clothes over her still-damp body. A middle-aged woman in a green bathing

28

suit came in. From the corner of her eye, she gave Mary a peculiar look, then quickly stepped into the shower. Without even bothering to comb out her wet hair, Mary fled the building.

Outside, she found her car in a small paved parking lot. Fumbling in her purse, she couldn't find her keys, and when she finally did, the key wouldn't go into the lock. Then she realized it was upside down. When Mary at last got the door open and slid behind the wheel, she was trembling so badly she couldn't drive. She simply sat there, shaking.

Oh, God, she thought. Why can't I remember? Why did I come here? What did I do to that woman? Unable to hold back her tears, she put her face in her hands and wept.

"What's wrong with me?" she sobbed. "What's wrong with me?"

Forty-five minutes later, Mary sat on the pseudo-Chippendale couch in her living room, trying to make sense out of what had happened to her. When she'd finally regained enough composure to drive, she discovered she was lost. Driving past unfamiliar homes and businesses, she'd eventually found some streets she recognized. She was near Dorchester.

Everything she'd done was so uncharacteristic. She didn't particularly enjoy swimming and she was hardly the type to display herself in a skimpy bathing suit. Why had she gone to an unfamiliar part of town to do something she wasn't fond of, dressed in a manner that embarrassed her?

I don't know, she thought miserably. I can never remember. It's as if . . . as if I'm out of control when it happens. She closed her eyes and clenched her fists, something deep inside her crying, *Help me, someone.*

Help me. But no one would come to her aid, because no one knew. She was unable to tell anyone.

Again, Mary tried to reconstruct what had happened. Having decided to rid herself of the bikini, she'd stuck it into her purse, intending to throw it away while she was out. Then she went into the bedroom and put on her sweat shirt. The next thing she knew, she was in a pool, some woman yelling that she had tried to drown her. The time in between was blank, and from experience, Mary knew that no amount of concentrating or worrying would pry loose a single memory. Although some of the events that occurred during a blank spell might be pieced together later, the time itself, in the personal sense that one had lived it, experienced it, was lost forever. A part of her life was gone, missing.

Well, she thought, at least I got rid of the bikini. She'd left it at the pool.

What did I do to that woman?

Suddenly, the quiet of the morning was shattered by the squeals of children. They were coming from next door; the Fentons had four kids, the two youngest not yet in kindergarten, and their yard was often the neighborhood gathering place for preschoolers.

The noise grew until it seemed as if there was a crowded playground next door, until it seemed the shrill voices were inside her head. Oh, stop it, she thought, covering her ears with her hands. The din, though muffled, still penetrated.

Finally, she went to the window to see what was happening. In the Fentons' yard were at least half a dozen youngsters and a new red-and-yellow swing set. It had three individual seats, all of them in use, kids swishing back and forth, shrieking with delight.

"It's my turn, Sally," a redheaded boy shouted at a

girl on one of the swings. Except for a defiant shake of her long black hair, she ignored him.

"It's my turn, and you better give it to me!"

The girl stuck out her tongue.

"Okay for you." The boy moved closer, then grabbed the chain as she swung by. Its movement rudely interrupted, the swing wobbled, nearly dumping the girl on the ground.

"You cut that out, Eddie, or I'll tell your mother!"

"Well, Eddie gets a turn, too!" another child yelled. And then they were all shouting. Oh, please, Mary thought, once more covering her ears. Please.

Moving away from the window, she suddenly felt weak and headed for the bedroom to lie down. She closed the door, which cut out some of the noise, then stretched out on the bed. She was shaking.

What did you do to that woman?

She rolled over, burying her head in the pillow. It wasn't that she disliked children; she just didn't like so many of them at one time. They reminded her of—

Don't think about that place.

What did you do to that woman? *What?*

I don't know, Mary thought. Oh, God, I don't know. Had she tried to kill the woman, to drown her? Did she lose *that* much control? Although the things she did during her blank spells were sometimes out of character, it was usually her inability to remember that bothered her, more than anything she'd done. But now she had reason to believe she might have tried to murder someone. She shuddered.

No, no. Maybe not. The woman could have been crazy, a paranoid. Perhaps all you did was bump her, and she screamed. Maybe *she's* the one who should be locked away.

What happens during the blank spells? Do you become a murderer, a monster? Oh, God, she thought, I don't know. I just don't know.

I need help, she thought. Professional help. A psychiatrist. And then she realized that it would be pointless for her to see a therapist because she'd be unable to tell the doctor anything. And yet, she was unable to totally dismiss the idea. Maybe a professional would know how to handle things like this. Maybe.

The doorbell startled her. Mary, her thoughts scrambled, responded in an almost-Pavlovian manner, moving into the living room and toward the door mechanically, simply because that was what one did when the bell rang. She opened the door without even considering who or what might be on the other side and found herself looking at Lynn. Mary unlocked the glass storm door and pushed it open. Her friend stepped inside.

"Where were you?" Lynn asked, obviously miffed. "I came by to pick you up, and no one was home."

And then Mary remembered. They'd had a date to go shopping. "I'm sorry, Lynn. It's just that I . . ." Having no idea what she had planned to say, Mary allowed her words to trail off.

"Hey," Lynn said, suddenly looking concerned. "What happened to you? Are you all right?"

Mary was still wearing the clothes she'd put on over her wet body at the pool, and her hair, which had dried on the way home, was a tangled mess. "I . . . I'm fine. Really."

"Well, you sure don't look it."

Before Mary could respond, Lynn had her by the arm and was guiding her toward the couch. Her friend sat down beside her, looking at her anxiously.

"Hey, kid, it's pretty obvious that something's wrong. You want to tell me about it?"

Mary was beginning to feel uncomfortable, as if she'd been caught performing some shameful act. She looked at Lynn, her friend's intense blue eyes almost pleading for a chance to understand, to help, and suddenly the emotion of the moment overwhelmed her. Clutching Lynn, she sat there and cried.

"Oh, if only I could tell you," Mary sobbed. "If only I could."

"Hey, come on. There's nothing you can't tell me. This is Lynn, remember? We know all each other's terrible secrets."

"There's one you don't know." She had her head on the other woman's shoulder. Lynn gently stroked her hair.

"I think it would be better for you if you told someone," Lynn said. "Whatever it is, is going to eat at you until you do."

And Mary realized that if there was ever a moment when she could speak of her problem this had to be it. And suddenly she not only wanted to tell Lynn, but she felt compelled to do it, as if she'd burst if she didn't. It was a wonderful feeling because she knew once she told Lynn, she'd have broken free; she could tell Tom; she could get the help she needed. Pushing herself away from Lynn, she quickly dried her eyes.

"Are you going to tell me?" her friend asked.

Mary nodded. "I've had it—this problem—all my life. You see, sometimes I . . ."

She felt the drool spilling from her lips, and then she was staggering toward the bathroom, her hand over her mouth. Reaching the commode, she dropped to her knees, hung her head over the bowl, and was sicker than she had ever been in her life.

When, finally, it was over, she flushed the toilet. Uncertain whether she had the strength to rise, she remained on the floor. Feeling decimated, beaten, she realized how foolish she'd been to think she could just blurt it out. Something inside her had stepped in to shut off the words, as it always would.

Lynn stood in the doorway. "Hey," she said, "are you all right?"

"I'm okay." She looked into Lynn's worried eyes. "But I can't tell you."

"I wish you would. It's not good for you to keep something like this bottled up inside you."

"I can't, Lynn. I just can't."

"Okay," her friend said. "It's up to you."

"It's not that I don't trust you, Lynn. If I could tell anyone, it would be you."

Her friend nodded. "Well, when the time's right, it'll come out. And if a sympathetic ear will help, you'll know where to find me. Okay?"

"Okay."

Taking Mary's hand, Lynn helped her up.

Four

MARGARET DONOVAN'S BASKET WAS FULL OF BROWN-shelled eggs when she left the chicken coop behind the barn. As they did each spring, the hens had been laying more than usual, responding to an age-old instinct that said this was the time of year for birds to reproduce. The Donovans' small flock was mixed, New Hampshires and Rhode Island Reds, both kinds being good for meat as well as eggs.

A slight woman in her midtwenties, Margaret had red hair and freckles. For her and her husband Les, living on this small farm tucked nicely into a little valley in rural Vermont was just perfect. Her only regret was that the place was too small to support them, which meant Les had to work in town while she tended the farm. This year their only child, five-year-old Jessica, had begun kindergarten, so Margaret had the place to herself.

She entered the barn through a small rear door and strolled across the floor to their battered tractor. She'd

35

been using it to do the spring plowing, and it had broken down three times—so far. They'd been saving for a new one but had less than half of what they needed. Soon, Margaret knew, there would come a breakdown that neither she nor Les could repair. Hang in there, tractor, she thought. Just hang in there.

Turning away from the rusty orange machine, she left the barn through the big double doors in front and headed for the house. Although it had been a little foggy earlier, it had turned into a beautiful day, the sky nearly cloudless, the sun warming the land in preparation for the rebirth that came each spring. Soon, everything would be green and beautiful. The farm had a tidy, well-kept look about it with its white fence, red barn, and newly plowed fields. The house was white, with a long screened porch that was a marvelous place to sit on warm summer evenings.

In the kitchen, she transferred the eggs from her basket to a large bowl, which she placed in the refrigerator. Later, she'd put some of them in cartons, for sale to people from town. Their egg business didn't pay the cost of feeding the chickens. Even so, it was worth it. Unlike the runny, colorless things you got in the grocery store, the eggs eaten by the Donovan family were thick-shelled with yolks that were bright orange.

She warmed the coffee on the electric stove, poured herself a cup, and sat at the big kitchen table of unpolished wood. Like the other rooms in the house, the kitchen was spacious, with sturdy furniture. For lack of a better term, she described the place as rural-rustic, which was just as she and Les wanted it. The environment was comfortable, honest, and filled with things that were plain but rugged, things that would last.

Taking a swallow of coffee, she glanced at the clock

on the wall near the hutch. It was after eleven; the mail should have come by now. She'd check the box after finishing her coffee.

She'd had another one of the dreams last night, another nightmare. It hadn't worked, what they'd wanted to do to her in that place when she was a little girl. It couldn't have worked; no one could alter another's behavior that drastically. In three weeks, Walpurgis Night would come and go. Nothing would happen.

And then, despite her efforts not to, Margaret recalled the *things* they had done to her, and she shuddered. Her foster parents hadn't believed her. Not that she blamed them; it was a bizarre horror story told by a seven-year-old girl.

"There were other children that these . . . these things were done to?" her foster mother had asked.

"Yes."

"Then why is it no one has complained, no one but you?"

"We weren't supposed to remember."

"But you remember."

"Yes."

"And no one else."

"I–I don't know."

So, grateful that she was no longer in that terrifying place and not wanting to upset her newly acquired parents, little Margaret had said nothing further about the Christian Home for Children. Later, with the orphanage closed and Sister dead, it no longer seemed important that she reveal what had gone on, since children weren't being hurt there anymore. And those who had undergone the horrors would remember as she had remembered and would never do the things Sister had wanted.

Suddenly, she saw an image of herself in a dark place, terrified. A shadowy figure was bending over her, strapping her arms and legs to the sides of a wooden table. She knew where she was: the punishment place. And she knew what was about to happen. She immediately pushed the image aside and stood up. With a shaky hand, she grabbed her cup and gulped down the remainder of her coffee. It was time to get the mail.

The mailbox was about three hundred feet from the house, at the side of the highway. She walked along the dirt drive, the sunshine warming her, taking away the chill of the punishment place.

"Hi, Joanna," she said to their milk cow. The animal eyed her indifferently from its side of the white board fence, then turned and walked away, its udder swaying gently.

Reaching the mailbox, she discovered the postman had indeed been there. Ignoring the magazines for the moment, she pulled out a handful of letters and began going through them. To Margaret, the postman's arrival was one of the high points of the day. Although she was in her midtwenties, she got a childlike thrill out of getting the mail. She went through the letters as if each one, rather than a bill or a piece of junk mail, would be an exciting surprise.

She was only vaguely aware of the car approaching on the highway.

Topping the rise in his Chevy pickup, Gordon De Grage saw the Donovans' farm and Les's young wife collecting the mail. Nice young couple, the Donovans. Pretty much kept to themselves—and put a lot of work into the farm. Les's ambition was to quit his job in town and become a full-time farmer. An odd notion for a

young man to have these days, but Gordon De Grage
approved. He owned one of the largest dairy farms in
the county and wouldn't give up his lifestyle for half of
New York and all of Boston. Sixty-two now, he expected to live another thirty years, while people his age
in the cities were dropping dead of heart attacks and
strokes—if the muggers didn't get them first.

Mrs. Donovan was still at the mailbox. It stood at the
very bottom of the small valley, the road climbing away
from it in both directions. As he descended toward
Margaret Donovan, he noticed another vehicle approaching her from the opposite direction. An old blue
Ford that looked as if it had escaped from a junkyard
somewhere. It was coming fast, probably another asshole from New Jersey or some such place who didn't
care how many animals or kids he ran over on his way
through. As far as De Grage was concerned, they
should build a wall along the Eastern seaboard to
separate the cities from the interior and keep all the
jerks where they belonged.

Suddenly, the speeding car swerved and headed for
Mrs. Donovan. De Grage blinked, unable to believe
what he was seeing. The blue Ford was deliberately
heading right for her. De Grage began urgently honk-
ing his horn, trying to attract either Margaret Donovan
or the lunatic driving the Ford. And then it hit her,
flipping her over the hood, letters flying through the
air, fluttering to the ground.

The car was back on the highway, coming toward
him. Stunned, De Grage watched as it sped by him. He
had a glimpse of the driver, a man with a crazed look on
his face, whose lips had been moving, as if he'd been
shouting something. Suddenly regaining his wits, De
Grage jammed on the brakes, then spun around and
looked out the rear window of the cab, watching the

receding Ford. It shrank until it was only a distant shape near the top of the hill, and then it was gone. But he had the license number: 815–TDE, Maine.

Pulling a ball-point pen from his pocket, he wrote the number down on the handiest place, the back of his hand. Then he quickly drove to the motionless form lying near the side of the road. It took him only a moment to determine that Margaret Donovan was dead. After driving up to her house and calling the sheriff, he returned to the highway and began picking up the mail.

Lieutenant Daniel K. Larson sat in his small, cluttered office at the Lewiston police station, ignoring the piles of neglected paperwork on the desk in front of him.

A picture of his wife, Joyce, peeked out at him from behind a stack of file folders. She was in her early fifties, a plump woman with graying hair and a warm smile, a woman who believed in hearty meals and who loved to cook. Larson adored her. Joyce was his second wife, the first having been unable to cope with marriage to a cop. Between the two of them, they'd given him four children, all of whom were grown now.

Ten years, he thought, and I'll retire. And then he wondered why retirement had come to mind. It was a topic he rarely considered, perhaps because it made him feel old. Well, what the hell, he told himself, letting out a long, slow sigh, you might as well admit it. You *are* getting old.

He was feeling melancholy, he supposed, because the John Edwards murder investigation had stalled after only two days, which meant it was quite likely the murderer would never be apprehended. The medical examiner's report had been no help. The weapon—still

unidentified—had penetrated the heart; death had
been nearly instantaneous. Time of death was unchanged from the ME's original estimate. Cause of
death . . . He'd forgotten the ME's medical gobbledy-
gook, but he knew what the cause of death was: getting
stabbed in the goddamn heart with something long and
sharp and deadly.

The victim's girl friend, Doris, had been eliminated
as a suspect. She'd been at work all day, leaving only
for lunch, which she'd eaten with two fellow employees
from the radio station where she worked in the traffic
department. The construction foreman Edwards had
assaulted had also been on the job all day. A check with
the victim's co-workers and friends had turned up no
new suspects.

Grant had found another of Edwards's neighbors
who'd seen the blue car parked down the street from
the victim's house: a teenage boy who remembered
walking past it on his way to catch the school bus. His
description of the driver matched those of the other two
witnesses. The boy, who knew cars, said this one was
an old and battered Ford. He hadn't noticed the license
number.

The man in the blue car was the only suspect, but
there wasn't a single worthwhile scrap of information to
go on. Three people had seen him parked there. One of
them had seen him go to Edwards's door about midmorning, then return to the car. No one had seen him
leave the neighborhood; no one recalled even a single
number from his license plate.

At least, two of the three witnesses had agreed on the
make of the car, which meant there was still one thing
he could do, although it was a long shot. He could put
out a regional alert requesting all law enforcement
agencies in New England to notify him of any incidents

involving aged blue Fords driven by tall, skinny men in their fifties. He knew the odds against accomplishing anything other than making a lot of extra work for himself were astronomical. Still, there was always the slim chance that the man in the blue Ford would be involved in something else that would bring him to the attention of the authorities somewhere.

Larson picked up the phone.

Later that day, Mary sat at her small breakfast table with a cup of coffee. After she had regained her composure, Mary and Lynn had gone shopping as planned, spending several hours but no money at two shopping malls—the kind of expedition Tom and Bob would have absolutely hated. Nothing more had been said about what had happened earlier, and Mary, once she'd pulled herself together, had managed to enjoy the day.

The resilience of the human spirit amazed her. Earlier, she'd been distraught, helpless, miserable. A few encouraging words from Lynn, and she'd bounced back, gone shopping, enjoyed herself. Soon, she would begin fixing dinner for Tom, something she could do only on her days off. She would deal with her problem as she had always dealt with it, by pushing the horrors out of her mind—until the next blank spell.

Just as Mary got up to refill her coffee cup, the phone rang. Leaving the cup on the counter, she hurried into the living room, sitting down on the couch as she grabbed the receiver.

"Hello."

"Hi, Mary." It was Maxine Caldwell, her foster mother.

"Hi," Mary said excitedly, glad to hear the solid,

reliable voice of this woman whose love had meant so much. "How are things in Evans Ridge?"

"How are things ever in Evans Ridge? The most exciting thing to happen around here in weeks was when Fred Ivers took a nap in the jail, and some kids locked him in and took the keys."

Mary laughed. Fred Ivers was the constable, a fat, usually disagreeable fellow no one liked very much.

"Had to get Hank Thomas to come over with his welding equipment and cut the lock off with a torch."

"They catch the kids?" Mary asked.

"Nope. They figure it was the Reynolds kids and maybe Kenny Miller, but nobody's admitting to anything."

For the next few minutes, they reminisced, discussed the possibility of Mary and Tom's coming up for a visit, talked of small-town happenings and mother-daughter things.

"Hey," Maxine Caldwell said. "When are you going to give me a baby so I can bounce it on my knee and get all misty-eyed and go 'goo-goo' and all that sort of thing?"

"You know the answer to that. We haven't decided whether to have children yet." And if she did, would her child be normal . . . or like its mother? She pushed the thought away.

"Oh, pooh. These days, everybody wants to think it over, decide, plan. One of these days, everybody'll decide they don't want any kids, and that will be the end of the human race."

"I don't think that's too likely."

"Well, maybe not. Hey, did that researcher ever get in touch with you?"

"What researcher?"

43

"Oh, some guy who called the other night. Said he was from some university down there by you and he was making some kind of a study on foster children who've grown up. Anyway, he said he wanted to get in touch with you, so I gave him your address and phone number."

"He hasn't called me yet."

"Well, maybe he got enough grown-up foster kids without talking to you. Listen, I better go before I run up the phone bill and get Papa in a dither."

When Mary hung up, she went into the kitchen to start dinner, thinking how much she loved Nick and Maxine Caldwell and how lucky she had been to have them for parents—foster or otherwise.

Five

It was nearly ten o'clock Monday morning when Lieutenant Daniel Larson sat down behind the desk in his small, cluttered office at the Lewiston police station. He was usually there bright and early, but this morning his alarm clock hadn't gone off. Eyeing the stack of papers awaiting his attention, he muttered quietly to himself.

Fifteen years he'd had that clock, and every morning since he'd bought it, he'd awoken before it went off. Every morning except this one, the one morning it failed to work. His wife, too, had overslept; but then Joyce, who liked to stay up and watch the late movie on TV, didn't share his love for early mornings.

Pushing these thoughts aside, he turned his attention to the papers in front of him. Most of them were forms—green ones, orange ones, white ones, copies to everyone, fuel for the bureaucratic machine. He flipped through them, stopping when he spotted a reply to his regional bulletin asking that he be informed of any incidents involving battered blue Fords. The report was from Vermont, where an old blue Ford had run down a young woman at her rural mailbox. Larson felt a tingle of excitement. This particular blue Ford had a Maine license plate and was driven by a man thought to be in his fifties. A witness to the hit-and-run said it was unquestionably deliberate, the car swerving off the road, aiming for the woman. And the witness had gotten the license number.

Quickly, Larson turned to the attached sheet. The license number reported by the witness belonged to a red AMC, not a blue Ford. The red car was owned by sixty-eight-year-old Phineas Sweeney of Bangor, and the authorities there had checked it out. He and his wife had been at a senior citizens' meeting when the young woman had been killed in Vermont. His license plates, number 815–TDE, had not been stolen. Bangor police had verified that they were still on Sweeney's car.

Studying the number, Larson looked for ways it could have been read incorrectly by a shocked witness. The most obvious way to get it wrong would be to mistake a three for an eight. Sliding a pad in front of him, he wrote down 315–TDE. A moment later, he added 315–TDF, 815–TDF, then changed the *T* to an *I* and added still more possibilities to the list. Finally, he picked up the phone and dialed a number in Augusta, the state capital. He read his list to the woman who answered, then he hung up and waited. Ten minutes later, she called back.

"Only one of those numbers belongs to a Ford," she reported. "Do you want the owner's name and address?"

"Give me the year and color of the Ford."

"White, brand-new."

"Nope, that won't help me. Thanks for your trouble."

"Anytime, Lieutenant," she said and broke the connection.

Replacing the receiver, he studied the license number in the report. For a moment, he saw something in the letters and numbers, but when he tried to focus on it, it slipped away. Damn, he thought, this seemed to be happening to him more and more lately. His body was in good condition, but was his brain going? He forced the thought out of his mind. The idea would come back to him eventually. A few hours or days or weeks from now, he would be lying in bed or driving home or just sitting here thinking and suddenly he would know what had been at the edge of his consciousness this particular Monday morning.

Leaning back in his desk chair, he sighed.

And brooded about getting old.

Mary stood at the kitchen sink, washing the dishes that had been soaking since breakfast. After feeding Tom and sending him off to work, she'd spent the morning reading. The afternoon before, Sunday, she and Tom had gone over to Lynn and Bob's for the first backyard barbecue of the season. After consuming some enormous steaks, they'd played bridge, Tom and she winning four of five rubbers. Her life, it seemed, had returned to normal, almost as if the events of the week before had never occurred. The doorbell interrupted her thoughts.

Grabbing a dish towel, Mary headed toward the living room, drying her hands as she went. She opened the door, revealing a tall, slender man with thin reddish hair.

"Yes," Mary said.

The man hesitated, looking uncomfortable, obviously waiting for her to open the locked glass storm door separating them—which Mary had no intention of doing. She had found that staying on her side of the glass was a good way to discourage the peddlers of consumer goods or religion—or anyone else who showed up on the doorstep uninvited.

The man's eyes dropped to the doorknob, then slowly rose to meet hers. He seemed nervous, tense. Suddenly, he smiled and said, "Hi, I represent American National Encyclopedias, and if I can come in, I'll have a free gift for you." He held up a black case, apparently indicating the gift was inside. His grin broadened. "It would take only a moment or two of your time, and I promise you it would be worth your while."

"I have a set of encyclopedias," Mary said. "I'm not really interested in having two."

"I'm sorry, but I can barely hear you through the door." He gave her a helpless look.

Mary repeated herself, more loudly this time.

"Oh. Well, that's no problem at all. We'll be happy to take your old set as a trade-in." He casually put his hand on the knob and gave it a gentle twist, as if it was a thing done absently and he had no real interest in opening the door. The locked knob refused to turn. "I'll only take a few seconds, and you'll really like the free gift. No obligation, none at all."

Mary shook her head. "I'm sorry. I'm really busy right now."

His eyes darted to the doorknob and, almost as quickly, they were again staring into hers—with an intensity that startled her. "The gift is either a free world atlas or twenty dollars in cash, your choice."

His whole being seemed to plead silently but desperately for her to unlock the door. Mary realized she was twisting the dish towel in her hands.

"N–no," she said, surprised at the weakness of her voice. She started to close the door.

"There's another gift I haven't told you about," the man said quickly, again grabbing the knob. He gave it a tug, and Mary involuntarily stepped back. She slammed the door and locked it.

Unsettled, she stood there a moment, trying to sort things out. Why had he been so anxious to come inside? And the offer of twenty dollars, she had never heard of such a thing. If he was a legitimate salesman, the man would go broke just giving presentations. *If* he was a legitimate salesman.

Suddenly, she was sure a salesman was the one thing he wasn't. Then what was he? What would he have done had she let him in? Was he a rapist, a murderer, both? She shuddered.

Mary stepped to the window, moving the curtain just enough to peek out. The man was nowhere to be seen. But was he really gone? Or was he out there somewhere, waiting? Stop it, she told herself, releasing the curtain. Just stop it. Even if the man wasn't a real salesman, you'll never see him again. He's gone; you're safe.

Heading back toward the kitchen, she stopped by the telephone, then hesitated, uncertain whether to report the incident to the police. All door-to-door salesmen were anxious to get inside. But not so eager they offered to pay for the privilege. She picked up the phone. When a male voice answered at the police station, Mary gave her name and address and explained what had happened.

"Did the man say anything threatening?" the police officer asked.

"You mean, did he specifically say he was going to hurt me?"

"Yes, ma'am."

"Well, no, but—"

"Did he make any threatening gestures?"

"No."

"Did he try to physically force his way into your home?"

"No. He . . . he just left, but—"

"Ma'am, I'm sorry, but there's really not much we can do. All you've reported is that a salesman came to your door, and there's no ordinance here against door-to-door selling."

"But . . ." Mary was beginning to feel very foolish. "Don't you think that was suspicious, that he tried to pay me twenty dollars?"

"It might be a little unusual, but it's certainly not illegal."

Realizing that calling the police had been a mistake, Mary ended the conversation. In the kitchen, she finished washing the dishes, then made a cup of coffee and sat down at the breakfast table, still feeling uneasy.

Shortly after arriving at work that afternoon, Mary was summoned to the office of Assistant Manager Walter P. Adkins. Stepping into his cluttered cubbyhole, she found a woman about her own age sitting in one of the two wooden chairs facing Adkins. The balding assistant manager was on the phone, talking to someone about a shipment of redwood lumber that was apparently overdue. He motioned for Mary to take a seat.

As she did so, she glanced at the woman in the other chair. Like Mary, she was slender with wavy shoulder-length dark hair. Just briefly, Mary wondered whether she was to be fired, the woman to be her replacement; then she realized that was pretty unlikely. She wasn't in any trouble that she knew of, and a sacked employee was hardly ever introduced to her replacement. The woman smiled at her. Uncertain how to respond, Mary nodded almost imperceptibly, then quickly looked away.

The office barely had room for the old wooden desk behind which Adkins was sitting, the designers of the building apparently having decided that retail space was entirely too precious to sacrifice very much of it for a lowly assistant manager. The room was strictly utilitarian—tile floor, cheap metal filing cabinets, no windows. Papers were stacked on the desk, the cabinets, wherever there was space.

Adkins's phone conversation was coming to an end, and Mary's attention returned to him. His plastic-framed glasses kept slipping down his nose; every moment or two, he'd reach up and push them back where they belonged. Mary had never really understood why Lynn disliked him as much as she did. Although he was undeniably a stuffed shirt, he wasn't a bad boss. Mary had never known him to be unreasonable or unfair.

"Ah, Mary," he said as soon as he had hung up. "Sorry to keep you waiting. I'd like you to meet Stephanie Flynn. Mrs. Flynn, this is Mary Taylor."

The two women nodded to one another, and Adkins continued. "As you know, Zel will be opening a new outlet soon near Worcester. So, what the company's decided to do is bring in some of the people who were hired to staff the new store and have them work a few weeks with some of the experienced people here in this

51

store." He paused, as if searching for just the turn of phrase a proper executive should use, and Mary thought: Yes, Walter, you are definitely a stuffed shirt.

"Mary," he went on, "I want you to take Mrs. Flynn here under your wing for the next few weeks and show her the ropes. She'll have your same schedule while she's here and she'll spend all her time with you. Any questions?" When neither Mary nor Stephanie asked one, he said, "Good. I'm sure the two of you will get along fine. And if you have any problems, just let me know."

As the two women rose to leave, he said, "Oh, Mary, I almost forgot. All next week, I have to leave early and I'm going to put you in charge of closing up."

Mary nodded. She'd done it before; it was no big deal, an easy half hour of overtime. After she'd led her new companion down a narrow hallway and out into the main store, there was an awkward moment of silence, neither woman knowing what to say. Finally, Mary smiled and said, "Well, this is it."

Walking beside her, Stephanie seemed a little awed by the rows and rows of tools and nails and pipe fittings. "Oh, boy," she said.

"Come on," Mary said, taking her arm. "There's nothing to it." Stephanie looked doubtful.

Mary gave her the tour, along with a crash course in nails and other carpentry items—this is a twenty-penny, this an eight, while over here we have finishing nails, which have these smaller heads. They examined table saws, chain saws, and coping saws, fittings for pipe and tubing, valves, and all the rest of it. As they stood before a display of circular-saw blades, Stephanie said, "I can do it. I know I can." She pressed her lips together, looking determined.

"It's a little overwhelming when you first see it all," Mary said, "but you'd be surprised how quickly you start getting the hang of it."

Stephanie eyed her skeptically. "How long did it take you?"

"I had the basic stuff pretty well down in a few weeks. You don't really have to know that much. Most of the people who come in here are amateurs; they only need to know a few basic things to get them started in the right direction." She smiled reassuringly. "Don't worry. No one's going to come in asking how to build a fifty-foot bridge that can support a tank or anything like that."

Stephanie rolled her eyes. "What if someone does?"

"Then you refer them to Adkins, and Adkins'll tell them to get a reliable contractor."

After Mary had explained a little about the various types of saw blades, Stephanie said, "I understand that they're planning to take me out back and have me use all the different power tools." The prospect obviously made her a little nervous.

"I don't know what they've got planned for you, but that's what I did." Afraid that she might cut off a couple of fingers—or worse—Mary, too, had approached the experience apprehensively. But nothing of the sort had happened, and once she'd conquered her initial fears, she'd enjoyed herself, as she expected Stephanie would.

They moved on to the aisle that contained wood filler, patching plaster, caulking compound, and the like. Mary pointed out a few of the items that were usually in demand; then, repositioning a small can of Plastic Wood, she said, "Well, Stephanie, about the only things you haven't seen are sinks, commodes, kitchen cabinets—the big stuff. And, fortunately, we don't have to handle any of that. If anyone wants a new kitchen or bathroom, get Adkins or whichever manager's on duty. Lowly employees like us don't mess with the big stuff.''

Stephanie nodded. Obviously, that was fine with her. "Call me Steph," she said, "if you wouldn't mind."

"Sure, whatever you like."

"On my last job, there were two of us. Two Stephanies. So I became Steph, and the other one became Stephanie. I had to train myself not to respond to anything but Steph." She grinned, her eyes finding Mary's for just an instant, then shifting to some object on the shelf. She had the bluest eyes Mary had ever seen.

"It was one of those state jobs," Steph added. "The Department of Motor Vehicles. I was one of those laid off in the latest round of budget cuts."

While Steph had been speaking, Mary had been studying the young woman. Roughly her own height and build, she had a round face, lightly freckled. And she had a grin Mary was certain could be quite seductive. She seemed nice; Mary was beginning to like her.

Glancing toward the front of the store, Mary spotted Lynn standing idly behind her cash register, waiting for the next customer to show up. "Come on," Mary said. "There's someone I want you to meet."

By the time Zel Home and Builders Supply was closing for the day, the two women were on their way to becoming friends. After getting their coats and purses from the employees' lockers, they found Adkins standing at the glass doors, waiting to let them out.

"Well, how did it go?" he asked. "Any problems?"

"There's a lot to learn," Steph replied shyly.

"We didn't expect you to learn it all in the first day. Just keep familiarizing yourself with things, and if you have any questions, ask Mary." He smiled reassuringly, the good manager bolstering the morale of the workers.

He unlocked the door, and the two women stepped out into the night. "Where you parked?" Mary asked.

"Over there," Steph replied, pointing into the darkness at the far end of the parking lot. "The first thing Adkins told me was where employees parked their cars. I had to come out and move it."

"Needless to say, that's where I'm parked, too," Mary said. They headed in the direction of their cars.

As they moved away from the building, the shadows in the unlit parking lot deepened. It was a dark night, neither moon nor stars visible in the black sky. A light mist hanging in the air caressed Mary's face almost as if she were walking through spider webs. The notion chilled her, and she shivered.

"You don't know how lucky you are to have your own place," Steph said, breaking the silence. "Even with both of us working, there's no way we could make the payments with today's prices and interest rates."

While Steph had been speaking, Mary thought she'd heard footsteps behind them. She turned to look, seeing only the empty parking lot and the building, its glass doors rectangles of light in the darkness. Adkins, who'd remained inside after letting them out, was no longer at the door. Blurred by the mist, the lights of the building seemed distant, unreachable.

"Something wrong?" Steph asked.

"No, I just thought I heard something." They began walking faster, Steph apparently sensing it, too. The night seemed hostile, unsafe—as if all sorts of crawly evil things had come out and were waiting in the darkness, just out of sight.

Quickly, Mary said, "Don't you have any hope at all of getting a house?"

Steph sighed. "When my parents are gone, my brother and I will inherit their house. Maybe we can make it into a duplex and both live there."

"And that's your only hope, to inherit a place?"

"That's it. And believe me, it's not just us. Most young couples we know are in the same boat. Only the ones with rich parents can look forward to having a place of their own." The last was said with obvious bitterness.

Finally, they reached the part of the lot where their cars were parked. "Mine's down here," Mary said.

"And mine's this way, I think," Steph replied, motioning in the opposite direction.

"Okay, see you tomorrow then."

"Good night."

Again, Mary thought she heard the sound of someone else moving across the darkened parking area. Suddenly, an engine fired up, and the lights of a car came on. A brown pickup pulled out from between two other vehicles and headed for the street. In its lights, Mary caught a brief glimpse of Steph, who was still walking away from her; then the darkness once more swallowed her up. She saw no one else. Obviously, the person she'd heard was whoever just drove off in the pickup. One of the people who worked in the yard, she supposed.

Hurrying to her car, she fished the keys from her purse and began fumbling for the right one. In the dark, they all felt the same. Just as she found the door key and slipped it into the lock, she thought she heard a noise, a muffled groan. For a moment, she listened intently, hearing nothing but the sound of a diesel truck rumbling along on the nearby expressway. Finally, deciding she must have imagined the groan, Mary unlocked the door and slipped behind the wheel of her small Plymouth. A moment later, she was driving across the asphalt parking area, the Horizon's headlights cutting into the darkness.

Glancing into the rearview mirror, Mary realized there were no lights behind her. Where was Steph? At the lot's exit, she stopped and looked back the way she'd come. Still no sign of Steph. Mary sighed. She'd have to go back and check on her. If Steph was having car trouble, she might need a ride.

There were only about six cars in the employees' end of the lot. Mary passed a Datsun, a compact Chevy, a station wagon. Had Steph told her what kind of a car she drove? Mary couldn't recall. She was driving in the same direction Steph had been walking. Ahead was a yellow compact, which seemed to be the most likely car for Steph to have been heading for. Mary slowed . . . no Steph . . . and no more cars ahead of her. Had Steph driven off without using her headlights for some reason? No, Mary decided, that made no sense. And then she had the answer. If Steph's car wouldn't start, she would have gone back to the store to use the phone. Of course. Mary's help wasn't even needed.

But as soon as Mary turned the car around and drove past the yellow compact from the opposite direction, she knew she was wrong about Steph's not needing help. The red smears on the car's side looked like blood.

Trembling, Mary got out of her car and walked to the compact, stopping a few feet from it. Up close, the smears were undoubtedly blood. Leaning forward, she peered inside and gasped. Steph lay on the seat, unmoving, one arm dangling on the floor, her clothes covered with blood. Her blue eyes stared at the roof of the car, seeing nothing. Mary had never seen a body before, but she knew with absolute certainty that Steph was dead. Hearing a noise behind her, she spun around, momentarily blinding herself because she was looking directly into her own car's headlights. Then she realized the noise had come from her car. It was idling; something had made a clunk.

Oh, my God, she thought, the full realization hitting her. Steph isn't just dead. She's been killed. Murdered. Here in this spot. Just a few moments ago. Mary ran to her car, slammed and locked the door, then frantically drove toward the rectangle of light that was the entrance to Zel Home and Builders Supply.

Six

AND THAT'S THE LAST TIME YOU SAW HER," THE DETECtive asked, "when the pickup pulled away?"

"Yes," Mary replied weakly. She could still see Steph as the headlights momentarily picked her out of the darkness, walking away from her, toward the killer.

The detective wrote something in his notebook. He was tall, slender, about forty, with thick brown hair. His name was Sergeant Steven Flanagan.

They were standing fifteen feet or so from the yellow car in which Steph still lay on the front seat, a man from the medical examiner's office bending over her. Nearby, another detective was talking to Adkins and Bill Henning, one of the men from the yard. Uniformed officers were on hand to shoo away the curious.

"Would you describe the truck, please," Flanagan said.

"It was brown." Mary shivered. She felt cold, vulnerable. She wished Tom were here.

"Compact or full-sized?"

"Regular size." She knew she probably wasn't being much help, but she didn't know what to say. She just wanted to be home with Tom, where it was warm.

"Do you know what make it was?" Apparently aware of the state she was in, the detective was being patient, for which Mary was grateful.

"No," she said. "I don't know one kind of a truck from another. I'm sorry."

"Did it have a camper or anything like that?"

Mary shook her head.

"What about the driver?"

"I didn't see the driver. I don't even know whether it was a man or a woman." She hesitated, then added: "Whoever was in the truck couldn't have done it. I saw her as the truck pulled away. She was alive then."

"We realize that," he replied, a touch of impatience creeping into his voice. "But the driver of the pickup might have seen something. We have to find out who he is so we can talk to him."

The other detective joined them. He was thirty-five or so, blond, muscular. "None of the employees who worked late tonight ordinarily drive a pickup," he said.

"Crap," Flanagan muttered. "If it was a customer, we'll never find him."

"Could be one of the employees borrowed it or something."

Flanagan grunted. To Mary, he said, "Were there any customers that left just as you were closing up?"

Mary tried to make her brain function. It was less than an hour ago that Adkins had unlocked the door, letting her and Steph out of the building. It seemed months ago. Finally, she said, "I think the last customer was a man who bought a trap for a sink. He left just a minute before we did."

60

"What'd he look like?"

"Uh, seventy, gray hair, six feet tall, and he wore those coveralls that have those thin blue and white stripes. Mr. Adkins had to unlock the door to let him out, I think. He might have seen what kind of a car the man was driving."

The blond detective trotted over to where Adkins was standing, presumably to ask him about that. Flanagan said, "Did you wait on him?"

Mary nodded.

"Did he say anything that might help us figure out who he is or where he lives?"

"He just complained about how poorly things are made these days." She hesitated, trying to recall her encounter with the man. "I think that's all he said."

Joining Mary and Flanagan again, the blond detective said, "It could have been the old guy all right. According to the assistant manager, he left only thirty seconds or so before the victim did. Didn't see what kind of a car he left in, but he thinks the old guy headed in this direction."

"Maybe he paid with a check," Mary said, trying to be helpful.

The blond detective shook his head. "I already thought of that. Adkins says the guy paid cash. Says he was standing right there by the cash register when the old guy came through the checkout."

"Why are all the cars parked so far away from the building?" Flanagan asked Mary. After she'd explained the parking situation to him, he said, "But the old man wasn't an employee. He could park wherever he wanted to. So, if it was him, then why did he put his truck all the way over here when he could have parked it right by the building?"

The two policemen looked at each other, neither

apparently having an answer for that question. The medical examiner joined them. "Not much I can tell you you don't already know," he said.

"Stabbed numerous times with an ice pick," Flanagan said. "Time of death: within the hour. How'd I do?"

The medical examiner nodded. He was maybe forty-five, balding, on the lanky side. "I can't say it was an ice pick, but it was certainly something along those lines."

Flanagan sighed. "When can I get the autopsy results?"

"Tomorrow afternoon, I hope."

After the medical examiner had gone, Flanagan told Mary she should go home and get some sleep. She declined Adkins's offer of a ride home. She was stunned but not in such bad shape that she couldn't drive.

There had been no chance to phone Tom, who would be worried because she was so late. He'd be totally unprepared for the tearful wife who would grab him, cling to him, and cry until she'd let it all out.

As he had for most of his sixty-nine years, Arnie Miller rose about five-thirty. Going to the window, he parted the curtains and checked on the day. Although the sun wasn't quite up yet, he could see this particular day was going to be a beauty. The sky cloudless, not a trace of fog. Yes, sir, she was going to be a beaut.

Not one to hang around in his bed clothes, he slipped out of his striped pajamas, folded them and put them on the small table beside the bed, then donned his customary outfit: gray work pants, a red flannel shirt, and his striped coveralls. After the obligatory stop in the bathroom, he got the *Globe* from his doorstep and carried it into the kitchen, where he put the coffee on to perk. Sitting down at the breakfast table, he opened the paper.

He'd very nearly sold the house when Noreen had died a few years ago. Knowing he'd have to give up his vegetable garden was what had stopped him. The garden had been therapy, something he could do to help him forget, and he wasn't sure he could have survived that summer without it. The hurt was gone now, but not the emptiness, not the hole in his life, that place where Noreen should be and wasn't. Sure, he knew that one batch of people had to make way for the next, that no one stayed here forever, but the whole damned process could be so very hard on those who stayed behind. Well, when his time came, he'd go willingly. It would be good to be with Noreen again.

Having found nothing of interest on the front page, he pushed the paper away from him. He was glad he'd kept the house. The only reason he'd wanted to get rid of it was to get away from all the reminders of Noreen, and the place held so many of them. The ever-present hint of a familiar perfume, the glassware her mother had given her, the things she'd bought for the house. But he'd stayed; the house in which Noreen had died would be the house in which he'd die, whenever that time came.

It was a good house, small but comfortable, plainly furnished. Built more than forty years ago, it had three bedrooms, one bath, a kitchen that was too cramped. He and Noreen had been its only owners.

On the counter, the coffee pot abruptly stopped perking. Arnie Miller got a cup from the cabinet, filled it with coffee, and returned to the table. While he drank the hot liquid, his eyes returned to the newspaper.

Today, he planned to start getting the soil in condition for this year's vegetable garden, which meant spending several hours laboring with a digging fork. It wasn't drudgery; it was a labor of love. There was almost nothing he'd rather do than be in his backyard, working in his garden.

A retired railroad engineer, he was in excellent shape for a person pushing seventy. Although his skin had that transparent, fragile look that seemed to come with old age, his body was wiry, his hair gray but thick. He had no problem putting in a full day's labor.

His coffee cup half-empty, he was near the back of the first section of the paper when he spotted the small story. Woman slain in parking lot, the headline said. The victim, twenty-two-year-old Stephanie Flynn, had been stabbed after getting off work at Zel Home and Builders Supply, her body found in her car in the store's parking area. No one arrested. No indications of robbery or sexual assault. The incident occurred about nine last night, when the store closed. Frowning, he pushed the paper away from him and absently sipped his coffee.

He'd been there at closing time and when he'd started his pickup, he'd noticed a young woman. He'd also seen a man getting out of a beat-up blue car, a man who'd seemed startled by the truck's headlights. Could the woman have been the victim, the man her attacker? If there was any chance at all that he could help, he should call the police.

He tried to recall exactly what had happened last night. The trap under his kitchen sink had sprung a leak, and he'd gone to Zel—the closest place—to get another. Having always believed that parking away from other vehicles in a large lot—especially at night— amounted to an invitation to thieves and vandals, he'd left his pickup where there were other cars, even though the spot was quite a distance from the entrance to the store. Now that he thought about it, the entrance itself was a busy place with people coming and going, and had he parked there, his truck would probably have been even safer, not to mention saving himself that long walk through the dark parking lot. Well, he hadn't thought about that at the time. Besides, he was a creature of habit. After all, if you did things the same way every time, you saved yourself a lot of unnecessary thinking.

Inside the store, he'd been waited on by two young women, both pretty brunettes, one of whom had been the woman he'd seen as he was pulling away in his pickup. Could she have been the victim, Stephanie Flynn? And the man getting out of the old blue car, had he been the killer? Had he been watching the woman when the pickup's headlights startled him? Or was it just an old man's imagination?

After mulling things over for a few minutes, he decided against calling the police. He didn't really know whether he'd seen anything worth reporting, and he didn't want to make trouble for people who might not have been involved at all. Oh, hell, he thought, at your age, you can afford to be honest with yourself. The truth is that you don't want to get involved; you don't want to risk having your life disrupted.

He wasn't being selfish, not really. The stability and tranquility of one's life was important. You spent a lot of years working for it. When your wife was gone, when your kids had children of their own, and when so many of your friends were dead, what besides tranquility did you have to hang on to?

He did feel a little guilty about his decision, as if just maybe he *was* being selfish. Well, dammit, he told himself sternly, you have every right to be. This murder last night is not your concern. And if everyone felt that way? some part of him asked. Hell, he thought, everyone does. He finished his coffee.

Detective Lieutenant Daniel K. Larson sat at a stained and scarred wooden table in a small grubby room at the Lewiston police station. Seated to his left was Detective Grant. Across the table from Larson was the young man who'd just confessed to the murder of John Edwards.

"Why'd ya do it, Paul?" Larson asked.

"I told you already." He was twenty-one, thin, dark-haired, and hadn't shaved for a few days. Though obviously trying not to let it show, he was extremely tense; twice he'd started trembling, stopping himself only by drawing on his last reserves of willpower. He'd walked into the police station a little while ago, announcing that he'd killed Edwards, that he was surrendering voluntarily.

"Tell me again, Paul," Larson said firmly.

"Oh, come on, man. I've confessed; I've made it easy for you. Why do you want to hassle me?"

"Again," Larson ordered.

"Oh, come on," the young man whined, his brown eyes darting from Larson to Grant. "Will you please just lock me up. Please." Again, he got the shakes and, again, he managed to control them. His name was Paul Mitchell; Doris Mitchell, John Edwards's girl friend, was his sister.

"It's not that simple, pal," Grant said. "You're going to be with us for a while, you can count on that, but just how easy things go for you while you're here depends on how well you cooperate. And right now, you're not cooperating for shit."

Mitchell looked away, refused to meet Grant's eyes.

"The sooner you start being helpful," Larson added, "the sooner this part of the procedure will be over."

Mitchell sighed. "Yeah, okay, whatever you say. Like I said, I did it for my sister, for Doris."

"You mean she asked you to kill Edwards?" Larson asked.

"No, no, no." He shook his head savagely. "Because of the way he was treating her, not because she wanted me to do it. She didn't know anything about what I had in mind."

"Hey," Grant said sharply, "you expect us to believe that you killed a guy because he beat on your sister a couple of times? That makes no sense, buddy. Not murder. Not just for that."

Mitchell's face reddened. "It was more than just a couple of times. And my sister's important to me. Nobody goes around hurting her."

"Oh, come on," Grant said disgustedly. "She was a big girl. She stayed there from choice. If she got pounded on, it was her own fault."

"No!" Mitchell shouted, half rising out of his chair. "It was *his* fault. He was hurting her!" Larson had been ready to push him down, but he sank slowly back onto the wooden chair.

"Sounds like she deserved to get beat up if she stayed and put up with it," Grant said.

Mitchell stared at the table top, sulking.

"Did you ever speak to Edwards about this?" Larson asked.

Without looking up, Mitchell shook his head.

"So you never threatened him?"

"No," Mitchell muttered.

"You never warned him, told him to stop?"

The young man shook his head.

"Instead, you just went over there and killed him."

67

"Yeah, that's right."

"Horseshit," Grant said. "Do you really think we're dumb enough to swallow that?"

Mitchell looked up, meeting his eyes. "Yes, dammit!" he said angrily. "Because it's the truth. If Doris had moved out, he'd have come after her. And he sure as hell wouldn't have stopped hurting her just because I told him to." His eyes, still fixed on Grant, smoldered.

"Tell us how you did it," Larson said.

"I went over there that afternoon, knocked on the door, and after he let me in, I killed him."

"Where'd you get the butcher knife?"

"I—wha—?" He sat there, frowning.

"Well?" Larson asked. The first time Mitchell had told the story, he'd said that he stabbed Edwards but hadn't said with what. Larson had decided to suggest a weapon and see what would happen.

"What butcher knife?"

Larson pressed on. "He was killed with a butcher knife. If you don't know that, then you didn't kill him."

Looking worried and confused, Mitchell said nothing. He began to shake again.

"That business in the papers about something long and pointed like an ice pick was a bunch of crap . . . just so we could trip up anyone who wanted to make a false confession." He shrugged. "There's always a few nuts around."

Trembling more noticeably now, Mitchell sat there, his eyes fixed on the wall behind Larson. He spoke, but so softly that Larson couldn't hear him.

"What? Speak up."

"I used an ice pick, man."

"You couldn't have. He was killed with a butcher knife."

"I used an ice pick," he said flatly.

If he was bluffing, he obviously intended to stick with it, so Larson shifted gears. "Where'd you stab him?"

"The stomach, the chest, that area."

"Why'd you stab him so many times?"

"So many?" Mitchell replied, looking even more nervous now.

"Yeah, why so many? Two or three would have done it, one if you knew what you were doing."

"I . . ." He trailed off. Beads of perspiration appeared on his forehead.

"You what?" Larson demanded.

"I . . . I'm not sure how many times I stabbed him."

"The medical examiner counted the wounds. How many do you think he found?"

After a long moment of silence, during which Mitchell's mind was obviously working frantically, the young man said, "I think I only stabbed him twice."

Grant snorted. "Let's toss this guy out of here. M.E.'s report says the victim was stabbed seven times."

"Twice," Mitchell said flatly.

"Let me remind you again," Larson said, "that, although you're not at this time under arrest, you have admitted committing a very serious crime, and you may wish to have an attorney present while we talk to you."

"I don't want no lawyer."

The two detectives questioned Mitchell for another half hour, failing to trick the young man into saying anything that would indicate he was lying. Finally, Larson called in a stenographer and had Mitchell dictate a confession. After he'd signed it, Grant took him to be formally booked, then joined the lieutenant in his office.

"Well?" Grant said, taking a seat.

Frowning, Larson leaned back in his desk chair. "I

don't know. I really don't. He got all the facts right, but then that was all in the newspaper. It would certainly have helped if he could have produced the ice pick." Mitchell had claimed he'd tossed it in the river after the killing.

"Why would he fake it?"

"Oh hell, Grant, who knows why the crazies do what they do. If he's faking it, the shrinks would probably say he's doing it because of some damn sexual hang-up with his mother—or his father or cousin or someone."

"So, what do we do?"

"We talk to his sister first, then maybe to his mother, his employer, whoever knows him. After that, we'll probably have to get his booking photo and find out if anyone in Edwards's neighborhood saw him that day."

Grant nodded. If he had an opinion about Mitchell's confession, he obviously had no intention of offering it. For now, Larson had no choice but to take the confession seriously. Still, something about it didn't ring true, although he wasn't sure just what. On the other hand, Grant's question had been a good one. Why the hell would Mitchell fake it?

"Come on," Larson said as he stood up. "We're sure as hell not going to learn anything sitting here."

Seven

Her legs tucked beneath her, Mary sat on the easy chair in her living room, staring at the paperback book in her hands. Unable to concentrate, she let the plot of the romantic-suspense novel fade in and out of her consciousness, her mind refusing to let go of what had happened last night.

When she'd arrived home, she'd told Tom all about it, and then the tears had come. She'd cried because of the horror of it all, for poor Steph's husband and the others who'd loved her, for the friendship that almost was and now could never be. Later, thinking she was ready to begin putting the event behind her, she'd gone to bed, only to find she couldn't get the horrid images out of her mind: the blood smeared on the car's yellow paint; Steph lying on the seat, her blue eyes open but unseeing, her clothes covered with blood. In a nightmare that had jolted her awake, screaming, Mary had seen Steph's eyes move, focus on her. And then the arm that had been hanging over the edge of the seat began reaching . . . reaching for Mary.

She'd spent the night clinging tightly to Tom, who'd done his best to soothe her, make her feel warm and protected. She was afraid to think what the night might have been like without him. Finding Steph like that had been the most gruesome experience of her life.

Or . . . or was it? She had the feeling there had been other terrible events, back in that time she was unable to remember. Suddenly feeling woozy, she realized her thoughts were entering forbidden territory. Why, she asked herself miserably, why does this happen to me? Suddenly, the room seemed to be spinning, and Mary put down her book, closing her eyes until the whirling sensation stopped.

Her internal censor had stepped in and said: No, you may not think about this. And the censor always had its way.

Something's wrong with me, Mary thought. Very, very wrong. And I'm powerless to do anything about it.

And then she recalled an idea that had occurred to her previously. She could seek psychiatric help, hope a professional would know what to do. But then, seeing a therapist wasn't as simple as it sounded.

First, there was the question of whether she would be able to tell the doctor anything. What good would it do to sit in the psychiatrist's office and get sick or faint every time she tried to explain why she was there? And then there was the problem of doing something behind Tom's back. How could she tell him? He'd want to know what was wrong, to help, and unable to tell him the truth, she'd have to lie. And going for therapy behind his back was like cheating on him, not in the sense that the expression was ordinarily used but in terms of trust. And if you didn't have trust in a relationship, what was left? A tear trickled down her cheek.

Trying to push all this from her mind, she reached for her book, then stopped herself. If there was any chance at all that a psychiatrist could help, then she had to take that chance. Before she could change her mind, Mary picked up the phone book and looked at the names of the psychiatrists listed in the yellow pages. Because they were all unfamiliar to her, she picked one at random. Dr. Helen Carpenter.

Quickly, before she could lose her nerve, she grabbed the phone and dialed.

"Dr. Carpenter's office," a woman said.

"Uh, I'd like to make an appointment with Dr. Carpenter."

"Your name, please."

"Mary Taylor."

"Have you seen Dr. Carpenter before?"

"Uh, no. This would be my first time."

"Let's see, I have an opening—"

"It's an emergency. I have to see the doctor right away."

The woman was silent for a few moments; then she said, "I have a cancellation this afternoon at 1:30. Can you make it then?"

"Yes. I'll be there."

Mary hung up, uncertain whether she'd done the right thing. She'd committed herself not only to seeing Dr. Carpenter, but also to doing so behind Tom's back. How easy it is to betray someone who loves and trusts you, she thought unhappily.

At least she wouldn't have to lie to her employer. She'd call in and say she was going to be late because she had a doctor's appointment. There was no need to mention what kind of doctor. As she reached for the phone, it rang.

"Mary, it's me, Lynn."

"Hi," Mary said, trying to sound a lot more cheerful than she felt. "What's going on? You at work?"

"Yes, I'm on early lunch break today. Listen, there was a cop here this morning, asking about you."

"Asking what about me?"

"Everything. He's investigating the murder last night."

"You mean . . . you mean he thinks I killed her?" Mary was dumbfounded. How could she be a suspect?

"Wait," Lynn said, "don't jump to conclusions. I'm only telling you this because I thought you should know what's happening." Then, doing a pretty good Bogart imitation, she added, "It's okay, sweetheart. No need to go on the lam yet."

"What did he want to know?" Mary asked anxiously. She was grasping the receiver so tightly her hand was beginning to hurt.

"Well, you know, how long I'd known you, what kind of a person you are, stuff like that. Don't worry, if what I told them gets around, you'll be the next candidate for canonization."

"Did they talk to anyone else?"

"It wasn't a they; it was a he. Sergeant Flanagan. I saw him speaking to a bunch of people. But I was stuck behind the cash register, so I didn't get to mingle that much and I don't know exactly what he asked any of them."

"Did he act like . . . like he suspects me?"

"Hey, listen, I don't think it's anything to worry about. The only reason I phoned is because otherwise I'd probably have had to wait for my afternoon break to talk to you. When a cop asks questions about a friend of mine, I figure the friend has the right to know. It's as simple as that."

Uncertain what to say, Mary was silent. After a moment, Lynn went on. "Flanagan's just doing his job. That's what a detective does; he checks on people. You were here last night, so you gotta be checked on. No big deal."

"You're probably right," Mary said hesitantly. An investigator would be negligent, she supposed, if he failed to check out the person who discovered the body. Still . . .

"When we do get a chance to talk," Lynn said, "I want to hear all about it. After all, this is the stuff novels and movies are made of."

Yeah, Mary thought, and nightmares. "I will," she promised.

"I gotta go. If I spend my whole lunch break talking on the phone, I won't have time to eat."

"Okay, thanks for letting me know, Lynn."

After hanging up, Mary sat there, her indignation welling up; then she got up and began to pace. A sad, terrible thing had happened last night. But, Mary thought, *I* didn't do it, and yet there's a policeman asking all sorts of questions about me. Okay, sure, Flanagan's got a job to do. But, dammit, he could be discreet; he doesn't have to barge into the place I work and make it clear to everyone that I'm being investigated.

I did the best I could last night. I don't deserve this. I don't, by God, I don't!

Having worked up sufficient anger, she sat down again, grabbed the phone book, and flipped it open to the city government listings. A few moments later, she had Sergeant Flanagan on the line.

"I want to know," she said, "why you're investigating me."

"Who said I was?"

"You were at Zel this morning," she replied flatly. Was this the right way to handle the matter? Suddenly she was unsure.

Flanagan sighed. "I wouldn't go as far as to say we were investigating you, but yes, we are checking you out."

"You're playing with words."

"No, not really. So far, there are no prime suspects, people we'd really investigate thoroughly. In fact, at this point, we only know of two people who had the opportunity to kill her. The man in the pickup and you."

"But—"

"In your case, all it takes is a little checking to put you in the clear—which I'm sure you'd want. The man in the truck will be harder, I'm afraid. We still don't know who he is."

"But, he left before . . ." She trailed off. Nothing would have prevented the driver of the truck from killing the lights, coming back to kill the woman he'd spotted walking alone in the dark parking lot. Then another thought struck her. "Sergeant, I couldn't possibly have done it. I would have been all . . . all bloody."

"Not if you'd worn a raincoat, then got rid of it before we arrived. You could have even put it in the trunk of your car."

Mary was stunned. This was unfamiliar territory, and she was uncertain what to say. Surely Flanagan couldn't think she'd had a bloody raincoat in the trunk of her car last night . . . could he?

"Look, Mrs. Taylor, I don't think you did it, okay? But I do have to check you out. I'd be a pretty lousy detective if I didn't."

Mary ended the conversation, uncertain whether she'd done the right thing in calling the detective. How had she seemed to Flanagan—irate, frightened, guilty? Well, she decided, heading for the bedroom to get ready for work, what's done is done. At least I let him know that I'm aware of what he's been doing and that I don't like it.

She shouldn't have let it upset her. The detective *was* just doing his job. And she certainly had nothing to fear from him; she'd done nothing wrong. She'd likely never see him again.

Larson and Grant sat in the small conference room of a Lewiston radio station. Doris Mitchell, who worked in the station's traffic department, faced them across the table.

"He did w–what?" she asked, shocked.

"He confessed to murdering your boyfriend," Larson said.

Doris Mitchell simply stared at them. She had short dark hair, brown eyes, very light skin. Her black eye was disappearing nicely. Finally, she shook her head. "No, it doesn't make any sense. He couldn't have."

"He says he did," Grant stated.

"He's making it up for some reason."

"Why would he do that?" Grant asked.

She hesitated, letting her eyes wander around the conference room. It was paneled, had a brown carpet, subdued overhead lighting. "He just couldn't have done it. He's not violent. He's never been violent."

"There's always a first time," Grant said.

She fixed her eyes on him, looking bewildered, lost. "Not for him. He wanted to be tough, but he wasn't. He couldn't hurt anyone."

"How did he get along with Edwards?" Larson asked.

"They . . . well, they didn't get along very well."

"Why not?"

"Paul thought Johnny . . . well, that Johnny didn't treat me right."

The two policemen looked at her, saying nothing, and her hand automatically rose to test the sensitivity of the bruised flesh around her left eye. "That was just the one time," she said quickly. "Oh, sure, there were times when he'd get mad and slap me or when we'd yell at each other, but that was the only time he'd ever done anything like this, the only time he really hit me hard."

"Why'd he do it?" Larson asked.

"Why'd he hit me?"

Larson nodded.

"It really didn't make any sense. I said something to him, and he didn't answer, so I said his name—John. Then, all of a sudden, he was screaming that John wasn't his name, that I should call him Jack. Before I could say anything, he came at me with his fists."

"Your brother says it was more than just that one time," Grant said. "He says you told him all about it."

She sighed nervously. "Paul and me . . . well, we're close; we talk to each other, tell each other things we wouldn't tell anybody else. So, if Johnny slapped me around, I'd tell him about it . . . you know, so I could talk it over with someone. Paul would get pretty upset, but I'd tell him there wasn't much he could do about it, not to worry."

"I think he worried," Grant said.

She shook her head. "Paul would never have confronted Johnny. He just wasn't tough like that. I think that bothered him sometimes."

"He could have found a way to become tough," Larson said. "All he needed was surprise and a long, sharp object."

Again, she shook her head. "You're wrong. He would never have faced Johnny. And he couldn't kill anything."

"Then why'd he confess?" Larson asked.

Her eyes shifted from one policeman to the other; she looked helpless. "I don't know. Some screwy reason that only makes sense to him, I guess."

Larson studied her. Here was an attractive young woman, just a little overweight maybe, but that hint of plumpness gave her a little-girl look that many men would find appealing. And yet she chose to live with a bum who slapped her around. Why, he wondered, why did the Doris Mitchells of the world seem so resigned to taking their lumps?

"Kid's a wimp," Dave Mitchell said. He and Larson were in the basement of a building in which Mitchell was installing the ductwork for a new heating system. Paul Mitchell's father was a heavyset man with dark curly hair. Dressed in dirty coveralls, he had a smear of grease on his cheek.

"A wimp?" Larson said. While he was interviewing the suspect's father, Grant was at the Mitchell home, questioning the mother.

"Yeah. You know"—he glanced around as if making sure no women were present—"a pussy." The two men stood beside the stepladder on which Mitchell had been working when Larson arrived.

"Why do you say that, Mr. Mitchell?"

Mitchell mopped his brow with a handkerchief,

which he tucked into the rear pocket of his coveralls. Above him, the shiny new duct he'd been installing stretched off into the shadows of the basement.

"Because," he replied slowly, "that's what he is and that's what he's always been. A pussy. As a boy, he was always getting beat up by the other kids and never fighting back. Told him again and again: 'By God, Paul, you get out there and kick some ass, and they'll leave you alone.' Of course, he didn't. He just let them keep beating on him. Never went out for sports, never did anything."

"What did interest him? Did he like to read or what?"

Mitchell snorted. "Nothing interested him. He wasn't a bookworm or like that. He made lousy grades. When he grew up, he couldn't hold a job. Spent most of his time drawing unemployment."

"Who were his friends?"

"Didn't have any."

"Not even one?"

"The only person he'd have anything to do with was his sister."

A drop of water fell from somewhere above Larson's head, hitting his shoulder. He looked up but was unable to find its source.

"They were pretty close, I take it," the detective said.

"Best friends to each other all their lives, I guess. Never did fight like most brothers and sisters do."

"Do you think Paul would kill Edwards for that reason, for taking Doris from him?"

Mitchell's eyes met Larson's and held them. "If you'd asked me that yesterday, I'd have said hell no, the kid couldn't kill anyone for any reason."

"And now?"

"Shit, he confessed, didn't he?"

"You believe his confession?"

"Well, yeah, of course. Why would he confess if he didn't do it?"

"It's happened before, people confessing to crimes they didn't commit."

"Yeah, the real loonies. But even if Paul's a pussy and kinda strange, he's not a raving loony, and only a raving loony would do something as stupid as confessing to killing somebody when he didn't." As if to emphasize the point, he began climbing the stepladder; a moment later, he was back at work.

Larson watched him a moment, thinking: Yeah, isn't it nice how everything's either black or white and only the guilty or the hopelessly insane confess to crimes. Above him, Mitchell began banging on something. Larson turned and left.

"There were five men on the project," Vic Archer said. "The four others ganged up on Paul and pretty much made life miserable for him until I laid him off." Archer was the owner of the landscaping firm that had been Paul Mitchell's last employer. He and Larson sat in the firm's office. Through the window, the lieutenant could see rows and rows of potted evergreens. The office itself was spartan—an old wooden desk, bare walls except for a calendar advertising a local bank, the inexpensive plastic-and-metal-tubing chair in which Larson sat.

"What exactly did they do to him?" the detective asked.

Cocking his head, Archer wrinkled his brow. He was about forty, blond, blue-eyed, slender. "As I recall, they used to tease him by calling him a girl and a homosexual."

"Was he?"

Archer smiled. "I can state flatly that he was not a girl. As to his sexual inclinations, I have no firsthand knowledge."

"How about a gut feeling?"

"You mean a guess. It's not the sort of thing I care to speculate about, Lieutenant. Besides, it's none of my business."

"What did Mitchell do for you?"

"He was a laborer, temporary help. I had the contract for landscaping four new city parks and I needed some extra hands."

"Why did the other workers pick on him? Couldn't he hold up his end of the work load or what?"

"No, he wasn't physically weaker or anything like that. He was . . . well, psychologically weaker, I suppose." Suddenly Archer's eyes grew intense. "He was a victim of our male-chauvinist society, Lieutenant. Other men can't tolerate one of their own who's not macho. Paul Mitchell's nature made it impossible for him to be macho, and as a result, he was teased, ridiculed, put down."

Certain that more was coming, Larson said nothing, and after a moment, Archer continued. "He simply didn't know how to handle the situation, Lieutenant. He came on the job, pretending to be just as macho as the rest of them, but it didn't take them long to see through his act. There were too many times when he was silent. Like when the conversation turned to football or hunting or things like that. He told tall tales about the women he'd had, but they saw through those, too. You see, he got the facts wrong. His sexual exploits were transparent fabrications. And once they'd pegged him as a phony, they started making life miserable for him.

"For example, they never called him by name. It was always, 'Hey, little girl' or 'fairy' or 'queer' or whatever cruel thing struck their fancy. I'm sure his whole life was like that, Lieutenant. Probably even worse when he was a boy. Nobody can be as cruel as children. Nobody."

"You sound as if you have personal experience, Mr. Archer."

The landscaper studied Larson a moment, then said, "Yes, Lieutenant, I have."

"I'm going to ask you a very personal question, Mr. Archer, one you're under no obligation to answer, and I hope you won't take offense—"

"I know what you're going to ask, Lieutenant," Archer said, interrupting him, "and I don't mind answering. Yes, I'm a homosexual—of course, the men who made things so miserable for Mitchell had no idea their boss was gay." He smiled.

"And Mitchell, was he gay?"

"You're asking me to speculate again, Lieutenant."

"I'm only soliciting your opinion as an expert on the subject."

Archer laughed. "All right, Lieutenant. In my expert opinion, Paul Mitchell was not gay. He may well have been one of the oldest virgins I've ever met. But then, that's pure speculation."

"Thank you," the detective said, rising, "you've been a big help."

Archer, too, stood up. "May I ask you a question, Lieutenant?"

"Sure."

"What has Mitchell done?"

"He says he killed someone."

Archer's eyes filled with disbelief. "Mitchell?"

"Signed a confession and everything."

"He's a screwed-up young man, Lieutenant. A confession from him might not be worth much."

"I know."

Eight

MARY PULLED INTO THE SMALL PAVED LOT AND PARKED beneath a large budding shade tree. She loved this time of year. Spring was a rebirth, a new beginning. Is it possible that Dr. Carpenter can give me a rebirth, a new beginning? she wondered.

Let me be normal, she begged of whatever force was out there controlling her life. Let me be like everyone else.

And then she saw Steph's bloody body, and any hopes that the psychiatrist could help her seemed to evaporate. For Steph, spring had brought only horror, death.

After locking her car, Mary headed for the entrance to the one-story modern structure that was the McClellan Medical Office Building. The place was set well back from the street, surrounded by trees and grass. In the foyer, she found that Dr. Carpenter was in number fourteen, which turned out to be at the end of a long hall.

"I'm Mary Taylor," she told the receptionist. "I have an appointment with Dr. Carpenter for one-thirty."

"Let me tell the doctor you're here," the young woman replied cheerfully. She did so, then smiled and said, "We've got a few forms to fill out; then the doctor will see you."

The paperwork completed, Mary found herself in a tasteful, modern office done in blues and greens. The cool, relaxing colors were intentional, she supposed, considering the purpose of the room. To her left was the traditional couch.

"Please sit down, Mrs. Taylor," the doctor said, motioning to a comfortable-looking chair in front of her desk. Mary took the indicated seat, surprised at how stunning the psychiatrist was. She'd expected a gray-haired German-looking person in her sixties, not this slender woman with just enough gray in her hair to give her a beauty no younger woman could possibly enjoy.

"In my drawer here, where you can't see it, is a tape recorder," the psychiatrist said. "Unless you object, I'll record all our sessions."

"I don't mind," Mary replied meekly.

"Good. Now, why don't you tell me what's bothering you."

"I can't."

"You can't?"

Mary shook her head. "If I try, I'll get sick or have trouble breathing."

"Why do you think this happens?"

"I–I don't know."

"Are you ashamed of what's troubling you, ashamed to admit it?"

Mary considered that. "Well, I'd prefer no one knew

86

about it, but that's not the reason I can't tell you. I don't know what the reason is."

"All right then, let's leave that for a while. Tell me about yourself. Start with your very first memory."

Mary's mind reached back, looking for the earliest thing she could recall. She found a vague image of somewhere dark, frightening, a place of pain, hurt . . . and of a figure . . . someone, something. And then her stomach was churning, and the memory was gone; the door that had briefly opened now was tightly closed. She saw another image suddenly, a clear, precise recollection. Her stomach settled.

"I see a white house," Mary said happily. "The house where my foster parents live. It's . . . it's the first time I've seen it. It's where I'm going to live."

"How long did you stay there?" Dr. Carpenter asked, studying Mary's face.

"Until I grew up. They were the only parents I ever knew."

"Were you happy there?"

"Oh, yes. Very."

"Were you happy before?"

"Before?"

"Before you went to live in the white house."

"I . . ." Her abdominal juices were seething again; her head seemed to be swirling. "I don't remember much about that time."

"Tell me what you do remember."

I won't be sick, Mary told herself. I won't. "Uh, I . . . I, uh, don't remember anything specific. Just vague impressions."

"Tell me about the impressions."

"I . . . I can't."

"Try. Tell me as much as you can."

87

"No!" Mary exclaimed, rising. "I can't, dammit! I can't!" She was shaking.

Dr. Carpenter said something, but Mary was uncertain what. The psychiatrist's voice seemed to be coming from a long way off.

"It was an orphanage," Mary said, her own voice equally distant.

"And what impressions do you have of it?"

Trembling, holding down the contents of her stomach, Mary forced herself to speak. "Darkness . . . pain . . . afraid . . . so afraid." And then she felt the foul-tasting stomach juices in her throat. "The bathroom. I'm going to be sick."

"To your left, the door by the bookcase," the psychiatrist said, her voice barely audible over the hum in Mary's ears.

Mary turned, trying to see the bookcase, the bathroom door, and then the noise in her ears grew louder, and she knew what it was: static, like on the radio. And she wondered why such a sound should be in her head, just as everything went black and the noise stopped.

"Mrs. Taylor, wake up." The voice was familiar. It was a reassuring voice, one she had confidence in. And yet, some part of her clearly didn't want to obey that voice because here in the darkness it was safe.

"Wake up now, Mrs. Taylor."

No, no, that part of her said. You'll just get sick again. And other things. Worse things. But that part of her was getting weaker now, and Mary was obeying the voice. She opened her eyes, blinked, and found herself on the floor, with Dr. Carpenter bending over her.

The psychiatrist smiled. "How are you feeling?"

"A little weak, I guess. What happened?"

"You fainted."

"Did I throw up?"

Dr. Carpenter shook her head. "You said you were sick, and that you needed to get to the bathroom and then you stood up and collapsed."

"I thought I was going to be sick."

"There was never a physical reason for you to be sick, and when you fainted, there was no longer a psychological need. You could no longer say things your unconscious didn't want said."

Forcing her brain to function, Mary tried to assimilate the psychiatrist's words.

"Let me help you up," the doctor said. "That floor's carpeted, but it still doesn't look very comfortable." She assisted Mary to her feet, then led her to the couch. Mary stretched out on it. Though a little light-headed, she was in one piece.

"I wasn't going to do this," Mary said, touching the blue vinyl surface on which she lay, "even if you asked me to."

"You mean lie on the couch?"

"Yes. It's just too . . ." Unable to find the right words, she trailed off.

"I know," Dr. Carpenter said, sitting down in a chair beside the couch. "You'd be surprised how many people feel that way." She smiled.

Mary found the older woman's eyes and held them. "What's wrong with me, Doctor? Please tell me."

"I don't know yet. These things take time."

"You started to tell me something before. About why I felt sick."

"I said there was no physical reason for you to be sick. The nausea, your fainting just now, the difficulty breathing you mentioned, those things are just the means your mind uses to protect you from something buried in your unconscious."

"Like what?"

"Something so horrible that your conscious mind can't deal with it."

"You mean that . . . like I saw my mother murdered or something like that?"

"Yes. But let's not play guessing games. It will take a lot of time and work to find out just what's locked away in your unconscious."

Mary considered this. "So, it would have to be something that happened when I was a child at the orphanage . . . because I can't remember anything about that time."

The psychiatrist frowned. "That's certainly an avenue we want to explore, but again let me caution you about jumping to conclusions. There are too many things we don't know yet. For example, why are you unable to tell me about the problem that brought you here in the first place?"

"I don't know."

"Neither do I. It will take time to find the answer."

Mary nodded, disappointed. Had she expected to walk out of the psychiatrist's office cured, never again to be bothered by blank spells? She hadn't really thought about it, but she supposed she expected at least something to be different after the session, and now she knew that nothing would be.

"How long will it take?" she asked.

Dr. Carpenter shook her head. "I don't know. You have to understand that treatment can go on for years and that there's no guarantee it will ever be effective. You won't walk out the door next week sometime and find I've removed your problem, as a surgeon would remove your appendix. Do you understand that?"

Mary said nothing, stunned by the knowledge that, after finally working up the courage to seek help, she would have to come here again and again, maybe for years, her blank spells continuing unabated, her . . . her *self* spinning out of control. And her behavior during the blank spells, would it continue to become more hostile, more frightening? Dr. Carpenter was looking at her. Mary tried to speak, but no words came out.

"Do you understand?" the psychiatrist asked again.

"Yes," Mary replied weakly.

"Good. You have to know what you're getting into, but I'm not trying to convince you that I can't help you. It's quite possible that I can. Nor does it necessarily have to take years to achieve some positive results. I'm only telling you what can happen and that there are no guarantees." She paused, then said, "I can tell you this. It's my professional judgment that you did the right thing in seeking psychiatric help. Even though the results you want may seem quite distant, even unattainable, I strongly urge you to continue what you started by coming here today."

An unspoken footnote seemed to hang in the air: *It's the only chance you've got. Pass it up, and it's the booby hatch, babe. Straitjackets, padded walls, electric shocks.* And then she realized that this addendum to Dr. Carpenter's words had been entirely her own creation. On the psychiatrist's face, she saw honest concern, nothing more.

"I want you to treat me," Mary said.

"And you understand there are no guarantees?"

"Yes."

"Good. I think I'll have you come in again later this week. We'll see how that goes; then we'll decide how to schedule your future visits."

"All right." Mary felt better now. Even though the results weren't going to be instantaneous, at least she was doing something besides passively accepting the situation as inevitable.

"How are you feeling now? Do you think you can make it home all right?"

Mary sat up. "I'm fine."

Alone in her office, Dr. Helen Carpenter considered the young woman who'd just become her patient. Although it wasn't unusual for patients to be evasive about what was troubling them, Mary Taylor was the first in her experience to state flatly that she was unable to speak of her problem. And Dr. Carpenter believed her. Had Mary Taylor made a serious effort to explain why she'd come here, she most likely would have fainted, just as she did when trying to remember her life at an orphanage.

Leaning back in her desk chair, Helen Carpenter frowned. Although she had to be careful not to draw any conclusions based on a single session, a scenario did seem to present itself rather forcefully. Something had happened to Mary Taylor at that orphanage, something shattering. And something that was directly linked to her present problems, which would explain why Taylor had the same reaction when she tried to recall her days at the orphanage or speak of what was troubling her.

What happened to you, Mary Taylor? the psychiatrist wondered. What monsters are buried in your unconscious mind? Whatever they are, they are monsters you will have to face and conquer.

The intercom buzzed, and when Dr. Carpenter pressed the button, her receptionist said, "Your next appointment, Mr. Andrews, just phoned to say he's had a flat tire and he'll be late."

"Thank you, Susan."

Again leaning back in her chair, the psychiatrist let her mind wander. Forty-seven years old, she had been in private practice for about three years now. The first two of those years had been lean, very lean, but she'd finally built up a practice. Prior to striking out on her own, she'd been a hospital psychiatrist, which had paid the bills but had always seemed a professional dead end. So, when her daughter had completed college and almost immediately married, Helen Carpenter, free of that heavy financial drain, had quit the hospital, rented an office, and hung out her shingle. As with almost every challenge of her life, it had been a struggle, but she'd made it.

The first challenge had come when her husband had divorced her, leaving her with a baby to raise and her own college education to complete. The child support payments hadn't come, not more than two or three of them, and Helen had worked two part-time jobs, studied a lot, and slept very little. But she'd made it through medical school and still more years of training in psychiatry. She'd overcome the problems of a woman in a male-dominated profession. And now she'd made it again, in private practice.

Single since her divorce, she had been going out with men since her daughter left for college seven years ago. For the past eighteen months, she'd been seeing quite a lot of a widowed lawyer named Jason. Although at times the relationship showed signs of getting serious, it never did. Perhaps all that was missing was for either Jason or her to give things a gentle shove. She wondered whether each of them was waiting for the other to do so.

Picking up the folder her receptionist had brought in before admitting Mary Taylor, Dr. Carpenter noted that her new patient was married, had no children, and had indicated her intention to pay in cash after each visit. Apparently, she didn't want her husband to know she was seeing a psychiatrist. If Taylor continued as her patient, the husband would probably find out. Eventually. Spouses almost always did.

She closed the folder.

Late that night in the quiet Boston suburbs, nine-year-old Gail Fenton stood at the window of her second-story bedroom, staring down into the shadows in her backyard. Around the neighborhood, all the houses were dark, including the Taylors' next door. Directly beneath her was the new swing. Red and bright yellow by daylight, it was gray now, a dim shape among the shadows.

Glancing over her shoulder, she saw no movement in Penny's bed. Unlike Gail, who liked to steal out of bed at night and spy on the sleeping neighborhood, her five-year-old sister was a sound sleeper. Nothing, Gail decided, not even a monster climbing into bed with her, could awaken Penny.

Gail was the oldest of the four Fenton children. She and her sister shared one room, their two brothers another. When she peered out at the night like this, Gail liked to pretend she lived in one of the dark houses, sometimes as a person who really dwelled there and sometimes as herself, grown-up. Staring at the McGraws' place, she imagined that she was getting up from bed there and going downstairs to start breakfast for her husband Bart, one of three make-believe spouses. The other two were Ed and Fred. All three loved her madly.

Bart was the best though. So strong, handsome, yet so tender, someone she could never dominate the way she did Fred, who let her make all the decisions. Well, she dominated Bart a little, but that was only because he worshipped her. With Fred, she simply bossed him around.

Sighing, she wondered whether the rather ordinary brown-haired girl she saw in the mirror could ever really grow up to have a man worship her like the imaginary Bart. Lightly freckled with a wide gap between her two front teeth, she could see herself as cute. Beautiful, on the other hand, was doubtful. And Bart was tall, muscular, dark-haired; he looked a whole lot like Superman in the movies.

The image of herself cooking Bart's breakfast in the McGraws' house faded away, and she placed herself in the Taylors' house as Mary Taylor. Again, she began to cook breakfast in the kitchen—bacon and eggs. Soon Fred—no, Bart—soon Bart would come in, hug her, kiss her, tell her how hungry he was, what a wonderful cook he had married. Immediately, she switched from being Mary Taylor to being her grown-up self. Bart was too good to share with Mary Taylor, and Mary's husband Tom wasn't the sort of mate Gail wanted. He was just too . . . ordinary. Like her father. Her pop was a good daddy, but who'd want to be married to him? Besides Mom, of course. He was just right for Mom.

Bart comes into the kitchen just as she's removing the bacon from the frying pan. He looks sad.

"What's wrong, my love?" Gail asks.

"I've been trying to find some way to tell you, but I haven't had the courage," he replies, looking away.

She goes to him. "There's nothing you can't tell me, my darling. You know that."

Bart sighs. "I've been fired. I've lost my job. Now we'll lose the house—everything."

"No, we won't!" Gail says, throwing her arms

around him, comforting him. "I'll get a job and support us. I'll go out and get one today!"

"Oh, darling! Would you?"

"Of course. It's the least I can do."

"Oh, my loving darling! What would I do without you?"

Suddenly, the scene in Mary Taylor's kitchen vanished. Below her in the shadows, something had moved. Peering into the darkness, Gail saw a black shape doing something by the swing. Her heart pounding, Gail tried to decide what to do. Should she tell Mom and Dad there was a prowler in the yard? If she did, they'd know she'd been up, looking out the window when she should have been in bed asleep. Well, she could always say she'd got up to go to the bathroom, that was no problem.

But should she wake up her parents at all? They might get mad if she did. After all, the prowler wasn't doing anything except crouching by the swings. There wasn't much harm in that. There probably wasn't even a law against crouching by swings. Uncertain how to handle the situation, Gail simply remained at the window, watching.

After a few moments, the shape began to blend into the blackness below, and Gail began wondering whether she had imagined the whole thing. Then she saw it again, slipping over the low fence separating their yard from the Taylors'. And then, plainly, very plainly, Gail saw the silhouette of someone entering the Taylors' house.

On the verge of panic, she was ready to run into her parents' room, screaming that someone had just broken into the Taylors' place, but then she realized the figure had simply opened the door and gone inside. It hadn't actually *sneaked* inside the way a robber would.

Gail was still puzzling this out when the light came on in the Taylors' kitchen. Suddenly, Mary Taylor, fully dressed, stood at the window, looking up at her. Gail slipped back into the shadows.

Did she see me? Gail wondered. Did she?

But what difference would that make? So what if Mrs. Taylor got up in the middle of the night and came over to look at the new swing? *I* can't sleep, Gail reminded herself, so, why should Mrs. Taylor be any different? Sure. She couldn't sleep, so she got up and came over to admire the new swing when she thought nobody was looking. We should have invited her over to see it. Will Mommy be mad because we didn't?

And yet there was something about that explanation, something that wasn't right. Well, Gail decided, yawning, it doesn't matter. Mrs. Taylor's not a bad person. With that thought, she slipped quietly across the room and climbed noiselessly into bed. Penny, as usual, was sound asleep, lost in her dreams, unaware of Gail's movements.

Nine

LIEUTENANT DANIEL K. LARSON LOOKED UP AS GRANT stepped into the office.

"Morning, Lieutenant," the detective said, sitting down.

Larson grunted.

Although he and Grant worked well together, they were entirely different in most respects. Handsome and athletic-looking, Grant was a confirmed bachelor whose only interests in life seemed to be his job and women. He drove a sleek, racy-looking car that cost a small fortune and got terrible mileage. Larson, on the other hand, had always had wife, family, the home mortgage, and he drove a compact that got thirty-six miles a gallon. Heavyset, he had never looked—or been—athletic.

"Well," Larson said, "what are we going to do about Mitchell?"

Grant shrugged. "We've got no hard evidence that would either prove or disprove his confession." A search of Mitchell's cubbyhole apartment had turned up nothing that would connect him to the murder. No one had seen him in Edwards's neighborhood the day of the killing. But then, no one could alibi him as having been elsewhere either.

"We do have his confession. But is it real? Did Mitchell do it?"

Grant held out his hand, rocked it from side to side. "His mother says he considers himself a failure, a guy who can't do anything right. Maybe this is his way of proving that he can do something after all."

"By really doing it, or by confessing to someone else's crime?"

"For him, it's the same either way, isn't it?"

Larson grunted. Grant was right; if Mitchell's aim was to get rid of his wimp status, then whether he actually killed Edwards was unimportant. All that mattered was that the world believed he had done so. He would have acquired the status of being a killer. That the real murderer might go free would probably mean very little to anyone as screwed up as this young man. Nor would the prospect of going to prison deter him, not if he was sufficiently unbalanced.

"Did I tell you that he tried to join the marines?" Grant asked.

"No." But it fit. A guy like Mitchell would try to sign up with the tough guys; hope doing so would make him seem rough.

"The corps rejected him. Psychological reasons."

"Figures." Sighing, Larson rubbed his forehead. Mitchell had refused to see anyone from the public defender's office; there seemed little chance he'd agree to see a shrink.

"Any chance the DA would take the case with just the confession?"

"Hell, no. If Mitchell suddenly rescinds it, decides to claim it was made under duress or something, then we've got nothing. You don't go to trial on a murder rap without some hard evidence."

"I imagine Mitchell would plead guilty."

"Probably, but a sharp lawyer could come along and say he wasn't competent to make the plea, which he probably isn't."

"So, what do we do?" Grant asked.

"I'm going to release him. I don't have the evidence to go ahead with a case against him, so there's nothing else I can do."

Grant nodded.

Arnie Miller pushed the digging fork into the dark earth, then lifted it, turning and crumbling the rich soil. It was another in a series of warm, sunny days, and the earth had dried just enough so that it was in perfect condition to be worked.

Pulling a handkerchief from the rear pocket of his striped coveralls, he removed his railroad engineer's cap and mopped his brow. Then, leaning on the fork, he surveyed his backyard. The garden took up most of it, expanding as it had over the years until the only grass that hadn't been turned under was a small patch by the back door. He already had his plan for this year; he knew where he'd put the broccoli, the lettuce, the peppers. He gave most of it away, of course, but that was part of the pleasure the garden gave him.

As he resumed working, his thoughts turned to a matter he'd been trying to avoid thinking about. The brief story in section two of this morning's *Globe* had been headlined: NO LEADS IN PARKING LOT SLAYING. He'd opened the paper, hoping to read that someone had been arrested in the case—or at least that

the investigation was making progress. Then he'd have
been off the hook, his silence concerning the man in the
blue car of no importance. But now he had to ask
himself whether a murderer was still free because of
him. And that question led to others. Would the killer
attack again? Would more people die because of a
selfish old man's determination to remain uninvolved?
What price would he put on his desire to be left in
peace? How many lives?

Ashamed and disgusted with himself, he kicked a
small rock he'd unearthed earlier. It sailed about ten
feet, coming to an abrupt stop when it landed in the
soft freshly turned earth. He gazed at the motionless
stone a moment, then headed for the back door. A
moment later, he was standing before the wall phone in
the kitchen.

But he didn't lift the receiver. Staring at the instrument, he began to rationalize that he didn't really have
that much to tell the authorities. He certainly had no
proof that the man in the blue car was the killer. And
he had no license number or anything that would
enable the police to identify the man. So, what good
was information like that? Not much, he decided.
Certainly not significant enough to justify involving
himself in a police investigation.

Back in the garden, he stood beside the digging fork,
which he'd left sticking in the ground, and wondered
whether he'd done the right thing. Finally, he grabbed
the fork and went back to work. Can't stand here all
day worrying, he told himself. Got too much to do to
waste my time like that.

Stretched out on her living room couch, Mary was
passing the morning by reading. She was on her third
consecutive romance; soon she was going to have to

read something serious or she would forget what good literature was all about. The trouble was that she was in no mood for serious reading. Because of the recent events in her life, she needed escape reading, something that took her away into a fantasy world, made it easy to forget the real one.

Mary was uncertain what she thought about yesterday's session with Dr. Carpenter. She wasn't convinced the psychiatrist could help her, but at least she was trying to help herself now, which had to be an important step in the right direction. She'd made a commitment; she would continue seeing the psychiatrist as long as doing so represented any hope at all . . . or until the censor made her stop.

As she'd left the psychiatrist's office the day before, she'd made another appointment for two days from then. Although she was paying cash for each visit, Mary was worried that Tom would find out. No bills would come, and no checks paid to a psychiatrist would turn up with the monthly bank statement, but psychiatrists were expensive; the disappearance of that much money wouldn't go unnoticed indefinitely. I feel like an embezzler, she thought.

The session having been interrupted by her fainting, Mary had never mentioned her discovery of Steph's body. It was unrelated to her main problem, she supposed, but it certainly had an effect on her, and it was something the doctor should know. She made a mental note to mention it to Dr. Carpenter during her next visit.

Work had not gone that badly after her appointment, all things considered. Although she was asked about the murder, no one had mentioned that the police had been checking her out, and no one had treated her like a murder suspect. Of course, how *did* one treat a

102

murder suspect? You couldn't be too obvious; you wouldn't want to antagonize a crazed killer. Oh, stop it, she told herself. Nobody thinks the police consider you a serious suspect. Flanagan was just doing his job; everyone knows that.

Mary was glad she hadn't been presented with another trainee, Steph's replacement. The day after Steph's murder, it would have been in poor taste. Eventually, there would have to be a replacement, she supposed. Mary hoped the new person would be assigned to someone else.

"Why don't you go higher, scaredy-cat!"

"I'm not a scaredy-cat!"

"You are too!"

"At least I'm not a sissy like you!"

The swing next door was already in use this morning, the children sufficiently raucous to make it difficult for Mary to read. Their voices were simply too shrill to tune out, and they had a tendency to communicate entirely by screaming. Turning the page, Mary tried to concentrate.

"Scaredy-cat, scaredy-cat, scaredy-cat!" The voice was singsong.

"I know a sissy." The response was also singsong, in that chant peculiar to children teasing one another, Mary sighed.

Suddenly, there was a loud crash, as if someone had just dropped a load of junk outside the house, and the children were screaming louder than ever. Putting down her book, Mary went to the window to see what had happened. She pulled the curtain back just in time to see Mrs. Fenton come running out of the house. Two children lay on the ground while the others stood back, looking helpless, confused. Lying beside the two boys were a number of red and yellow pipes. All at once,

Mary realized what had happened. The swing had collapsed. She ran out the back door, stopping at the fence separating her property from the Fentons'.

"Can I help?" she asked. "Is there anything I can do?" But no one seemed to have heard. Mrs. Fenton, a small woman with reddish-brown hair, was tending to the two downed boys. One, a blond youngster, was whimpering; the other, a dark-haired child, was bellowing. The dark-haired one was Billy Fenton. Mary was unable to identify the blond boy.

"Can I help?" Mary asked again, louder this time.

Mrs. Fenton looked up, but before she could speak, her youngest daughter, Penny, ran up, tugging at her mother's arm, saying something with great urgency. Mary caught the phrases "Gail said" and "last night." Mrs. Fenton, who was bending over her still-bawling son, gave Mary a peculiar look. Abruptly, she scooped the boy up in her arms and ran inside with him.

Mary watched, confused, as the woman returned a moment later and helped the other boy to his feet. He seemed unhurt. Taking him by the hand, she ordered the other children to go home, then quickly steered the blond boy and her daughter into the house, without speaking to Mary or even glancing in her direction.

Thoroughly bewildered, Mary returned to her living room. Hearing a screech of tires, she hurried to the front window and peered out. The Fentons' station wagon was disappearing down the street. Was Mrs. Fenton taking Billy to the hospital? Was he hurt that badly? When she returns, Mary decided, I'll have to go next door and find out how Billy is.

Mary turned from the window, still disturbed about the events of the past few minutes. Why had Edna Fenton looked at her that way? There had been something almost accusatory in her eyes. Returning to the couch, Mary sat down and picked up her book, forcing herself to concentrate on it.

An hour later, Mary's reading was interrupted by the doorbell. Laying her book aside, she got up from the couch, hoping it would be Edna Fenton stopping by to tell her everything was all right. Instead, she opened the door to find herself face-to-face with Sergeant Flanagan, with whom she'd hoped to have no further dealings.

"May I come in, Mrs. Taylor?" he said through the locked glass storm door.

She unlocked it and let him in. In the living room, she returned to her place on the couch. The detective sat down in the easy chair, facing her.

"Have you caught the person who killed Steph?" she asked, hoping that's why he was here, to tell her the murderer was behind bars, unable to hurt anyone else.

The detective shook his head. "No, the murder investigation isn't going to get wrapped up quite that quickly, I'm afraid. I'm here because of what happened next door."

Mary was confused. "Next door? What are you talking about?"

"There was an accident. The swing." Although his dispassionate expression revealed nothing, his eyes studied her intently.

What's going on here? Mary wondered. Why is a detective sergeant investigating the collapse of a child's swing? Billy Fenton got banged up pretty good, but his injuries were hardly fatal. Why isn't this guy out there trying to catch Steph's killer instead of concerning himself with a broken swing?

"Normally," Flanagan said, "a uniformed patrolman would handle something like this. The matter was brought to my attention because you're involved in a case I'm working, and I decided to handle it personally."

Mary still had no idea what was happening. Because Flanagan seemed to be waiting for her to speak, she said, "How's the Fenton boy?"

"Broken leg. His mother took him to the hospital, where he's being patched up. He'll be in a cast for a while, but he'll be fine."

"That's good—I mean that he'll be fine, not that he broke his leg."

Flanagan regarded her silently for a moment; then he said, "Mrs. Fenton doesn't think it was an accident."

"What do you mean?" Mary asked, still uncertain where this was all leading.

"She had reason to believe the swing had been tampered with."

"Was it? Did you check?"

"Yes, just a few moments ago. And it had been tampered with."

"Oh," Mary said, feeling herself begin to relax. Flanagan probably only wanted to know whether she'd seen anyone fooling around with the swing. How terrible, she thought, that someone would purposely do something that would result in a little boy's leg getting broken.

"Would you mind telling me what you were doing last night around midnight?"

"What?" she asked, rattled. The question had been totally unexpected.

"What were you doing at midnight last night?"

"Why? Why do you want to know?"

"I'm investigating what happened at the Fentons' today."

106

"But . . . but what does that have to do with me?"

Flanagan frowned. "It's a simple question. Why are you so reluctant to answer it? You don't have anything to hide, do you?"

"Anything to hide! Sergeant, last night I went to bed about ten-thirty and stayed there until I got up this morning."

"Can anyone verify that?"

"My husband can."

"Is he a sound sleeper? Would he know if you got up after he'd fallen asleep?"

"You'll have to ask him." She didn't understand this; she didn't understand at all. "Sergeant," she said as firmly as she could, "unless you tell me what this is all about, I'm not answering any more questions."

"All right." He fixed his eyes on hers. "You were seen last night doing something to the swing."

"I . . . I was what?"

"You were seen. In the Fentons' yard. By the swing."

"But . . ." And then she recalled the scene right after the swing had collapsed, little Penny Fenton tugging at her mother's arm, saying something about last night. But that was impossible. She hadn't got up from bed, gone next door. And then a dizziness swept over her, the result of a jolting realization. She tried not to react outwardly because Flanagan was staring at her.

She couldn't say with certainty that she hadn't gotten up last night, gone over to the Fentons'. She did things she was unable to recall having done. She had blank spells. During her last one, she had attacked a woman at a public swimming pool.

The children had bothered her with their screaming. She hadn't liked having the swing there, so close to her

107

house. Had those feelings motivated her during a blank spell? Had she slipped out of bed last night, gone next door, deliberately sabotaged the swing? Was *she* the terrible person who caused a little boy to break his leg? Oh, God, she thought. Oh, please, don't let it be me. Please.

Flanagan was still watching her, and suddenly she knew what he was thinking: that there was something peculiar about a person who would sabotage a kid's swing, that such an individual just might be the sort to stab a woman to death for no apparent reason, the motive buried in the twisted workings of a sick mind.

And, for a moment, she wondered whether it was possible, whether she could have killed Steph. And then, filled with relief, she realized that she couldn't have. Her blank spells were just that: blank, episodes of which she could recall absolutely nothing. And she remembered the night Steph died quite well. There were no blank spots, dammit! There weren't.

Flanagan still gazed at her, his expression neutral, his eyes accusing.

"Get out," she said. "I have nothing further to say to you unless I'm being arrested."

"It would be better for all concerned if you cooperated with us, Mrs. Taylor."

"Am I under arrest?"

He sighed. "No, you're not, but if you can help us clear this thing up, I think you should."

"I'm not saying anything else until I've had a chance to consult with my husband and a lawyer."

He stood. "As you wish, Mrs. Taylor. If you should change your mind, you know where to reach me. I'll show myself out."

She heard the front door close, and for the next several moments, she remained on the couch, staring at the carpet. She should get up, make sure the door was locked, call Tom—especially call Tom. But then she couldn't tell him the whole story; she couldn't tell him that she had blank spells, that she really might have tampered with the Fenton kids' swing.

Suddenly, Mary found herself grappling with a new horror that had crawled unbidden into her consciousness. The time required to kill Steph would have been so minimal that the missing minutes of such a short blank spell could go unnoticed. If she'd blanked out just long enough to kill Steph, reawakened in the same parking lot, unaware of what she'd done. . . .

Was there a blood-soaked raincoat in the trunk of her car—or some other garment she had used to keep herself from getting bloody? No, no, no, she thought. No, there can't be. I never put anything like that there. Still, before she called Tom, she would have to see what was in the trunk of her car. Just to be sure.

Tears rolled down her cheeks. She was shaking uncontrollably.

Through the grimy window in the detached garage, Paul Mitchell watched his parents' house, waiting for his mother to come out and drive off in her red Chevy, which was parked in the street. He knew she would because she always did. Bored after a morning of cleaning and daytime TV, she had to get out of the house. She'd window shop, visit friends, sometimes take in a movie. It was 1:10; she should emerge from the house at any moment.

Leaving the window, he began to pace the cement

floor, avoiding the center, where years of dripped oil and grease had accumulated. This was where his father's new four-wheel-drive pickup spent its nights. Because it was only a one-car garage, his mother's Chevy stayed in the street.

Everything here was dusty, cobweb covered. No one ever cleaned the place. It was filled with old garden hoses, tires, broken tools.

At first, when the police had let him go, he'd been furious. Walking aimlessly, he'd wanted to grab a stop sign and pull it down, break a window, anything to vent his wrath. They hadn't believed him, hadn't thought a weakling like him could really kill anyone. They'd probably laughed, described him with words like "candy ass" or "pussy"—the same terms his father used. And being disbelieved by the cops would make things even tougher. Anyone crazy enough to confess to a crime he didn't commit would be viewed as below a candy ass, even more pathetic than a pussy. And scarce, so very scarce were things like sympathy or understanding or kindness.

It was always the same: *Get out there and kick ass; don't be a crybaby, a wimp.* They all knew he couldn't do that and they all laughed behind his back. Except his sister. Doris understood. But he'd never done anything for her. He'd never been able to stand up for her, protect her, and the one time he'd tried to make it seem like he had, he'd failed miserably.

He'd walked, angry, frustrated, hurt. And then his rage had died, replaced by a sad, hollow, lonely feeling. He'd felt so terrible that he considered suicide. He'd thought about it before, but this time he'd decided to actually do it. He'd planned to come here, wait as he was doing now, then get one of his father's hunting rifles, put the barrel in his mouth. . . .

It was only after he let himself in through the side door of the garage and began watching the house that a much better idea had come to him, a way he could prove he *was* capable of doing something, and that he wasn't the candy ass the cops and his father thought he was. He'd show them all. The men on the landscaping crew who'd taunted him, called him queer. Bobby Knute, the bully who used to beat him up after school. All of them.

Hearing a car door slam, then an engine start, he hurried to the window. He couldn't see his mother's car from here. If it was she, the red Chevy would appear to the left of the house. And there it was, his mother behind the wheel. She was in her forties, heavyset, brown hair. She had always been a neutral part of Paul's life, neither ridiculing him nor protecting him from those who did. Live and let live was her philosophy. Even when life for her son was sheer hell.

Dismissing his mother from his thoughts, he stepped from the garage, closed the door behind him, and headed for the house. A narrow two-story structure, the white frame home in which he'd grown up was still in fairly good shape. The neighborhood was slowly deteriorating—lawns with a few more weeds each year, paint that was starting to flake here and there—but it was still middle-class, nice for the most part and likely would be for a few years yet.

At the back door, he fished his keys from his pocket, found the right one, and inserted it into the lock. A moment later, he was at the closet in his parents' bedroom, pulling down a long wooden case from the shelf. He put it on the bedspread, which like most things in the house was flowered. His mother, the decorator, had picked out furnishings in a variety of styles, blossoms being the one thing they had in common.

Inside the case were two hunting rifles, cleaning equipment, ammunition. He closed and latched it, picked it up, and headed for the door. He hoped Doris would understand.

Ten

OH, THANK GOD YOU'RE HERE," MARY SAID, THROWING her arms around her husband as he stepped through the front door. After she'd phoned him, told him about Sergeant Flanagan's visit, Tom had said he'd be right home.

She clung to him a moment, drawing strength from him; then he pushed her back, holding her at arm's length, his eyes on hers. The concern on his face made him seem older than thirty-two, as if, sometime after leaving for work this morning, he'd suddenly and unexpectedly slipped into middle age.

"Do you have any idea who's supposed to have seen you in the Fentons' yard last night?"

"Flanagan didn't say, but I think it was Gail." She told him what she'd overheard Penny Fenton say to her mother.

"A child? You mean that cop had the nerve to come over here and accuse my wife on the basis of what a little girl saw in the middle of the night?"

113

"I can't be sure, Tom. That's how it looks."

He frowned, obviously angered.

"Tom . . ." Her words trailed off. Oh, how do I ask this? she wondered. How?

"What, honey?"

"Last night, did I . . . did I get out of bed as far as you know?"

Giving her a peculiar look, he said, "No, of course not. Why?"

"Well, I thought just maybe I'd gone sleepwalking or something, ended up outside. . . ." She shrugged.

"But you've never done that before."

"I don't think so," she said, suppressing a shudder. It was true; she wasn't a sleepwalker—but something far worse. If only I could tell him, she thought. If only I could.

"Could I have left the bed without your knowing it?" she asked, desperately hoping he'd say no.

He hesitated, frowning. "Well, yeah, I suppose so . . . but I don't think you did."

"But," she replied, trying to hide her disappointment, "what you think won't impress Flanagan at all. If you can't say for sure that I never left the bed. . . ." Again, she shrugged.

Muttering something incomprehensible, he shook his head. Once more, she slipped her arms around him, holding him tightly. No one, not even Tom, could save her from herself. Mary realized she was sobbing. Tom stroked her hair.

After she'd had a good cry, her husband gently pushed her away from him. "I'm going to get to the bottom of this," he said. "I'm going next door and find out just what they've been telling the police. If we're being harassed on the basis of some story told by a child, I'm going to be very upset."

114

And then, still standing by the front door, Mary was alone. She hoped Tom wouldn't make a scene, which would do no good at all. He won't, she told herself; he'll be calm, rational; he'll try to get to the bottom of all this.

Moving into the living room, she lowered herself onto the couch. Of course, Tom would be unable to get to the bottom of things. How could he when he didn't know all the facts? For instance, he didn't know about his defective wife, who had blank spells, who attacked strangers at swimming pools, who . . . who might even be a killer.

Before calling Tom, she'd checked the trunk of her car, but hadn't found a bloody raincoat or anything else that would indicate she had stabbed Steph. And then she'd realized that, had there been such evidence, she could have removed it during a blank spell. She knew the case for her being Steph's murderer was a weak one; too many things would have to have happened during very brief and perfectly timed blank spells. And yet there was no way she could prove to herself that she was innocent. Through logic, she could render her culpability improbable but not impossible. And even the remotest possibility that she had slain Steph was nearly unbearable.

And now, she had apparently sabotaged the swing, an act that resulted in a child's leg being broken. The evidence wasn't as conclusive as waking up in a swimming pool, your victim pointing an accusing finger at you, but there seemed little doubt that she had done it. Tom was unable to say that she couldn't have left the bed last night, and why would the Fenton girl lie? None of those kids had anything against her.

Why, she demanded, why did I do something that would injure an innocent child? She had no answer; she almost never had one when the question concerned her blank spells. They just occurred, taking her where they would, causing her to do what they would. And suddenly they were changing. No longer the frightening but basically harmless episodes such as buying a skimpy bathing suit, the blank spells were becoming more sinister. Her behavior during them was becoming hostile, violent, dangerous. She had attacked a woman, broken a child's leg, and, just maybe, though the possibility seemed remote, just maybe she had murdered someone.

Please, God, she thought. Please let it be someone else. I couldn't live if I found out I was the one who killed Steph.

And why, why had she done those things? Her only clue was her irritation over the noise the children had made when they used the swing. Oh, God, what was she, a monster—ready to attack, destroy, injure simply because of some noise that occasionally interfered with her reading? No, no, she told herself; to do such a thing simply isn't me. It isn't. I'm not a monster; I'm not.

And she really didn't know for sure that she'd been in the Fentons' yard last night. Children had active imaginations; they were vindictive for reasons adults didn't understand. No, there was no proof, not really.

And the woman in the pool?

I don't know, she thought. I just don't know. The woman could have attacked me, for all I know. Maybe I was just defending myself.

And maybe the sky's green with pink polka dots, too.

No, there was too much evidence pointing to her blank spells becoming more frequent, her behavior during them more violent. And there was nothing she could do about it. She couldn't even seek help. If she tried, she'd choke on the words, reveal nothing.

Then she recalled that she was seeing Dr. Carpenter tomorrow. I hope she can help me, Mary thought. Please let her be able to help me. Please.

She felt the tears start to come in earnest, but then Tom was there, looking very displeased, and she choked them back.

"What's wrong?" she asked.

"Mrs. Fenton. She wouldn't even open the door to me. She said we were trying to kill her children and she wouldn't let me in her house."

Mary just stared at him, knowing that her voice would crack and she'd burst into tears if she tried to speak.

"The woman's mad," Tom said. "Totally nuts."

No, Mary thought, I know who's insane here, and it's not poor, confused Edna Fenton. And then the tears came despite her efforts to hold them back. Tom sat beside her on the couch, taking her in his arms. She leaned against him, crying uncontrollably.

In Lewiston, Maine, Lieutenant Daniel K. Larson crouched behind a patrol car, peering up at the third story of an abandoned brick building. Once a large house, it had become an apartment building as the neighborhood had deteriorated. Now it stood uninhabited, derelict, vandalized, awaiting the arrival of the wrecking crew. And on the third floor was Paul Mitchell, armed with a rifle that he'd already used to fire at cars, pedestrians, whoever or whatever was in sight. Neighboring buildings that might become targets were being emptied. So far, no one had been hurt.

Crouched beside Larson were Grant and Captain Vincent, the officer in charge at the scene. The captain handed him a piece of paper. "That's the note," he said.

Unfolding the sheet, Larson read:

To the police:

I didn't kill Edwards and I couldn't make you believe I did. One for you. But you can't say I'm not really up here doing this. One for me.

> Your Pal,
> Paul R. Mitchell

PS—You should have believed me. Look how much simpler things would have been.
PPS—Doris, I hope you'll understand and forgive me. I love you.

"Tossed it out the window, wrapped around a piece of wood," the captain said. "This is the guy who confessed to the Edwards murder?"

"Name's the same. I haven't seen who's actually up there." He returned the note to the captain.

"What do you know about him that might help?"

"Not much. His confession was questionable, although we couldn't get any real evidence to either back it up or tear it down. Because the confession was all we had, I had to let him go." He rubbed his eyes, then resumed watching the third floor, hoping to get a glimpse of the gunman.

"He's a guy with a lot of problems," Larson continued. "Mostly with his self-image, I guess. Everybody put him down, picked on him, made him out to be a sissy, that sort of thing. He really resented it, but he kept on taking it. I guess I believe what it says in the note, that his confession was a phony. I'd say he saw confessing to Edwards's murder as a way of changing his image in the eyes of the world. When we released him, we took away that chance, and it must have been quite a blow. In any case, he's apparently found a way of making the world see him in a new light."

"There are better ways to prove yourself to the world," Captain Vincent said disgustedly. A tall, slender man in his fifties, he had a lean face with a hawkish nose, thick dark hair. In his hand was a two-way radio.

"For you and me, there are better ways. For him . . ." Larson shrugged.

"Can we talk him out of there?"

"It's doubtful. He doesn't plan to fail again. The way I see it, our best chance is to get his sister over here, Doris. She's the only one he might listen to."

The captain nodded. "Get her."

After sending Grant to fetch Doris Mitchell, Larson surveyed the scene. A number of patrol cars were on hand, lights flashing, officers using the vehicles as shields. Farther away, still other cops were keeping the curious away, far enough back so they wouldn't become targets for the man on the third floor of the abandoned brick building.

The structure itself was typical of the neighborhood: bricks discolored by grime accumulated over the years, peeling paint, neglected lawn. This was the first building in the block to be vacated; others would no doubt follow. Because it was unoccupied, it had been hit by vandals. A number of ground-floor windows were broken. Someone had written B. LOVES SANDRA in white spray paint on the wall by the front door.

"Have you tried to communicate with him at all?" Larson asked.

Vincent shook his head. "We were waiting for you."

"You want me to give it a try while we're waiting for Doris to get here? I don't suppose it can hurt any."

The captain reached in through the window of the patrol car and pulled out a microphone, which he handed to Larson. Keying the mike, the lieutenant heard an amplified click come from the speaker atop the car.

"Paul, can you hear me? This is Lieutenant Larson."

After a few moments passed with no response from Mitchell, Larson again keyed the mike. "Come on, Paul. Talk to us. What have you got to lose? Wouldn't you like us to know why you're doing this?"

Suddenly, one of the twin red lights atop the cruiser exploded, pieces of glass falling to the pavement around the car. Instinctively flattening himself against the cruiser, the captain said, "Oh, Jesus."

Larson tried to determine which window the shot had come from. Two were open; it could have been either. The third floor was fifty yards away. Although hitting something from that distance hardly required a marksman, it was apparent that Mitchell knew how to handle a rifle. Before now, Larson would have guessed that Mitchell had no interest in firearms. But now that he thought about it, he realized it was obvious that the young man would know how to shoot. It wasn't just that guns had macho value; they were also great equalizers. With one in your hand, you were the master of anyone without one. Point a gun at a bully and the tables are reversed. *He* cowers before you.

Another shot rang out, and the chrome-plated speaker jumped off the rack on which it had been mounted between the twin red lights. It landed about fifteen feet away and rolled under another patrol car.

"Shit," Larson muttered. "What's he got, do you know?"

"I'd say a deer rifle of some sort. Now I know how the deer feel."

Larson realized he was still holding the microphone. He flipped it through the window into the car. Without a speaker, it was useless.

"One-eighty-eight to three-fourteen," a man's voice said over the two-way radio in Vincent's hand. He raised it to his lips.

"Go ahead."

"I'm in position, Captain."

"Ten-four. Can you see the subject?"

"Negative."

"Okay, ten-four." Then to Larson he said: "That's Clark. He's on the roof of the building behind us. Mackey's on the roof of the place next door, to the right." The two were the department's sharpshooters. Sam Clark was a burly patrolman with bright red hair. Kathleen Mackey was a detective, twenty-nine years old, mother of three. Of the two, she was probably the more expert shot.

Keeping low, a uniformed officer hurried over to Larson and the captain. "Detective Grant's on his way with the subject's sister," the young patrolman reported.

"Hey," Larson said, "I think I saw movement at one of the first-floor windows. He might have moved downstairs."

Suddenly, the captain's two-way radio came to life. "He's coming out!"

"Hold your fire," Vincent ordered.

Paul Mitchell, a rifle held across his chest, had just emerged from the building. He stood on the small open porch, nervously surveying the scene before him.

"Shooters, report," the captain said into his radio.

"Can't see him. The corner of the building's in the way." Mackey's voice.

"I've got a clear shot, Captain." Clark.

"Hold your fire." Then, peering over the hood of the car, he shouted: "Paul Mitchell, this is Captain Vincent of the Lewiston Police Department. Drop your weapon. You're surrounded and outnumbered. Drop the gun. Now."

Suddenly, Mitchell raised the rifle, and a bullet slammed into the patrol car. Then another.

"Clark," the captain yelled into the radio, "shoot to bring him down, not to kill."

Larson, his snub-nosed .38 in his hand, kept his head down. Two more shots rang out from Mitchell's direction; then an urgent voice came over the radio:

"He's running, heading for the street!"

The captain lifted his two-way radio, but before he could speak, a shot sounded from behind them, and someone yelled: "He's down! Hold your fire."

Larson raised his head enough to see over the hood. Paul Mitchell lay facedown on the lawn, the rifle on the grass in front of him. Two uniformed officers, their shotguns trained on the downed man, approached cautiously. Holstering his own weapon, Larson hurried to the spot where Mitchell lay, Captain Vincent right behind him.

When he got there, a patrolman was bending over Mitchell. The officer rose, pushing his hat farther back on his head. "He's dead, sir. Looks like the slug caught him in the chest."

Larson nodded. On the back of Mitchell's shirt was a small red spot, which marked the exit point of the bullet. The hole was tiny, made by a bullet that was meant to pass cleanly through whatever it hit, designed to stop a person, not tear him apart. Still, if it hit in the wrong place, as this one obviously had, it could kill. And now, Paul Mitchell lay among the half dozen or so beer cans someone had dumped on the lawn, just another object the world had used up, discarded.

Most of the people who'd known him wouldn't care. They'd shrug, dismiss him as someone who didn't fit in and was therefore unworthy of their concern. Only his sister, Larson thought, only Doris gives a shit.

"I did the best I could, Captain," said a voice behind him. Larson turned to find a large red-haired man with a sniper rifle. It was Clark.

Captain Vincent nodded. "I know you did. He was moving, and I ordered you to stop him. You did what had to be done."

Clark said nothing, but the look in his blue eyes said he wouldn't sleep well that night, maybe not for many nights to come.

"He killed himself," Larson said. "It was a suicide. Instead of turning the gun on himself, he used us."

Clark remained silent, the pained look in his eyes unchanged.

"And instead of going out as a wimp, as his father called him, he went out as a crazed gunman. He got everything he wanted."

Clark frowned, indicating he had no idea what the lieutenant was talking about.

"Someday over a beer," Larson said. "When you feel like talking about it."

Eleven

THE NEXT MORNING MARY KEPT HER APPOINTMENT WITH Dr. Carpenter. Sitting in the same comfortable chair as before, she told the psychiatrist about Steph's murder, the collapse of the Fentons' swing, her visit from Flanagan.

She had heard nothing further from the policeman. Nor had she contacted a lawyer, Tom having advised her to wait and see what would happen. The collapsed swing still lay in the Fentons' yard, a bunch of red and yellow pipes in the grass. Soon, someone would have to move them; otherwise the lawn couldn't be mowed.

She hadn't seen Billy Fenton since the accident—nor any of the other Fenton children for that matter. Apparently, they were being kept away from the horrible neighbor woman who preyed on small children. For the first time she could remember, the yard next door was quiet, constantly quiet. The silence, however, instead of being a relief, was a continual reminder.

When Mary finished relating the events of the past few days, Dr. Carpenter studied her a moment, then said, "I take it that the child who claims to have seen you tampering with the swing was mistaken."

Mary hesitated, choosing her words carefully. "To the best of my knowledge, I had nothing to do with what happened to that swing."

The psychiatrist frowned. "To the best of your knowledge. Why did you phrase it that way?"

"I . . . I can't tell you."

"I see. So there's at least a possibility that you could have done it without knowing about it."

"Y—yes." Mary's stomach did a flip-flop, then settled down.

Dr. Carpenter considered that a moment. "As far as you know, you weren't responsible for what happened to the swing, but there's at least a chance you could be. And you can't tell me why that is."

"No, I can't. If I tried, I'd faint again. Or get sick. Or something."

"Do you have lapses of memory?"

Instantly feeling dizzy, Mary didn't answer. If I just take my time, she thought, maybe I can answer. Instead of trying to speak, she thought the word. *Yes.* The room seemed to spin and dim. Mary gripped the edge of her chair.

The doctor's question hung there, demanding an answer she was unable to give. *Do you have lapses of memory?* One word, Mary thought, just one word. If I could just say it, the doctor would know. Vaguely, she sensed that the psychiatrist was beside her, holding her, giving her strength. Unwilling to give up, Mary reached for the word that might save her: *Yes. Yes, I have lapses of memory. Help me! Please help me!*

She heard Dr. Carpenter speaking, but the words didn't register. "Mary, I've got you. Everything will be all right."

I have to talk, Mary thought desperately. I have to tell her. And then she heard her voice.

"Walpurgis Night. You have to help me before Walpurgis Night."

A searing pain shot through her body, and she heard herself cry out. As everything went silent and black, she sensed that she had beaten the censor, but she was unsure how because she hadn't been able to speak the word that would have answered the doctor's question.

"Mary," Dr. Carpenter said.

"Yes." Mary opened her eyes. She was sitting in the chair. The psychiatrist was beside her, studying her.

"Are you all right?"

"I . . . I think so. Did I faint?"

"Only for a moment."

"I . . . I'm sorry I couldn't answer."

"You didn't have to. It's obvious that you suffer lapses of memory and that you're unable to tell me about them."

Suddenly, Mary felt elated. She'd succeeded. The doctor knew. Now she could get help. "Now that you know what's wrong . . ." The doctor's serious expression caused Mary to allow her words to trail off.

"Mary, I know almost nothing. There's much, much more I have to learn before I'm sure what your problem is. We've barely begun."

Although Mary could understand that, she was still disappointed. All this time she'd been wishing she could let someone know about her blank spells, and now that someone finally knew, nothing had changed.

"Do you ever find out later what you've done during your memory lapses?" the psychiatrist asked.

Instantly feeling nauseous, Mary said, "I can't tell you."

Dr. Carpenter nodded. "What is Walpurgis Night?"

"What is *what?*"

"Walpurgis Night."

"I've never heard of it."

"Just before you passed out, you mentioned it. You said I had to help you before Walpurgis Night."

Vaguely, Mary recalled her words and the feeling that she'd somehow beaten the censor. And then something else tugged at her memory, something from those years she was unable to remember, and suddenly the nausea was back. Mary shook her head. "I don't know what I meant."

Dr. Carpenter turned to the bookshelves behind her, removed a volume from a set of encyclopedias, and opened it on her desk. "According to this," she said, studying the book, "Walpurgis Night occurs on the last day of April. Legend has it as a night of witches, and it's a major religious day in witchcraft and Satanism, almost as important as Halloween."

Mary gave the psychiatrist a bewildered look. She had no idea what any of this had to do with her.

For the rest of the session, they talked about Mary's childhood after the orphanage, the Caldwells, her life with Tom. And as Mary told the psychiatrist about these parts of her life, she could see that hers was basically a happy story. A little girl who, though orphaned, loved her foster parents and was loved by them. A young woman who adored her husband and was adored in return.

The blank spells ruined it of course. They hung over

Mary's happy story, dark and ominous. And because of them, she had deceived the people who loved and trusted her.

While she talked to the doctor, two words seemed to float in the back of her mind: Walpurgis Night. Although the words meant nothing to her, she realized there was a part of her for which they did have meaning. A part of herself she wasn't allowed to know.

At the conclusion of the session, Mary asked, "Do you have a calendar?"

"Yes." The psychiatrist indicated the desk calendar by her phone.

"How many days until Walpurgis Night?"

Glancing at the calendar, Dr. Carpenter replied, "It's two weeks from tomorrow." The psychiatrist's gray eyes studied her.

Picking up her purse from beside her chair, Mary rose, unable to shake the feeling that something would happen in two weeks. Something terrible.

"I'll see you next week," the doctor said.

Mary nodded.

Later that day, Mary drove along Scones Boulevard, on her way to Zel Home and Builders Supply even though this was Thursday, one of her days off. A little while ago, Rod Hoffman, one of the assistant managers, had called saying they were short-handed, could she please come in. No problem, Mary had replied dutifully.

Walpurgis Night. Ever since her session with Dr. Carpenter, the words had floated in and out of her thoughts. Words that were very important to her, yet words whose significance she didn't know, couldn't know.

And then, as she stopped for a red light, Mary suddenly saw an image of a woman dressed in black, her eyes reflecting the flickering glow of the candles that illuminated her. The black-clad figure seemed sleek and beautiful, yet dangerous, like a panther.

There was something else about the figure, something that was hard to put into words. It was the feeling you got looking at a black widow spider hanging upside down in its web, the red hourglass visible on its abdomen. The spider wasn't just dangerous; it seemed something more . . . something almost evil. The name "Sister" came into Mary's thoughts, and she realized that Sister had been at the orphanage. She shivered.

Behind her, a horn sounded; the light was green. Stepping on the gas, Mary glanced in the rearview mirror. Directly behind her was a battered blue car and behind that a red van that cut off her view. Her eyes returned to the road for a few moments, and then she found herself looking into the rearview mirror again. There was something about the man driving the blue car, something familiar. The old sedan was still behind her, but about three or four car lengths back now, too far away for her to make out the driver.

And then she forgot about the man in the blue car because it had suddenly occurred to her that something unusual had just happened. Her internal censor hadn't stepped in when she'd recalled something about the orphanage. Why hadn't she experienced nausea or dizziness? Could it have been because the image and the name Sister had come to her unbidden, because she'd made no conscious effort to enter forbidden territory?

When she arrived at Zel Home and Builders Supply, Mary still had no answer for that question.

When she left work that night, the parking lot wasn't dark, because lighting had been installed. Her car was parked directly beneath one of the tall poles that now dotted the area. A lot of good the new lights will do Steph, she thought as she started the car and drove out of the parking area.

Zel Home and Builders Supply was located near a freeway, which Mary took as far as the Scones Boulevard exit. Scones would take her to within a few blocks of her house. The trip never varied; it was the most direct route between home and work.

At the first red light on Scones, she glanced into the rearview mirror, seeing a battered blue car directly behind her, one that looked very much like the wreck that had been behind her that afternoon. In fact, the longer she looked at it, the more certain she became that it was the same car. She tried to see the driver's face, but it was obscured by shadows.

Someone honked; the light was green. As she began pulling away from the blue car, she got a better look at it. Pieces of the grille were missing, as was the chrome around one headlight. It was undeniably the same car.

Coincidence, she decided. Someone who worked the same hours she did and who lived in the same part of town. Dropping farther back, the car stayed behind her until she left Scones. The old sedan continued straight ahead, proving that it wasn't following her—not that she'd had any reason to think it was.

Still, having the same car behind you, on the same street, both when you went to work and when you returned . . . well, it was unusual; it made you just a little uneasy.

Ahead was her house. The porch light was on. It looked warm and inviting. She hoped Tom, as he did sometimes, would come out and meet her in the driveway.

The next afternoon, as she drove along Scones Boulevard on her way to work, Mary found herself eyeing the rearview mirror more than she usually did. It had been raining lightly all day and the windshield wipers swung back and forth, keeping the drizzle away.

She glanced in the rearview mirror. After passing a veterinary hospital, two motels, and a gas station, she checked it again. Still no blue car.

Nothing further had come of the incident with the swing. The Fentons, children included, still seemed to be keeping out of sight. Before, she and the Fentons had had a relationship of polite disinterest; now it was one of hostility and mistrust—at least on the Fentons' part—and it seemed unlikely that it would ever again be otherwise. As for her possible role in what had happened to Billy Fenton, Mary had pushed the matter from her mind. She would never know for sure; it was best not to dwell on it.

As she passed a McDonald's, she checked the mirror again. Still no blue car.

Flanagan continued to leave her in peace. She was beginning to hope, really hope, that she'd seen the last of him. Mary disliked the detective and was fairly certain the feeling would only intensify should she be forced to have any further dealings with him.

Walpurgis Night and the name Sister continued to haunt her, although she still had no idea why. If she concentrated, tried to search for the answer, she became woozy. Despite her unbidden recollection of Sister, the censor had not stopped doing its job, though she wondered whether it might be weakening. The wooziness she felt when thinking about Walpurgis Night or Sister seemed less severe than the attacks of nausea and dizziness she was accustomed to. Or was that just wishful thinking?

Her next appointment with Dr. Carpenter was on Monday morning. She planned to see the psychiatrist twice a week, and though uncertain how much good the doctor would be able to do her, Mary found she looked forward to the sessions. Perhaps it was because it was good to be with someone who knew, even if only superficially, what her problem was . . . someone who wanted to help.

Her main regret continued to be that she was doing it behind Tom's back. But she still didn't see how she could tell him. He'd want to know why she was seeing a psychiatrist, and she'd be unable to answer his questions. He'd be confused, hurt, and Mary would feel no less guilty for having told him. She'd be withholding so much information that she'd still be deceitful, a betrayer of his love and trust. Unable to deal with these thoughts, she tried to empty her mind.

Once more, her eyes found the rearview mirror. There it was, maybe four or five cars back. An old blue sedan, rusty, missing chrome around the headlight. What's going on here? she asked herself nervously. Can he really be following me? Why? What does he want?

The car was totally unfamiliar to her. She was certain she'd never seen it before yesterday. The driver, however, *had* seemed vaguely familiar, although she'd only caught a glimpse of him in the rearview mirror, just enough to be sure it was a man, probably middle-aged.

She shuddered, thinking of the kind of people who might be apt to follow a woman . . . and what one of them had done to Steph. The car was still there, hanging well back. It followed her onto the freeway.

Worried now, she forced her eyes to leave the mirror and look where her car was going. Why her? Why, with millions of women in metropolitan Boston, had he chosen to follow her? He obviously knew the route she used to get to and from work, and her hours, so he probably knew where she worked. Did he know where she lived? Her name?

And then a question occurred to her that opened up a whole new set of unpleasant possibilities. Could the driver of the blue car be someone she'd encountered during a blank spell? Had she done something to this man—or with him? If so, the man would be aware of everything that had transpired between them; events that, as far as she was concerned, had never occurred.

In the mirror, she could still see the old blue sedan, six, maybe seven cars behind her. Oh, God, she thought, if he's really following me, he has to want something.

The possibilities were terrifying.

The rain had stopped. Mary switched off the wipers and rolled down the window. The interior of the car had suddenly become suffocating.

Then she saw flashing red lights ahead; a police officer had pulled someone over. Signaling, she pulled into the emergency lane and rolled to a stop behind the police car. A pickup, four cars, and a van sped past her, and then the blue sedan, its driver looking straight ahead, as if he had no interest in her or anything else except getting to where he was going. Although she caught only a glimpse of it in profile, the face again seemed vaguely familiar.

The license number, something inside her was

screaming, get the license number! But she was too late; the blue car was too far away. Oh, damn, she thought. Damn.

"Is something wrong?" A female voice asked, startling her. The police officer, a heavyset woman with dark hair, was standing beside Mary's car.

"I . . . I stopped when I saw your police car. I thought I was being followed by someone in a blue car."

"What happened when you pulled over?"

"The car went on by."

The officer smiled. "You did the right thing. If it happens again and there are no police cars handy, just pull into some place with people around, find a phone, call us, and wait till we get there."

Mary nodded. "Yes, I will. Thank you."

Back on the expressway, Mary found herself tensing whenever she came to an interchange, waiting for the blue car to appear. When, after five interchanges, it hadn't, she began to relax. Perhaps he thought the police would be waiting up ahead, waiting to grab him should he be foolish enough to resume following her. And then a new thought struck her. It could be the police who were tailing her. One of Flanagan's men in an unmarked car. No, she told herself, no. They wouldn't use the same car every time; they'd switch them around to keep the person being followed from becoming suspicious.

And how did she know they weren't doing exactly that? Just because the blue car wasn't behind her now didn't mean some other vehicle hadn't taken over. Glancing in the rearview mirror, she saw an eighteen-wheeler, a number of compact cars, a green bus. . . . It could be any of them. Or none of them.

If Flanagan was having her followed, it wouldn't

be because of an incident involving a child's swing.
It would be because he suspected her of Steph's
murder.

Confused and afraid, Mary drove on. Ahead was the
exit that would take her to Zel Home and Builders
Supply.

That night, she took a route home that bypassed
Scones Boulevard. It made the trip longer, but she saw
no sign of the blue car. The next day, Saturday, she did
the same thing both going to work and coming home,
again seeing no blue car. Monday, after her next visit
with Dr. Carpenter, she would try her regular route
again and see what happened. So far, she had not
mentioned any of this to Tom.

"What was the name of the orphanage?" Dr. Carpenter asked.

Uncertain how far the censor would allow her to go,
Mary said, "It was called the Christian Home for
Children. It's not too far from Evans Ridge, the town in
Maine where I lived with my foster parents."

"Is it still there?"

"No. It burned down a long time ago."

Mary had just begun her Monday session. She sat in
the usual chair, Dr. Carpenter at her desk. The censor
had shown no interest in her conversation so far, so
Mary plunged on.

"Uh, I think the place was run by a woman called
Sister." Mary hesitated; so far, so good. "I remembered her a couple of hours after my last appointment
with you. All of a sudden, I saw her in my mind and
remembered her from the orphanage."

"Were you trying to remember, or did it just come to
you?"

"It just came to me. I was driving, and my mind was wandering."

"Did this recollection make you dizzy or sick?"

"No. Only when I *tried* to think about it later."

"And Walpurgis Night? Have you tried to think about that?"

"I can't," Mary said. "I'll get sick or faint. But I know that it's important. I know that in less than two weeks something's going to happen." Her stomach churned, then relaxed. A warning.

"What will happen?"

Mary shook her head; she didn't know. And then she heard herself say: "The change will take place. This year. On Walpurgis Night."

Dr. Carpenter watched her expectantly, her gray eyes fixed on Mary's face.

"I . . . I don't know why I said that," Mary said. "I don't know what it means." Suddenly feeling woozy, she gripped the chair.

"Are you going to be all right?" the psychiatrist asked.

"Yes, I'm fine now."

"All right, let's try something then." The psychiatrist held up some cards. "Each of these has a shape on it. I want you to study each shape as I show it to you and make up a story that goes along with it."

Mary nodded, and the doctor held up a card on which was a stop-sign-shaped figure filled with dark lines. "It's a maze," Mary said and made up a story about a little girl who got lost in it but finally found her way out.

Shown a star shape, Mary made up a short tale involving a sheriff's badge that was now in a museum. And then Dr. Carpenter showed her a black square. Mary shivered.

"It's the punishment place," she said in a weak, distant whisper. "It's horrible. No one should have been made to go there." She was trembling. The punishment place terrified her.

"I don't know what the punishment place is," Mary said. "I don't know why I mentioned it. I don't know why I'm so afraid of it." She began to feel light-headed. The censor had decided that she was moving into forbidden territory.

Dr. Carpenter was silent a moment; then she said, "I think this is a good sign, these things starting to come out like this. It means the protective wall you've built around certain memories is starting to crumble. That's what we have to do; we have to get that wall to crumble, get you to remember the things that are locked away in your unconscious. Once we've accomplished that, the battle will be half won."

"You mean that's all I have to do, just remember?"

"No, that's not all you have to do, but it's probably the most important thing. Once we bring everything out in the open, you'll have no more reason to get sick or faint when you try to remember. You can't protect yourself from knowing what you already know.

"And knowledge is also the key to your recovery. Once you see the root of your problem, you can understand what's been happening to you; you can begin to deal with it."

"I can see that," Mary said.

"Good. It may not seem like it, but believe me, considering that this is only your third session, you're making remarkable progress."

I hope so, Mary thought. Oh, how I hope so. "I have the feeling that the reason I'm starting to remember things is because Walpurgis Night is so close, and . . . and after Walpurgis Night, it won't matter."

"Why do you think that?"

"I don't know. It's just a feeling."

When the session ended, Mary made an appointment for Friday morning and then drove home, Walpurgis Night and Sister and the punishment place swirling in her thoughts. Terms from the past, a past so terrible she had hidden it from herself.

Driving home, she realized she hadn't told the psychiatrist about the man in the blue car. It seemed there was always so much to say, and the fifty-minute sessions were so brief. Later that day and again on Tuesday, Mary followed her normal routes to and from work. To her relief, there was no sign of the man in the battered sedan.

At 9:10 Wednesday night, Mary stood at the glass doors of Zel Home and Builders Supply, ready to let Howard Cummings out of the building. A balding man in his thirties, Cummings was the nighttime head cashier, whose job it was to collect the cash drawers from the registers at the close of each day and put them in the safe. This was the week Mary was in charge of closing up because Adkins had had to leave early. Even when Adkins was here, he wasn't allowed to collect the cash drawers, just as Cummings wasn't entrusted with the keys to the building. Mary had no idea what the reasoning behind this was; she simply accepted it as the way things were done.

As Cummings approached, she turned the key in the lock, pushed the door open. "Good night, Howard."

"Good night, Mary." He stopped halfway out the door and stepped back inside again.

"Say, Mary, who's going to lock up tomorrow night? Thursday's your day off isn't it?"

"I don't know, Howard. Adkins never said."

"You don't suppose he forgot about your being off on Thursdays, do you?"

"I doubt it." Adkins was entirely too efficient to overlook that sort of thing. "If you're worried about it, why don't you check with him tomorrow?"

He nodded, apparently to himself. "Okay, Mary, thanks. I'll see you Friday."

As soon as Cummings was outside, Mary locked the door behind him, then set about making sure that the coffee pot in the employees' lounge was unplugged, that all the lights were switched off except those designated as night lights, that no one was left in the building. Only a week ago, she would have left the place in the hands of the janitors, but they didn't come at closing time anymore. Now they cleaned somewhere else first and didn't arrive at Zel until dawn.

Once she was satisfied that all was in order, Mary headed for the door to let herself out. In the dim night lighting, some of the bins and shelves cast shadows across the floor. There was something a little spooky about a place like this when it was empty and dimly lit. Her footsteps echoed in the stillness.

At the door, she was startled to see a man on the other side of the glass, watching her. It was J.M. Styles, the night yard foreman, who all this week had been waiting for her and walking her to her car after she'd locked up. He was a burly fellow with huge hairy arms that could probably squash—literally—the average mugger or rapist or murderer. He hadn't made any bones about why he was escorting her to her car each night? "We lost one girl here, and I don't plan to let anything happen to you."

"Hi, J.M.," she said, locking the door behind her. It was a clear but chilly night. She buttoned her jacket.

"You all done?" he asked as she inserted a key in the wall switch that activated the alarm system.

"Yep, all done." With that, they headed for her car, walking leisurely through the now brightly lit parking area. She would shut these lights off, too. The key-operated switch was at the exit.

The lights were the only thing outside the building Mary had to be concerned with. Locking up the yard was entirely Styles's responsibility; Mary wasn't even supposed to check.

"What does the J.M. stand for?" Mary asked. "I've never heard you called by anything except your initials."

"That's all my parents gave me, initials."

She started to ask him whether he knew why his parents hadn't given him a regular name, but then she decided it was really none of her business. A moment later, they reached her car.

She drove to the lot's exit, where she got out of the car, inserted a key into the lock at the base of a light pole, and plunged the parking area into blackness. And then, her last duty done, she was on her way home.

Pulling onto the freeway, she glanced into the rear-view mirror, seeing no blue car behind her. It hadn't been there all week, even though she'd resumed using her usual route to and from work. She immediately pushed these thoughts aside. Considering the blue car forced her to pose too many questions for which there were no answers, only frightening implications.

In all, her life seemed to have returned to normal the past few days. She'd heard nothing from Sergeant Flanagan. She'd had no further blank spells—none that she was aware of, in any case. The only indication that anything was amiss occurred when Mary and Edna Fenton had stepped into their respective backyards at

the same moment. Mrs. Fenton had turned away but
not until she'd given Mary a pointedly icy look.

These thoughts, too, Mary pushed aside. Tomorrow
was her day off. She and Lynn were going shopping,
and Mary was looking forward to it. She was also
looking forward to getting home, finding out what Tom
had made for dinner, being alone with him for a while,
just the two of them, snug in their little yellow house.

When she left the freeway at Scones Boulevard, her
eyes were again drawn to the rearview mirror. Whoever he is, he's gone, she reassured herself; you won't see
him again.

Twelve

"WHY DO WE ENJOY THIS SO MUCH?" MARY ASKED AS she pulled into the mall's spacious parking area. Because they'd used Lynn's car last time, it was Mary's turn to drive.

"Shopping?" Lynn was checking her face in the mirror of a compact.

"If you want to call it that. We never buy anything."

"Humph," Lynn replied, dropping the compact into her purse. "Buying things is for people who make more money than us poor slobs who work at Zel. All we can do is look, drool on the merchandise, torment ourselves."

Mary piloted the car into a parking space and turned off the engine. As they climbed out, she resisted the impulse to scan the parking area for the old blue sedan. She hadn't looked for it once since leaving the house and she would not allow herself to start now. That particular paranoia was behind her.

It was one of those days that looked warm but wasn't.

From inside a building or car, one peered out and saw the bright sunshine; then one stepped out and felt the penetrating chill of the breeze, a reminder that winter was only a few weeks behind you, summer still months away.

In the mall, they began in a large department store, checking out the summer fashions, sometimes shaking their heads when they inspected the price tags, occasionally nodding sagely, frequently exchanging knowing looks. Suddenly, it occurred to Mary that they hardly ever spoke in stores anymore. They had no need to; they'd been doing this for so many months now that they'd developed a nonverbal form of communication. She knew exactly what Lynn thought about a particular garment without Lynn's having to say a word, and vice versa. Curious to know whether other shoppers did the same thing, she looked around for any nearby customers and found herself staring into the eyes of a man who immediately looked away, a man she'd seen somewhere before.

He stood maybe twenty feet away, separated from her by three or four racks of women's garments. A tall, thin man, who appeared to be keeping his back to her. Then, with just a quick glance in her direction, he started walking away from her. Suddenly, she knew where she'd seen him. He was the salesman who'd come to the house the week before. The encyclopedia salesman.

In the next instant, she realized she'd seen him somewhere else, too. In the rearview mirror, behind the wheel of the blue car. He was almost to the exit now; another moment and he'd be out of sight. Trying desperately to unscramble her thoughts, Mary started after him.

She had a momentary doubt. Was this the right thing

to do? Yes, something inside of her said. He knows
what this is all about. He has the answers.

She lost sight of him for a moment, but when she
entered the main mall, she spotted him easily in the
sparse Thursday morning crowd. He glanced over his
shoulder, his eyes quickly sweeping the area behind
him. Mary ducked behind a chunky bald man; he didn't
see her. She began walking faster, closing the gap.

Passing a toy store, then a men's shop, the man
abruptly stopped in front of a Radio Shack and hesitated as if uncertain whether to enter. On the other side
of the mall, standing in front of a bookstore, was a
security guard, whose presence gave Mary the courage
to act. She approached the thin man, who was still
looking at the display in the window.

"Why are you following me?" she demanded, stopping about three feet from him.

He slowly turned, his eyes meeting hers, holding
them. "I beg your pardon."

"W–why are you following me?" she stammered, her
courage fading. Why had she done this? Why hadn't
she at least grabbed Lynn, who was no doubt still back
in the department store, wondering where she had
gone?

"I have no idea what you're talking about. If you
persist in accusing me like this, we'll have to go to the
police and let them sort it out."

She stared at him, speechless. She wasn't wrong.
This was the man who had come to her house claiming
to be an encyclopedia salesman. This was the lean,
beady-eyed face she'd seen behind the wheel of the
blue car. She took a step backward. This had been a
mistake. It was foolish to think the man would tell her
anything. Taking another backward step, she started to
turn.

"Wait," he said, and she froze. His eyes left her, looked across the mall to where the security guard had been standing. Mary looked, too. The guard was leaving, walking slowly away. She took another step away from the thin man, ready to run, scream.

"Wait," he said again. "I can tell you what you want to know. But not here. Come outside with me, where we can discuss things privately." His eyes seemed to plead. "It's important. Very important."

"No," she said. "Oh, no." Fear of this man had completely replaced her desire to know why he had been following her. Again, she began moving away from him.

"Please. It's urgent. You must be told. I can see that now. It's the only way."

Mary shook her head.

He sighed. "Very well, but before you run away, let me tell you this much." He paused, his eyes again locking onto hers. "I know you, Mary/Mara. I know what you are."

For a moment, she stood there, staring into the stranger's eyes, seeing in them something peculiar, something so intense it frightened her. A shiver caused her to break the eye contact, and she fled, dashing madly back toward the department store. Suddenly, someone grabbed her.

"Mary! What's happening? What's the matter?" It was Lynn.

Mary threw her arms around her friend. "Oh, God, Lynn. It was the man."

"What man?"

Realizing she had mentioned the man in the blue car to no one, Mary quickly related the essential details.

"Mary . . ." Lynn trailed off, looking concerned, bewildered. "What's happening to you? There are things about your life you're afraid to discuss with even me. People follow you. I mean, what is it with you, Mary? What's this all about? Is this man somehow connected with the things you won't talk about?"

"I don't know," Mary said weakly. "I just don't know."

Lynn sighed. "Okay. If you want to tell me, you will, and if you don't, you won't. You feel like continuing our mad shopping spree?"

Releasing her friend, Mary nodded. She didn't want to be alone, even at home. The strange man knew where she lived.

As they walked along the mall, automatically heading toward a small expensive dress shop on their right, Lynn said, "Do you think you ought to tell the police about this guy following you?"

"There's nothing they could do. He hasn't really done anything. I don't even have his license number."

Lynn, apparently sensing that Mary would prefer to drop the subject, didn't say any more about it.

In the expensive dress shop, Mary paid little attention to the clothes, trying instead to organize her thoughts. At least now she knew for certain that the man had not been following her on orders of Sergeant Flanagan. The man had come to her house before Steph's murder, before the detective had ever heard of Mary Taylor. Then who was he? What did he want? Questions without answers. Her whole life was made up of questions without answers.

And why, Mary wondered, posing yet another question for which she had no answer, had he referred to her as Mary/Mara? *I know you, Mary/Mara. I know what you are.*

She snatched a dress from the rack and tried to

concentrate on it. The name Mara meant nothing to her. And yet . . . and yet it seemed to trigger something deep in her unconscious, something that could not be brought to the surface for study and analysis even if she wanted, which she didn't. Whatever was down there, she'd learned long ago, was best left undisturbed.

But I *have* to remember, Mary thought, suddenly recalling what Dr. Carpenter had told her. I have to try to tear down the mental barriers I've been using to hide things from myself.

And then she wondered whether she *could* face whatever was locked away in her unconscious. If her mind had gone to so much trouble to protect her from her memories, perhaps they were better left undisturbed. But that would mean simply going on as she had been, which would be unbearable. She had to trust in Dr. Carpenter.

Mara, Mara, Mara. She turned the name around in her mind, again sensing just a hint of familiarity. Suddenly, bitter stomach juices filled her throat, and Mary quickly emptied her mind. After a moment, her stomach settled. She realized that, by prohibiting her from thinking about certain things, the censor was telling her that those things were important. The knowledge seemed useless.

Oh, damn, she thought, blinking back her tears. Oppressive governments with their secret police and torture chambers could make you do anything, say anything. The one thing they were unable to do was control what you thought. But Mary had a secret policeman right in her brain. As long as she followed the officially accepted behavior patterns, everything was fine. When she tried to do anything that was frowned upon—even *think* anything that was frowned upon—the secret policeman instantly put a stop to it.

But I'm going to defeat you, she told the censor, suddenly feeling determined. I'm going to find out everything you don't want me to know.

Then she noticed the dress in her hands. It was a hideous thing, purple with yellow flowers, four sizes too large. She hastily returned it to the rack, hoping no one had noticed her interest in it.

As she selected another garment to examine, Lynn whispered in her ear, "Yuk! For a moment there, I thought you had lost all your taste."

"I just didn't believe it was real," Mary replied. "I couldn't believe a class shop like this would display a thing like that."

Lynn chuckled. "It just goes to show you that people with money have bad taste, too."

They moved on to another rack, scrutinizing the shop's offerings, checking the price tags, communicating through exchanged glances. Although she tried to appear interested, Mary participated halfheartedly. In her mind, she saw the intense, frightening eyes of the thin man, heard him say: *I know what you are.*

And what am I? Mary wondered. Unable to shake the feeling that the question had a very horrible, terrifying answer, she once more turned her attention to the clothes displayed before her. This time, she selected something appropriate. A lightweight jacket, beige, water-resistant, a hood with drawstrings. The price tag read $136.95. Looking suitably horrified, she held the tag for Lynn to see. Her friend nodded sagely.

Having finished with the expensive dress shop, they moved on, hitting all the interesting stores on one side of the mall, eating lunch at a cafeteria, then catching the shops on the mall's other side. And all the while, the question tumbled through Mary's mind: What am I? What am I that a stranger follows me because of it, calls me by a name that's not mine?

"Now where?" Lynn asked as they left the mall and headed for Mary's car.

"A movie?" Mary said hopefully, still not wanting to be alone.

"Okay," Lynn replied enthusiastically. "How about the horror flick over at the other mall?"

"What horror flick?" Somehow, a scary movie wasn't what she'd had in mind. Real life was scary enough. For Mary, an escape movie would be *Bambi* or maybe *Lady and the Tramp*.

"You know, the usual madman-escapes-from-mental-hospital-and-stalks-young-woman type thing."

Oh, God, Mary thought, just what I need. "Isn't there anything else?" she asked, making a face.

Lynn shrugged. "That's the only one I can remember, but there are four theaters there, so let's drive over and see what the other offerings are."

"Sounds good."

After a moment's panic, they found the small green Plymouth two rows over from where they thought they'd parked it. Mary drove to the freeway that would take them to the other mall, about six miles away. Walking to the car, she had seen no sign of the thin man, nor had the blue Ford appeared in her rearview mirror as she left the mall's parking area. After she'd been on the expressway two or three minutes, she checked again.

"He's behind us," Mary said, feeling herself tense.

"Where?" Lynn turned to look.

"The blue car. The one that's all beat up."

"I see it, but it's too far back for me to get the license number." She grabbed the sleeve of Mary's jacket. "Slow down. Let him get closer."

Mary eased up on the gas, but the blue sedan grew no larger in the mirror.

"Come on!" Lynn said, staring through the car's rear window. "Come on up here, you jerk. And bring your license plate with you."

But still the blue car kept its distance.

"Stop," Lynn said. "Pull over to the side."

"On an expressway?"

"It's an emergency, isn't it?"

Reluctantly, Mary steered the car to the emergency lane and applied the brakes. Behind her, the blue sedan also pulled off, slowed.

Exasperated, Lynn slapped the seat. "Damn! Well, you might as well keep going. If we stop, he'll stop."

A few minutes later, they pulled into the parking lot of the shopping mall. The sign out front indicated that, besides the horror film, a love story and two comedies were showing.

"Well," Mary said nervously as she parked the car, "what should we do?"

"I thought we came here to go to a movie."

"But what about the man in the blue car?"

"I'm not letting some jerk run my life."

"But . . ." But it will be dark in there, Mary thought, and practically empty on a weekday afternoon.

"If anyone hassles us, I'll yell 'rape' and 'pervert' so loud they'll hear it two blocks away. He wouldn't dare do anything."

Though unconvinced, Mary decided to go along with her friend's judgment. That anyone would attack Lynn seemed inconceivable. She was the sort such things just don't happen to. And being in her company seemed to extend the same protection to whoever was with her. Such logic, Mary supposed, was a precarious thing on which to base actions involving one's safety, but then when in her life had she ever truly been safe— especially from herself?

"Okay," she said, "let's go to a movie."

"Which one appeals to you?" Lynn asked.

"How about a comedy?"

"Why not."

Getting out of the car, Mary scanned the parking lot for the blue sedan. Though certain it was there somewhere, she was unable to spot it. As they walked toward the theater entrance, they decided which of the two comedies they would see. There was still no sign of the thin man.

Stepping into the darkened theater about five minutes after the show had started, they hesitated while their eyes adjusted to the reduced light, then took seats about midway down the aisle. There were maybe a dozen people in the theater, most of them kids—who Mary assumed were either truant or enjoying a school holiday with which she was unfamiliar. Who, Mary wondered, who will step forward to rescue me when Lynn yells rape and pervert? She chuckled because she had a momentary vision of some brave sixth-grader stuffing his bubble gum in the villain's ear. Then her eyes drifted to the double doors leading to the lobby. They'd just been opened, and silhouetted there was a tall, thin man who appeared to be looking for someone.

"Lynn," she whispered urgently, "it's him."

"Where?" The door had just closed; the silhouette was now a shadow.

"By the door, standing there."

"It's too dark to see."

The shadow started moving slowly down the aisle. Mary braced herself. Lynn could scream if she wanted to, but Mary planned to fight, to kick and bite and scratch.

"I can't tell for sure if it's him," Lynn whispered.

The shadow approached deliberately, looking from side to side. Looking for me, Mary thought. It was only the knowledge that she'd immediately reveal her location that kept her from jumping up and running. She was trembling.

"Look straight ahead," Lynn warned. "You're too obvious. I'll watch behind us."

Mary complied, almost surprised to discover there was a movie in progress. She felt as if someone were standing behind her with a club. The blow would come; the only question was when.

"He's stepping into the row behind us," Lynn whispered. "I still can't tell if it's him."

Then, behind her, Mary heard a male voice, speaking just above a whisper. "They didn't have Diet Pepsi, so I got you a Tab. Is that okay?"

A woman's softly spoken response was unintelligible.

"It's not him," Lynn said, stating the obvious.

"Lynn," Mary said slowly, the thought having just occurred to her, "you've never seen him up close. How were you going to identify him?"

"You told me what he looked like, silly. And if there had been any doubt, I'd have had you turn around and check."

Well, maybe, Mary thought. Lynn was a good friend, but putting too much faith in her judgment might be unwise.

"Relax," Lynn whispered. "He's not here. Forget him and enjoy the movie."

Easy for you to say, Mary thought. It's not you he's been following.

Throughout the film, Mary turned to look whenever the doors to the lobby opened. Occasionally, she would get caught up in the movie, but during most of it, she found herself unable to concentrate on the screen; the comic antics of the actors seemed frivolous. Lynn, on the other hand, was completely absorbed and seemed to be chuckling continually. But then such was Lynn's way, no problem too big to be promptly sloughed off and forgotten.

Mary knew that when Tom came home she would have to tell him. She dreaded that because she could only recount the part about the thin man in the blue car. About the rest, about all the implications of his words, she would be able to say nothing, for her internal censors would never permit it. She would have to lie to Tom. Not by looking him in the eye and uttering untruths, which she doubted she could do, but by omitting so much of the truth.

And if she continued to deceive him by omission, how much longer would it be before she could go all the way, before she could meet his gaze, smile, say whatever was convenient, feeling no guilt at all when her words were entirely false?

As she and Lynn left the theater, Mary pushed the question from her mind and began looking for the thin man. She didn't see him. Nor did his old blue car appear in her rearview mirror.

The following day, Friday, Mary had her next session with Dr. Carpenter. Sitting in her customary place, she began by telling the psychiatrist about the man in the blue car.

"And he called you Mary/Mara?" the doctor asked.

"His exact words were, 'I know you, Mary/Mara. I know what you are.' I have no idea what he meant."

The psychiatrist considered that. "Could the man be someone you encountered during one of your memory lapses?"

Mary hesitated, uncertain how much the censor would allow her to say about her blank spells. "It's possible," she said, and when nothing happened, she wondered again whether the censor might be weakening.

"Sometimes I do violent things," she added quickly. Instantly, a pain that felt something like a charley horse gripped her stomach, bringing tears to her eyes. "Oh, God," Mary gasped. "I shouldn't have said that." The censor might have relaxed a little lately, but it certainly wasn't dead.

"Would you like to lie down?" Dr. Carpenter asked.

Mary shook her head. "I'm okay now."

After a moment's silence, the psychiatrist said, "To the best of your knowledge, have you ever harmed anyone during one of your memory lapses?"

"I . . . I'd better not try to talk about it."

"I understand. Has anyone ever called you by another name before, a name you wouldn't normally respond to?"

"You mean like Betty or Jane or something like that?"

Dr. Carpenter nodded.

"No, not that I can recall."

"All right, how do you feel about trying the cards with the shapes on them again?"

Mary said that was fine, and Dr. Carpenter held up a card with a crescent shape on it.

"It looks like the moon, but I can't think of any stories to go with it."

"Let's try this one then," Dr. Carpenter said, holding up a stylized silhouette of a woman similar to the figures sometimes used to identify men's and women's rest rooms.

"It's a woman," Mary said. "But it only appears to be one person. It's really two, in one body."

"How did the other person get in there?"

"I don't know. I just know she's there."

"Do they get along?"

"I don't know."

"Is there any more to the story?"

Mary thought for a moment. "No," she said finally, and she wondered what the meaning was of the story she'd just told. Or did the stories she made up to go along with the cards have any meaning, even to Dr. Carpenter?

The next card showed a rectangular grid. "It's a calendar," Mary said. "It's for this month, this year. And the last day of the month is circled. Walpurgis Night." Suddenly, Mary was trembling. "Doctor, please, you have to help me before Walpurgis Night. Please. It'll be too late if you don't."

Oh, God, she thought, staring at the grid. Walpurgis Night is a week from today. What's going to happen to me on that date?

"Why?" Dr. Carpenter asked. "Why will it be too late?"

"I . . . I don't know. But that calendar is in my head. It's part of me. It's like a timer, ticking away, with no way to stop it. Don't you see, that's why I can talk about it. Because there's no way to stop it." Tears were running down her cheeks now. She heard herself sobbing distantly, as if she were listening to the misery of another, a stranger.

When Mary's tears subsided, Dr. Carpenter said, "The next time you come, Mary, I'm going to hypnotize you—with your permission of course."

"You've got my permission, but do you think it will help?"

"It might. Hypnosis is one way to get into the unconscious. Sometimes hypnotized patients will reveal things they would never tell me otherwise, things I need to know if I'm to help them. But keep in mind that hypnosis is like everything else in psychotherapy. There are no guarantees."

It will help, Mary thought. It's got to help. But did she really believe that, or was she just trying to convince herself? Time's running out, some part of her kept insisting, and there's absolutely nothing you can do about it.

Thirteen

Y OU SURE THIS'LL WORK?" THE MAN ASKED, EXAMINING
the object in his hand. It was a four-inch toggle bolt.

"On the kind of wall you describe, yes," Mary
replied. "You drill a hole just large enough for the
toggle to fit through with its wings folded back against
the shaft; then it snaps open once it's through the hole,
and you can tighten it with a screwdriver. How thick's
the surface you have to penetrate?"

"I don't know." The man was about sixty, white-
haired, a little on the paunchy side.

Trying not to be obvious about it, Mary let her eyes
wander to the clock on the wall near the checkout cash
registers. It was 8:59, a minute before closing time on
Friday night. The man was the only customer still in the
building, and she wanted to get rid of him so she could
close up and go home.

From one of the compartmented metal bins holding
various types and sizes of fasteners, she grabbed a

six-inch toggle bolt. "Here," she said, handing it to
him. "This has to be long enough. If it's too long, if it
won't go in all the way, you can cut it off with a
hacksaw."

He stood there, studying the object in his hand,
frowning. Then he slowly nodded. "Yep, that'll do fine.
If it's too long, I'll just cut it off."

"How many do you need?" Mary asked, glad she was
about to get him out of the store.

"Two."

Smiling, she handed him another one. "There you
go, sir."

The man headed in the direction of the checkout
registers. Mary, taking a different aisle, made it there
ahead of him and took up her position by the door,
ready to chase away any late-arriving customers. As
soon as the man with the toggle bolts left, she locked
the door behind him and immediately began the routine of locking up for the night.

Ruth Bennett, a squat dark-haired woman of about
thirty, was still at her cash register. She couldn't leave it
until Howard Cummings showed up to collect the
money.

"When you need out, give me a holler," Mary said.

"Oh, I will," Ruth replied. "I don't want to spend a
single second more in this place than I have to."

Passing the discount counter, on which inexpensive
tools and other such items were displayed, she headed
down one of the main aisles leading to the rear of the
store. Looking to her left, down an aisle whose shelves
held small power tools, she could see a display of toilet
seats on the wall. To her right were cans of paint and
varnish and thinner. Moving deeper into the building,
she passed aisles where one could find nails, wire,

plumbing supplies, shovels, crowbars, chains, locks, sledge hammers. . . .

Against the rear wall was a vertically mounted glass cutter used primarily for trimming window panes to the sizes specified by customers. Beside the device was a big plastic garbage can filled with pieces of scrap glass, some of which were long and jagged. Walking along the back wall, she passed shelves holding aprons, tool belts, safety goggles. At the door leading to the yard, she stopped to make sure it was locked. It was. A few feet away another door led to a janitor's closet. It, too, was locked.

"Hey, Mary! Let me out!" It was Ruth.

Mary headed for the front of the store. As she pulled the key ring from the pocket of her jeans, Cummings showed up.

"The offices are all secure," he said. They were his responsibility, as the yard was Styles's, the store this week hers.

"Okay, Howard, thanks," she said, holding the door open. "Good night, Ruth." And then they were gone; she was alone in the store.

Mary quickly relocked the door and slipped the keys into her jeans. That she could dress casually was one of the things she liked about working here. Employees, management had wisely decided, should look as though they worked with the things being sold here. A person in a suit and tie or a trendy dress simply did not look as though he or she knew a damn thing about crowbars or chain saws or cement.

Still standing by the door, she surveyed the store. Empty like this, the place always seemed eerie to her. There should be people here, picking things up, checking the prices, asking questions, in the background the

159

ringing up of purchases, the rumble of trucks and forklifts from the yard. There was something vaguely disquieting about being in a place like this and knowing you were the only one here.

Well, she told herself, the only way to stop being the only one here is to finish up so you can go home. She headed for the only spot she hadn't checked: the employees' lounge. Walking past the customer-service counter, she entered a hallway that led to a door marked OFFICES. Just to be on the safe side, she tried the knob. The door was locked. On her left was another door, which led to the employees' lounge and locker room and the only rest rooms in the building.

Pushing the door open, she looked into the room before entering it. There was no one inside, waiting to pounce on her, but the empty building had this sort of effect on her. Murderers and rapists lurked in every shadow. And in light of what had happened to Steph, her fears weren't entirely groundless.

The lounge was nothing more than a small room with a table, vending machines for candy, soft drinks, and the like, and a row of metal lockers along one wall. Mary went to hers and twisted the dial on the combination lock. When she closed and relocked the gray metal door, she had slipped into her jacket and her purse hung from her shoulder. Before leaving the lounge, she checked the men's and women's rest rooms. Both were empty.

As she stepped into the hallway, closing the door behind her, Mary recalled how she and Steph had come this way after their meeting in Mr. Adkins's office, neither of them having any idea that Steph's first day on the job would also be her last. Mary was unable to recall what she had been thinking as she and Steph walked down this hallway, and it bothered her, although she wasn't sure why. There was no reason she should recollect that particular instant in her life. And yet not remembering made her feel callous somehow, as if Steph's death hadn't mattered.

The light switches were behind the customer-service counter. To simplify setting the night lights, the dozen or so switches on the wall came in two colors. The brown ones were switched off at night, the white ones left on. As she set the switches, the store grew progressively dimmer. The night lighting was sufficient for someone outside to look through the glass doors and tell whether anyone was inside, which, Mary supposed, was all that was necessary. She flipped down the final switch, and a group of lights somewhere in the back of the building winked out.

Letting herself out through the gate in the counter, she headed for the door. Once she'd let herself out of the building, she would activate the alarm system, using the key-operated switch on the wall. A security-patrol firm would check on the place periodically throughout the night. To Mary, this didn't seem like much protection for a place with such quantities of easy-to-dispose-of merchandise—like power tools—but then to her knowledge it had never been burglarized, and she was no security expert.

She was fishing the keys from her pocket when something crashed to the floor in the rear of the building, startling her. She whirled, staring in the direction from which the sound had come, seeing nothing unusual. Something—she had no idea what— had apparently fallen from its shelf. Although she knew she should go and see what had happened, she simply stood there, gazing at the rear of the store, her heart pounding. Get hold of yourself, she thought. Something fell; that's all.

161

Finally, she began moving down a main aisle, her footfalls on the floor tiles sounding like crashes in the dead quiet of the store. She thought she heard a noise somewhere ahead of her, the rustle of clothing, a shoe sole slipping on a tile. Stop it, she told herself. Your imagination's playing tricks on you. There's no one else here. There couldn't be, because you looked everywhere there was to look.

And then she had doubts about that. What had she failed to check? Where had someone been able to hide, wait until she was alone, vulnerable?

Stop, stop, stop! she commanded. Don't do this to yourself. There were simply no cubbyholes to hide in; the architects of the building hadn't allowed for any. Every square inch possible had been devoted to retail space. There wasn't even a storeroom. Computers kept track of the merchandise. When an item ran low, it was ordered, and when the shipment arrived, it was put right on the shelf. If things got screwed up and you got too much of something, it still went right on the shelf, stacked three or four high sometimes, or piled on the aisle floor, wherever there was room.

What about the office? How well did Howard Cummings check things out before locking up? Someone could have hidden in one of the offices, then, after Cummings was gone, let himself out. The doors wouldn't even be locked to anyone on the inside. The locks were designed to keep people out, not in.

And then she realized that no one could have moved from the offices to the back of the store without going right past her, which no one had. No one here except the boogeyman, she thought. And he only lives in the imaginations of children . . . and a few panicky adults.

And if someone had come out of the offices while you were checking out the rest rooms in the employees' lounge, would you have seen him then? No, she decided. And the boogeyman suddenly seemed less imaginary than he had a moment ago.

Mary was all the way to the last aisle before she found what had fallen: three large cans of glazing compound, which had tumbled off one of the middle shelves. What she couldn't figure out was why they'd fallen. Nothing on the shelf was stacked precariously; there was plenty of room for everything. She picked up the cans and put them back. Sometimes customers rearranged things, Mary concluded, and that was what must have happened. She sighed, relieved. So much for the boogeyman.

And then, as she was turning to go, she saw it. The door to the janitor's closet was open about an inch. Backing slowly away from it, she realized what had happened. Someone had got into the closet somehow, and when she'd tried the knob, found it locked, the person had been in there, waiting. And the cans had been knocked off the shelf on purpose, to get her to come back here, close to the closet. She continued backing away, knowing the door would burst open any moment.

Run! something inside her urged. Run while you can. But when she turned to do so, the lights went out.

Mary froze, listening intently, hearing only the thudding of her heart. It wasn't completely dark. Outside, the parking lot lights were still on, some of their brightness seeping in through the glass front door. But the light didn't reach the very back of the store. Where she stood, it was almost totally black.

Realizing that as long as the lights were out she'd be invisible here, she remained motionless, trying not to panic. Think, she told herself. Use your head.

The cans had indeed been knocked from the shelf to

lure her to this part of the store, but not so someone could pounce on her from the closet as she'd first thought. The idea had been to trap her here. She had to assume she was in great danger.

Behind her was the door to the yard. Unlike some of the building's other doors, it had locks that could not be opened from within without a key. And Mary had one, which she had no intention of using, for beyond that door was part of the store's security she'd forgotten about earlier—a guard dog, a Doberman.

It arrived each night in a van and was turned loose in the yard just before J.M. Styles locked the gate. On the other side of that door was a lighted compound surrounded by a high chain link fence, patrolled by a dog that had every reason to think she was a burglar if she showed up out there. For a moment, she toyed with the idea of tricking whoever was in the building into going through that door, but then she realized it wouldn't work. She'd forgotten something else. Immediately beyond the door was a fenced enclosure with a gate that would be locked with a padlock right now, its purpose to keep absentminded employees from stepping through the door and remembering too late about the dog. J.M. Styles locked the enclosure's gate each night before allowing the dog to be put in the compound.

Styles! The big man with the enormous arms that could crush almost anything. He'd be waiting for her; he'd notice that the lights were out, realize something was wrong. All she had to do was move closer to the front of the building, then dash for the door, pound on it. Styles would come to her rescue.

As quietly as she could, Mary headed toward the glass door. She was moving out of the cloaking darkness and into the dim light. Ahead, she'd be clearly visible. Ahead, someone waited.

Who? And why? What did whoever was here have in mind? She saw Steph's bloody body lying in the front seat of the car and shuddered. Had the same killer come back for another victim?

Her composure crumbling, Mary rushed to the door. Styles wasn't there. Through the glass, she could see part of the lighted parking lot, including the spot where employees parked. There was only one car in that spot: hers.

Styles was gone.

She and whoever had turned out the lights were the only ones here.

Although she didn't remember pulling her keys from her pocket, they were in her hand, and she was trying desperately to insert the one that unlocked the front door. It refused to go in. Frantically, she turned the key over and tried again. When that failed, she tried another key, then another. Finally, she realized something was wrong with the lock. Running her fingers over its surface, she felt the end of something that had been jammed into the mechanism and then broken off. And, at that moment, she became certain that whoever was here was closing in on her, about to . . . to what? Dropping the keys, she whirled to defend herself, finding no one. Is someone playing some kind of a game with me, she wondered—a bizarre, sick game?

Mary considered getting a hammer and trying to break the door. But it was made of thick tempered glass. The glass was so strong that even banks used it; she was sure it wouldn't break from a single hammer blow, and whoever trapped her here would hardly sit idly by while she pounded on it.

Grabbing the keys from the floor, she moved away from the door. Somewhere, whoever was here had to be waiting for her. No other explanation made any sense. Why else would anyone hide in the janitor's closet, lure her to the back of the store, jam the lock? Uncertain where she was heading, Mary stopped. She couldn't wander aimlessly, or she'd step right into her adversary's arms. To her left were the cash registers. Ahead was the customer-service counter, which, it suddenly dawned on her, had a telephone with an outside line. Moving quietly, cautiously, she headed for it.

Although the area around the counter was open, providing no place to hide, a person could easily be concealed behind it, waiting for her to come, try to use the phone. And once back there, she'd be trapped. Still, she continued moving slowly forward because getting to the phone was her only chance.

Reaching the counter, she peered over it, seeing shadows, the shape of a desk, a chair. Though still in the front of the store, she'd been moving laterally away from the door, which was the only source of light. There were three phones here, one on each of two desks, a third under the counter, out of reach from this side.

Having no choice but to enter the enclosure, she began inching her way toward the gate, listening intently.

The gate creaked as she pushed through it, then swung silently back into position. Mary stood motionless, ready to turn and flee at the first sign of trouble, but nothing in the shadows moved, and the only sound was her own nervous breathing. Okay, she told herself, get to the phone. Quickly.

She slipped along the counter until her fingers touched the cord; then, squatting before the phone, she lifted the receiver and put it to her ear. The phone was dead. Again, her fingers found the cord, and she began pulling it to her. A moment later, the end of the wire, neatly cut, passed through her fingers. Instantly, she had the feeling that someone had been waiting for her, was behind her right now. She scrambled desperately away from the counter, stopping when she reached a desk, bracing for the attack that didn't come.

Panting, she crouched beside the desk and looked around her, peering into the shadows in which nothing moved. Calm yourself, she thought. You've got to have your act together if you're to have any chance at all of defending yourself. Her hand touched another phone cord, which she grabbed. It, too, had been severed. Checking the third phone, she knew, would be pointless.

Okay now, she thought, don't panic, think. The only other phones were in the offices, for which she had no keys. There were two doors for which she did have keys, but one led to a locked fence gate with an unfriendly Doberman on the other side, and the other had a jammed lock. So, how was her adversary going to get out? By removing the obstruction from the lock, using her key? Well, she could do that, too. There were certainly enough tools here. A pair of Vise-grips would likely do the job.

And something else was abundant here as well: weapons. On the shelves could be found axes, hammers, things that could be used as garrotes or clubs, things that bent, chopped, made holes. She shuddered. This could be the creative murderer's best place to shop—specially stocked for killers with a sadistic bent. She realized suddenly that she was sweating, and yet she felt very cold.

Come on, come on, she thought. Think about what

you're going to do. You've got to find two things: a pair of Vise-grips and a weapon. This cat-and-mouse business won't go on forever. Sooner or later, something's got to happen, and you'd better be ready for it.

Suddenly, she almost wanted to laugh, because she'd just realized why J.M. Styles hadn't been outside waiting for her tonight. This was Friday, one of Styles's days off. The yardman tonight would have been Quentin McGinnity, whom she barely knew but who would certainly never think of walking her to her car after work. He was a middle-aged man who, rumor had it, beat his wife and children. No one at Zel seemed to like him very much.

Changing her mind about not bothering to check the third phone, she straightened from her crouch, moved to the other desk, and reached for the instrument. Rather than picking up the receiver, she grabbed the cord. As she'd expected, it had been cut. And then, from under the desk, a hand grabbed her ankle. She heard herself gasp.

Instantly, she was falling, her head hitting a waste-basket, a dark shape emerging from under the desk, coming at her. Stunned, her thoughts swirling, she was momentarily unable to act. And then some protective instinct took over. She lashed out with her feet, and the man yelped, staggering backward. Her right foot had hit him in the stomach; the left one had caught him squarely in the crotch.

Frantically scrambling to her feet, she ran for the gate in the counter. To her right, she saw the dark shape of a man, doubled over but moving along the wall, trying to intercept her. She veered to the left and threw herself onto the counter, sliding across it on her stomach. Her bag, which somehow had stayed on her shoulder, snagged on something. The strap snapped, and it was gone. And Mary was on the floor.

She lay there a moment, dazed by the impact with the hard surface. Then the counter gate was flung open with a bang, and Mary was on her feet, running.

She raced down the nearest main aisle, toward the rear of the store, into the darkness. Before reaching the back wall, she turned into another aisle, stopped, and looked back the way she had come. Silhouetted by the light from the front door, her adversary was coming. But slowly. He was hobbling, obviously still in pain from the kick to his crotch. Mary had no idea who he was or even what he looked like. The silhouette was tall, thin, unquestionably male, although on that point there had been absolutely no question after she'd heard him cry out. At least, in his present condition, she would have no trouble eluding him. She suddenly found herself filled with loathing for this man, wishing she'd kicked him in the testicles so hard she'd squashed them, ruined them, inflicting more agony than he could endure. The raw intensity of the emotion surprised her.

But she had no time to analyze her feelings. She still needed the Vise-grips and a weapon. Peeking around the corner of a shelf, she saw that her pursuer, still moving awkwardly, had covered only about half the distance from the front of the store. Mary slipped along the shelves, then, using another main aisle, moved toward the front of the building. She turned right, hurried along past shelves containing all sorts of hand tools, and stopped in front of the Vise-grips. Although this far from the door it was too dark to see things clearly, she had no trouble finding her way around. Her familiarity with the place was an advantage over her adversary, and she'd have to remember to use it. She slipped the Vise-grips into the rear pocket of her jeans. Now she needed a weapon.

Returning to the main aisle she'd just used, she looked in both directions, seeing nothing. She crossed the aisle and moved to the one where she'd last seen her pursuer, again checking both directions. There was no sign of him. Fighting down the panic that was starting to well up, she reminded herself that she knew her way around better than he did and could out-maneuver him. Now, find a weapon, she thought. Defend yourself.

The trouble was that, though she knew the store and the things in it, she had never thought of the tools as weapons before. A radial saw could slice off a hand without difficulty, but one could hardly carry it around. All sorts of things had sharp edges, but most of them were unwieldy or too small or suffered from other faults that rendered them pretty useless as weapons, which of course they were never intended to be. And then she had the answer: a gun . . . a stud gun to be precise.

The device was loaded with a twenty-two caliber charge and shot specially hardened nails into concrete. It had a safety feature that prevented its being fired unless pressed tightly against a surface, but she was fairly confident she could defeat that. She'd get the gun, nails, and charges, go somewhere he'd be sure to find her, and wait. When he showed up, she'd shoot him.

The stud guns were in the rear of the store, near the spot where she'd stopped and watched the man hob-bling toward her. She would have to move into the darkness, with the light behind her. She'd be silhouet-ted by the light from the door while anyone waiting in the shadows would be invisible. Mary, thinking her adversary would most likely watch the central aisles, decided to take one that ran along a wall.

And on the shelves just ahead were some good interim weapons. Wood-splitting tools, including hatchets and axes. Once more checking for any signs of her adversary and finding none, she crossed the aisle, grabbed a hatchet from the shelf, and hurried to the far wall, where she turned and headed for the back of the store.

She could think of no way to get help. The phones were useless, and she couldn't set off the security alarm because it wasn't activated. The key-operated switch was on the wall outside the front door; she knew of no way to switch on the alarm from inside the building. Nor could she set off the fire alarm, not without starting a fire. The only other way of setting it off would be to find a stepladder high enough to reach the ceiling and hold something that was burning under one of the system's sensors. It seemed unlikely that her assailant would stand idly by while she did all that.

As Mary moved silently down the aisle, she stopped every few feet to listen, holding the hatchet ready. Each time it was quiet, unnervingly so. Where was he? What was he doing?

When she reached the stud guns, she found the one that was out of its box for display purposes, set it and the hatchet on the floor, and felt around on the dark shelves until she found a box of nails and another of twenty-two caliber charges. Squatting, she opened up the gun. There was so little light here that she had to load it primarily by feel, but she finally succeeded. The stud gun looked something like a large power drill, except that instead of a chuck to hold a drill bit it had a metal cup at one end. This was the shield, and one had to rest it on a surface and push down on the gun, or it wouldn't fire. This was the safety mechanism she had to defeat if the gun was to be an effective weapon.

Realizing that she had been in this spot too long and that she might have made enough noise to reveal her location, Mary quickly stuffed some nails and charges in her pockets and grabbed the gun, leaving the hatchet behind. As she neared the main aisle, she stopped and listened, hearing only silence. But when she stepped into the main aisle, leaving the protection of the shelves, she heard a gentle metallic clunk. Close. Very close. She dived forward, throwing herself at the floor, and something swished over her head, crashing into a shelf, scattering its contents.

Mary, still clutching the stud gun, rolled over in time to see the silhouetted shape of her assailant lift something with a long handle and swing it at her. She rolled again, something metal striking the shelf just inches from her head, boxes tumbling into the aisle. The man was off-balance, and she lunged at him with the stud gun, trying to press it against some part of him—any part of him—so she could pull the trigger. Unable to get to her feet, she found herself on her stomach, sliding over the debris on the floor. The man stepped back quickly, but then he gasped and fell, and Mary realized what had happened. The objects on the floor were main electric fuses, little cylinders that acted like rollers if you stepped on them. She scrambled forward, reaching out with the stud gun. He kicked at her but missed. She shoved the gun against his leg and pulled the trigger. The gun fired. He bellowed.

And then he must have kicked again because the gun was knocked from her grasp and slid across the floor, into the shadows and out of sight. Quickly, she tried to crawl away, slipping on the fuses, but a hand grabbed her ankle, and then he was on top of her, reaching for her throat. She tried to keep his hands away, but he was stronger than she was, and his fingers closed around her neck. Her blows fell short when she tried to strike him in the face; his arms were much longer than hers. Pulling the Vise-grips from her back pocket, she reached for his face, found it, and squeezed the handles. Releasing her, he screamed.

The man was still on top of her, so she began savagely pounding him with the tool in her hand.

"Stop it, you bitch!" he yelled. "Stop it." And then he was off of her, both of them trying to get to their feet. Mary made it to hers just as the man's feet slipped out from under him. She ran.

"Bitch!" he hollered. "Bitch!"

Frantically turning corners and plunging down dark aisles, Mary tried to put as much distance between herself and the man as possible. When she stopped, crouching in the shadows, trembling, out of breath but trying to control her breathing so the sound wouldn't give her location away, the Vise-grips were still in her hand.

Oh, God, she thought, slipping the tool back into her pocket. It was the only thought that would come, and it repeated itself over and over in her mind: Oh God, oh God, oh God. . . .

Finally, her brain began to work again. She knew what her adversary had attempted to clobber her with. A weed cutter. Swung with enough force, it could decapitate someone.

Somewhere in the building, something crashed into something else, and then it was silent. Although Mary was certain she had shot the man in the leg, she had apparently not rendered him harmless. Could he be the man in the blue car? Mary wondered. She still hadn't had a clear look at his face, but the man she'd seen silhouetted by the light from the door had been tall and thin, as had been the man in the blue sedan. Because her assailant had only yelled or groaned so far, his voice was no help in identifying him. But then identifying him was unimportant at the moment. For now, all she needed to know about the man was that he was stronger than she was and that he apparently wanted to kill her.

By now Tom would be wondering why she was late. Would he try to phone the store, perhaps call the police when he got no answer? Not for a while yet, she thought. It's too soon. He'd wanted her to call the police last night after she'd told him about the man in the blue car. She'd talked him out of the notion, thinking it would just bring another visit from Sergeant Flanagan, whom she particularly wanted to avoid. A tear trickled down her cheek. Would she ever see Tom again? Or was this it? Would she die here tonight? Oh, no, she thought. Oh, no, no, no.

The realization that she might never leave this place, might never see Tom again was devastating. She wished she could stretch out on the floor and escape into a dream from which she'd awaken to find everything was all right again.

Suddenly, a bright glow came from an area a couple of aisles away from her, then disappeared. He'd found the flashlights, which were conveniently displayed next to the batteries. With a light, he could walk down a main aisle and illuminate the cross passages in both directions, eliminating the shadows, including those in which she now hid. Knowing she had to get out of this spot and quickly, she moved along the shelves, abruptly stopping when her hand touched something smooth and cylindrical. She grabbed it, felt around on the shelf for an igniter, and took both objects to the end of the aisle. Again, the light came on and then went out, closer now. Mary hurriedly took the two objects to the other end of the same aisle. The man should come this way.

Crouching, she held the igniter ready, waiting. The light came on, went out, very close now. Then she could hear him breathing, only a few feet away, moving toward her. She turned the knob atop the metal bottle and immediately struck a spark with the igniter. Flame squirted from the torch. Springing up, she pushed the fire into the man's face, which twisted in shock, horror. He swung the flashlight at her, hitting the torch but not moving it. The light flew from his hand and hit something behind Mary. She twisted the knob, trying to get the flame to go higher. Instead, it went out. She'd turned the knob in the wrong direction. Not knowing what else to do, she raised the small gas bottle over her head and tried to bash him with it, but there was nothing there to strike; he was gone. The bottle, which had slipped from her grasp, hit the floor, rolled.

Dazed, she simply stood there, shaking. She could hear him moving away, retreating into the shadows at the back of the store. It was the man in the blue car; she'd seen his face clearly in the light from the torch. Suddenly, she turned and ran for the front door, pulling the Vise-grips from her back pocket.

At the door, she quickly adjusted the tool, then tried to get it to grab the object that had been jammed into the lock. After two more adjustments, she got the Vise-grips locked on; there was just enough of the object sticking out for them to grip. When she pulled gently, nothing happened, so she pulled harder. The Vise-grips slipped off the object. Don't panic, she told herself. Clamp them on again. You can do it. When she'd done so, she pulled again on the object jammed into the lock, and it came out. Before she could determine what it was, there was a loud noise to her left.

Startled, she looked in that direction, seeing only shadows, but knowing he was close. Too close. If she tried to get the door open, he'd be on her. But if she left this spot, would he jam the lock again—did he even know she'd succeeded in removing the obstruction? If I can lure him to the back of the store, she decided, then I can get back here and have a few seconds to unlock the door. She began moving to her right, away from the noise she'd heard. Entering a main aisle, she looked to see whether the man had gone to the door. He hadn't. She heard another noise and began moving faster. Suddenly, her legs were knocked out from under her, and she was on the floor.

Uncertain what had happened, she sat up, looking for her adversary. This close to the door, there was enough light to take in her surroundings, and the man was nowhere to be seen. She saw what had caused her to fall, a rope that had been stretched across several aisles so it would trip her no matter which one she took. As she started to get up, a pain shot through her left shoulder, and she hesitated. Nothing broken, she decided, but it hurt.

And then the man was there, limping but still advancing on her rapidly. Trailing a long extension cord behind him, he had an electric chain saw in his hands. He switched it on.

Momentarily unable to move, Mary stared in horror

at the blur of metal teeth. Then she was half crawling, half running down the aisle, the saw's howling abruptly stopping as her pursuer switched it off and came after her. Her feet struck something lying in the aisle, and she fell. The man was nearly on top of her. Grabbing an object from the shelf—a small can of something—she hurled it at him. Bouncing off his arm, it had no effect. Suddenly, the saw was howling again, the deadly teeth once more a blur. She reached for something to defend herself with, finding nothing. He stopped about two paces from her and smiled, looking pleased with himself. The game was over, and he had won. Stepping toward her, he raised the saw deliberately. It died in his hands.

They stared at each other, the confusion on his face obvious even in the dim light. Then Mary saw it. By his foot was the saw's plug, connected to nothing, nothing at all. He'd run out of extension cord, taken one step too many, unplugged the saw. Instantly, Mary was on her feet, running. From behind her came a crash. She thought he'd thrown the saw at her, although she wasn't sure. In her headlong plunge into the darkness at the rear of the store, she nearly slammed into the wall. Stopping just in time, she sank to the floor, her heart pounding madly. Had the extension cord been a few inches longer. . . . She deliberately left the thought uncompleted.

Mary heard a noise, close, maybe an aisle or two away. He was searching for her. Quickly, she began feeling around in the dark for a weapon. She found only cloths, the carpenter's aprons. Think, she told herself, think. What's in this aisle? Tool belts, safety goggles . . . what else? The glass cutter. She grabbed one of the aprons and moved to the plastic garbage can which held scrap glass. Gently fingering the sharp pieces, she selected a long one about six inches wide, wrapped the cloth around it, and withdrew it.

The man must have heard her because he was there almost instantly, a dim shape coming toward her. Using both hands, she swung the glass as hard as she could. It hit him, shattering. He gasped.

Dropping what remained of the glass, Mary dashed to the end of the aisle. As she tried to turn the corner, she lost her footing and crashed into a shelf. Reaching for something to hold on to, she found herself clutching a window. It was a chest-high portable display that showed how a wooden-sash window worked. Her fingers brushed something cold and hard, a counterweight. Hearing the man's footfalls as he came after her, Mary grabbed the cord to which the cylindrical weight was attached, waited until the man was almost on top of her, then swung it with all her strength, pulling the display over onto the floor. The weight hit solidly and the man dropped to the floor, moaning. Mary raced for the front of the building.

At the door, she pulled the keys from her pocket, desperately trying to determine which one was the right one. Selecting one, she jammed it into the lock, but it wouldn't turn. Frantic now, she tried another one and realized she was attempting to put it in upside down. She turned it over; it slipped in, turned, and the door was open, Mary running through it into the parking lot.

Glancing behind her, she saw him in the doorway and tried to run faster. Suddenly, there were lights in front of her. Headlights. Still running, she waved her arms, tried to yell, but she was so out of breath that words were impossible. As she reached the car, a door opened and a uniformed man climbed out. It was the security patrolman who checked on the store at nights.

"Hey," he said as Mary collapsed against him. "What's wrong? Why are all the lights out inside the building?"

"Go after him," Mary said, gasping for breath.

"Who?"

"The man. He was behind me. Didn't you see him?"

"I'm sorry, but I didn't see anyone. Now, see if you can tell me what happened. First of all, who are you?"

Fourteen

AND YOU'RE SURE THIS WAS THE SAME MAN WHO WAS
following you, the man you confronted at the shopping
center?" Flanagan said. He and Mary sat on metal-and-
plastic chairs behind the customer-service counter.
Tom was there, too, sitting beside her, squeezing her
hand.

"Yes," Mary replied. "I'm sure." From where she
sat she could see a detective dusting the chain saw for
fingerprints. Because she had had access to no working
phones, the security patrolman had radioed his dis-
patcher, requesting that Tom be notified. Although he
was apparently trying to remain calm for her sake, her
husband looked pale and drained. Holding his hand,
she could almost feel the tension in him.

"And," Flanagan said, "you have no idea who he is
or why he would want to harm you."

"No. The first time I saw him was when he showed
up pretending to be an encyclopedia salesman. Or

maybe he really is an encyclopedia salesman, for all I know."

Flanagan frowned. "I doubt it, but we'll check and see if any encyclopedia companies have anybody working for them who matches the description."

"Did you call Mr. Adkins?"

"Who?"

"The assistant manager."

"Oh, yeah. He'll be here any minute now."

A uniformed officer stepped up to the counter, waited until Flanagan looked his way. "There's blood smears in quite a few places back there."

"Extensive blood loss?"

"Hard to say, Sergeant." He was a tall young man, slender, blond hair. "There's no puddles of it or anything like that."

"Could any of it be yours?" Flanagan asked Mary.

She shook her head. "My shoulder's pretty sore, but that's it."

The detective snorted. "This guy better find another line of work. He tries to jump a girl, and she sends him home bloody."

He studied Mary's face, apparently awaiting her reaction. She could tell by the way Tom squeezed her hand a little more tightly that he resented Flanagan's attitude. So did Mary, but she didn't let it show. She just looked at the detective tiredly.

Flanagan shifted his eyes to the uniformed officer. "Besides the blood, what does it look like back there?"

"There are places where things have been knocked off the shelves, and there's some things on the floor that might have been used as weapons. A weed cutter, a hatchet, the chain saw there"—he glanced at it—"an axe, a funny-looking thing that sort of looks like some kind of a gun."

"It's a stud gun," Mary said, "for shooting nails into concrete."

"Oh."

"Where'd you find the axe?" she asked. She shuddered; she hadn't known the man had had one.

The patrolman glanced at Flanagan to see whether it was okay to answer. The sergeant nodded, and the young officer said, "In the far corner there." He motioned toward the back of the store. "There's a window lying on the floor there. It's right next to that."

Oh, God, Mary thought, he had it in his hands when I hit him with the glass, then clobbered him with the weight. How close did I come to dying tonight? How close? She shivered, and Tom again squeezed her hand more firmly.

"Sergeant," Tom said, "do you mind if I take my wife home? She's been through quite a lot tonight, and I'd like to take her home and put her to bed."

Mary doubted she could sleep, but she did want to get out of here, away from Flanagan. At some point tonight, she supposed, her emotions would all come out. She'd cry until the terror didn't taste so fresh, so real anymore. So far, she hadn't reacted to her experience at all; she'd simply been numb.

"All right," Flanagan said. Then, looking at Mary, he added, "Tomorrow morning sometime I'd like you to come in and look at mug shots. Maybe we'll get lucky."

Mary said she'd be there about nine-thirty. As she and Tom rose to go, the detective said, "Once you realized you were being followed, did you report it?"

"There was nothing to report," she said wearily. "He hadn't really done anything."

"I see." He eyed her knowingly, as if they shared some secret.

Oh, my God, Mary thought. He still suspects me of something, of . . . of being involved in all this in some way other than as a victim. Well, dammit, tonight I *was* a victim, and I damn near got killed.

The trouble, she realized unhappily, was that Flanagan might be right. She was aware of her role as a victim. But she also did things of which she was unaware. And the thin man hadn't selected her at random; there was a connection between them, a link that had to have its roots in her blank spells. Inwardly, she shuddered.

It was dreary and overcast the next morning when Mary drove to the police station. She found a parking space in the free public parking lot that separated city hall from the police station. Both were modern three-story brick buildings. Here in the suburbs, local governments lived happily, prosperously, on their nice fat tax bases.

At the front desk, a young uniformed policeman told her she was expected and directed her down a long beige hallway to room 107, where another uniformed officer explained that Sergeant Flanagan was out on a case and wouldn't be here to deal with her personally.

"Sit down," the officer said, indicating a chair at a modern table. She was about thirty, blond, slender.

Mary did as instructed. The room was small, containing only the table at which she sat, another one just like it, a few chairs with plastic seats. The officer left, returning a moment later with a large loose-leaf notebook, which she laid on the table in front of Mary.

"The pictures you'll see here were selected by the computer after we told it what we know. All of the men will be about the right age, height, so on. And all of them have proven themselves capable of violence."

Mary opened the notebook, flipped through the pages. It contained hundreds of photos, each with a number. None of the faces were identified.

She looked up at the cop, whose name tag read Lorene Ball. "I didn't know there were this many bad guys here, not in a nice quiet community like this."

Officer Ball smiled. "The suburbs just get a better class of criminals, the more successful ones. But you're right; we don't have that many criminals here who fit what we know about your assailant. These pictured come from all over the metropolitan Boston area. Before I leave you with them, do you have any questions?"

"If I find one that looks like the guy, what should I do?"

"Just hang tight. I'll be back to check on you in a few minutes."

As soon as she was alone, Mary turned her attention to the book. It contained page after page of middle-aged men, usually with numbers hanging from their necks, often standing beside other numbers that showed their heights, their black-and-white faces looking dejected, defeated. Occasionally, one would peer belligerently at her, sometimes with transparent bravado, sometimes with such menace that Mary felt like averting her eyes. The one she found most frightening was the photo of a man with tangled gray hair and a sly smile on his face. It was the man's eyes that first caught her attention. In them, she'd seen the same frighteningly intense look she'd seen in her attacker's eyes when she'd been face-to-face with him at the shopping mall. You stared into those eyes, and you knew beyond a doubt that this person was insane. She could see that face in the picture approaching a control panel somewhere, a hand reaching out pressing the button that launched the nukes and ended everything.

Finally, she reached the end of the book. Some of the faces had had similar eyes or noses or chins, but none had been the right face. She turned to find Officer Ball standing behind her, looking at her expectantly.

Mary shook her head. "He's not in here. I'm sure."

"Okay," Officer Ball said, smiling reassuringly. "We've got plenty more pictures. Don't give up yet."

But the next batch of photos included men who were obviously too young or too old and presumably less likely to be the suspect in other ways as well. These were the long shots, and there were three books of them. It was noon when she finished.

Officer Ball sighed. "Well, that's the way it usually works. It just means we're not going to luck out and get him the easy way."

Mary left, grateful she hadn't had to see Flanagan. As she had done on the way to the police station, she kept an eye on the rearview mirror. There was no sign of the battered blue Ford.

Fifteen

UNCERTAIN WHERE SHE WAS OR HOW SHE HAD GOTTEN there, Mary stared at the darkened houses. Dressed in jeans and a shirt, she was standing on a sidewalk that ran along one edge of a small park. The homes, the park, the street were all vaguely familiar. This was her neighborhood, she concluded, a part of it she rarely visited. But what was she doing here, alone and in the middle of the night? And then, her head clearing, she knew the answer to that question. She'd just come out of another blank spell.

Suddenly feeling weak, she took a few steps into the park and sat down on the cool damp grass, her thoughts swirling. For a few moments, she simply stared at a large house across the street, its windows dark except for one on the second floor. Some part of her mind, apparently searching for some piece of reality to grab on to, concluded that one dimly lit window was in a hall, the weak glow coming from a night-light.

Pulling her eyes away from the faint yellow rectangle, she took in the rest of her surroundings. She was in the middle of the block, in the darkness between the pools of illumination from two streetlights. The park itself was a collection of shadows, black shapes that by daylight might be bushes and benches and trash cans, shapes that in darkness seemed certain to be muggers and rapists and things that stalked you, breathing heavily. She shuddered, remembering the faces she'd seen that morning in the mug book—and the face of the man who *had* stalked her last night, in a store full of potential weapons.

She remained where she was. Not because she was unafraid but because it was pointless to run from the monsters. If determined enough, the flesh-and-blood monsters would get you eventually. And the other kind . . . well, those monsters were part of you, and there was no way to flee from yourself. Which do I fear the most, she wondered, the man in the blue car or the monster within myself?

Leaving the question unanswered, she tried to reconstruct her day so she could determine when the blank spell had begun. She recalled going to the police station, then to work, Tom waiting for her when she got off and following her home in his station wagon, dinner, going to bed with Tom. So she had gotten out of bed, dressed, and left the house. To do what? The last time she'd left bed in the middle of the night, she'd apparently sabotaged a child's swing. What had she done tonight?

Then an even more frightening question occurred to her. What if this weren't Saturday night at all? What if she'd slipped into the blank spell days ago? Could this be Wednesday, Thursday? It had happened before, when she was a child. Two whole weeks had vanished, fourteen days that, as far as Mary was concerned, might as well have been stricken from the calendar.

Feeling cold, she folded her arms across her chest. She wasn't wearing a jacket, and April nights were chilly in Massachusetts. In the distance, a siren wailed. The sound faded, then began growing louder. Something with flashing red lights screamed by a couple of blocks away.

Still looking toward the intersection where she'd seen the emergency vehicle go by, she saw something moving in the shadows of the next block. A man. He was coming toward her. And then the streetlights went out. Instantly, Mary's mind returned to the store, the lights going out, the man coming after her. Was it he on the next block, the man who wanted to kill her?

Getting quietly to her feet, she began moving into the park. The black shapes were gone now, swallowed up by the darkness, along with the houses, the street, the world. The sky was overcast, not a single star penetrating the thick clouds. Glancing behind her, Mary noticed that even the dim rectangle of yellow light was gone.

Suddenly, she cried out, terrified, blindly striking out at the thing that had just grabbed her. Abruptly, she stopped, breathing heavily, feeling very foolish. She'd just fought with a bush.

And then she heard footsteps, someone hurrying along the sidewalk. Whoever it was was close, very close. She had to get out of here. She'd made too much noise during her scuffle with the shrub. Moving as silently as she could, Mary began heading away from the footsteps.

Within moments, she had lost all sense of direction, but she kept going, feeling her way around the trees and bushes that kept popping up in her path. Some-where in the darkness, a twig snapped.

Mary froze. Had the sound come from behind her, her right, her left? She kept hearing that snap over and over in her mind, and each time, it seemed to come from another direction. She listened intently, hearing only the sound of an approaching vehicle.

Its headlights appeared in the street, some of their brightness momentarily spilling into the park. Enough light for her to see the shape of a man maybe fifteen feet away. The vehicle continued on its way, taking with it the illumination it had briefly provided.

Don't panic, Mary told herself. If you run, you'll crash into something. He can't get you. In this dark-ness, fifteen feet's as good as a mile. She heard him then, moving, almost close enough to touch her. Oh, God, she thought, trying to control her breathing, what if he bumps into me?

"Mary, is that you?" a very familiar voice asked rather tentatively.

"Tom?"

"Mary! My God, what are you doing out here?"

"I . . . I just woke up and went for a walk." Oh, God, she thought, here come the lies. Because I can't tell him. I can't.

His hand found her shoulder, and she resisted the impulse to pull away. It wasn't that she found his touch repugnant; it was warm and comforting. Still, some part of her mind seemed to scream: *How do you know it's his hand?* And then he had her in his arms.

Mary wanted to cry then, to hug him and sob. But she wouldn't, because then she'd have to explain the tears, and she was unable to do that without telling more lies.

"I woke up and realized the bed was empty, so I

called your name," Tom said. "When you didn't answer, I got up and I saw you through the window. You were walking away from the house."

"Why did you come after me?"

"Well, it's a little unusual, isn't it, getting up at three in the morning to go wandering in the dark? I didn't want anything to happen to you." He fell silent, apparently awaiting an explanation.

When she didn't offer one, he asked, "Is anything wrong?"

Girding herself to tell more lies, she replied, "It was what happened last night. I couldn't get it off my mind, so I decided to get up and get out of the house. I thought a walk might calm me down."

"But it's not safe out here," he said, squeezing her more tightly. "What if . . . you know, what if the guy who attacked you last night was out here waiting for you?"

I thought he was, Mary thought. I thought he was. She knew for sure now that it was Saturday—or rather early Sunday morning. Apparently, she had left the house only minutes ago.

There were more sirens now, close. "Must be a fire somewhere," Tom said. "Let's see if we can find our way out of here."

Taking her hand, he began leading her out of the park. Mary knew they had come to the street when the surface under her feet changed from grass to concrete.

"Look," Tom said.

But Mary had already seen it. To their left, an orange glow silhouetted the trees and rooftops. Something was burning. "What's over there?" she asked.

"I don't know. Let's go down to the next block. Maybe we'll be able to see something."

Although Mary had never cared for being one of the

onlookers at the scene of a mishap, she realized that it was human nature to spectate so she went along without any resistance. Now that they were out of the park, the orange glow above the rooftops provided enough light for them to see where they were going. The streetlights were still out, the houses dark. Recalling how frightened she'd been when the lights had gone out, Mary felt foolish. It was nothing but an ordinary power failure.

When they reached the end of the block and rounded the corner, they saw the fire. A fairly large building was engulfed in flames, the glow bathing the block in orange. In the street was a spectacular display of flashing red lights. Firemen were connecting hoses, spraying the flames, yelling things to each other. A police car arrived, adding its flashing lights to the others.

After she and Tom had moved a little closer to the blaze, Mary realized that this was what had caused the power failure. A line was down, one of its wooden poles lying in the street, charred and smoking. As they continued to move closer to the fire, Mary began to feel the heat on her face. Ahead, a policeman stood on the sidewalk, and a middle-aged woman in her bathrobe was waving her arms as she spoke to him.

"I was looking out the window," she was saying, "and I saw someone over there, doing something with some square object. Anyway, I left the window for a few moments, then came back. Well, at first I didn't see anything. Then, suddenly, I saw flames, spreading like crazy. And I saw someone run away from the church."

Glancing at Tom, whose face was orange in the light from the fire, Mary noted that his hair was uncombed, his clothes rumpled. They knew what was burning now, a church. And then Mary knew which church. Sure, she'd passed it numerous times. It was a white frame structure with a steeple. She had often wondered to which denomination it belonged, because the sign out front indicated the times of the services and that was all. A portion of the building collapsed, sparks and flames leaping skyward.

"Can you describe this person you saw?" the cop asked.

"No. I'm sorry. All I saw was . . . well, the shape of someone."

"Do you know if it was a man or woman?"

"I'm sorry."

Taking a quick look behind her, Mary discovered that she and Tom were at the forefront of a growing group of spectators.

"How about the object this person had?" the policeman asked the bathrobe-clad woman. "Can you identify that?"

"It was a gasoline can."

"If it was too dark to see the person, uh, how can you be so sure about the object?"

"Well, what else could it have been?"

An unbidden thought made its way into Mary's consciousness: We have a square gas can in the garage, for fueling the lawn mower. Then, without knowing why she did so, Mary reached into her pocket and withdrew the only object her fingers found. She stared at it, horrified. There, in the palm of her hand, glowing orange in the firelight, was a crumpled book of matches. And she didn't smoke.

Her eyes shifting from the matchbook to the inferno that had been a church, she wondered: Was it me? Am I an arsonist?

Wait, she told herself; just hang on now. There's no proof that you set the fire. Half the people here probably have matches with them; it's not exactly a crime. And, Christ, who in suburbia doesn't have a gas can for filling up the lawn mower?

And if you get home and yours is missing, what then? The prospect simply left her feeling numb. Why get upset? she asked. If you attack people and destroy things and you can't stop, can't even tell anyone about it, then accept it, live with it. Get what pleasure you can from life before they come for you, lock you away where you can't hurt anyone.

Or is life even worth living under such circumstances?

Before she could address herself to that question and all its implications, a young policeman was in front of her, urging the crowd to move farther back.

"Come on, folks," he said loudly, "everybody back to the end of the block. If you want to watch, you can watch from there." Behind him, a wall of the church collapsed. Almost nothing was left of the structure now.

"Let's go," Mary said, taking Tom's hand. "I want to get back to bed."

When they were again in the darkness of the power outage, Mary flipped the matches into the street.

"Mary . . ." Tom said as they moved cautiously through the blackness.

"What?"

"I hope you don't do this again. It's so dark out here you can't see where you're stepping. You could have hurt yourself."

"The fire caused a power failure. It wasn't this dark out here when I left the house."

"Even with the lights on, I'm surprised you'd come out at night after what happened to you last night. And after what happened to that woman in the parking lot."

193

"You're right. I guess I wasn't thinking."

Tom fell silent. It wasn't his nature to belabor a point once it had been made. They picked their way cautiously through the night until they came to a block that hadn't been affected by the power outage. From there, it was only a block and a half to their house. When they reached it, Mary thought the house seemed warm, friendly, and inviting. The porch light was on, her small Plymouth in the driveway, Tom's station wagon at the curb.

As they started up the driveway, Mary said, "I think I'll put my car in the garage tonight."

"The night's nearly over," Tom replied. "It's close to four in the morning."

"With people going around the neighborhood, burning down churches, I'd feel better if I put it inside. And you should get yours out of the street."

Tom sighed. "Okay. I'll open the garage door for you."

"First, let me into the house. I don't have my purse, so I don't have my keys."

She found her bag on the living room couch, ending her fears that she might have lost it somewhere—possibly at the scene of an arson-caused blaze that destroyed a church. Grabbing her car keys, she returned to the driveway. The garage door was open, and the light was on; Tom was climbing into his station wagon.

Mary slipped behind the wheel of her Plymouth, almost afraid to find out what was—or wasn't—in the garage. Her desire to put the car inside, of course, had nothing to do with its welfare. She had to find out whether the gas can was there. As she pulled into the garage, her heart sank. Without getting out of the car, she could see the lawn mower and, beside it, the spot where the gas can should have been . . . and wasn't.

Again, she felt anesthetized. It didn't really matter. Nothing did. Nothing at all.

Suddenly, Tom was there, standing beside the car. "Hey," he said gently, "are you falling asleep right there or what?"

"I—I'm just upset about everything that's happened. It'll be a few days before I'm myself again."

"You probably shouldn't have gone to work today," he said, opening the car door. "Come on. I'll take you to bed."

"Tom," she said in a rush. "I—" The words died in her throat.

"Do you want to tell me something?"

Oh, she so desperately wanted to tell him something. Before things got any worse. It no longer mattered that she'd be admitting to hiding things from him. She was on a downhill run, she could see that. He had a right to know. If for no other reason, so he could protect himself from her.

Oh, God, she thought. I'm dangerous. Even to the man I love. I've got to have help. And she had to at least try to warn Tom, to the extent her internal censors would allow. If she hurt Tom . . . she couldn't live with that. And suddenly, her numbness was gone, for she had something vitally important to do. She had to tell Tom enough so he'd be on guard, so he could protect himself.

"Yes," she said, "I do want to tell you something. But I don't think I can." A wave of nausea rushed through her. "Something . . . something inside won't let me."

Tom looked puzzled. "I—"

She stopped him by holding up her hand. "I might . . ."—the nausea was getting worse—"might be dangerous to you."

"Dangerous? Mary, what are you talking about?"

"I . . . I might hurt you. I—" Suddenly, she was unable to breathe, her lungs struggling for air that didn't seem to exist.

"Mary!"

Unable to speak, Mary felt as though she'd had the wind knocked out of her. Then, just when she thought she'd suffocate solely from the inability to make her lungs function, the first ragged breath came, then another. A moment later, air, blessed air was flowing in and out of her chest.

Tom stared at her, his face ashen. "Mary, what's happening to you? Do you need a doctor?"

"No," she gasped, again feeling nauseous. "I—I don't think so."

And then, fighting down the nausea, using every ounce of willpower she had, Mary grabbed her husband and said, "I lied, Tom. Do you understand? I lied."

"Honey, I don't have any idea what you're talking about."

"Goddammit!" she screamed. "I lied. I'm defective, and I lied. I lied. I lied. I lied."

The whole world seemed to be sick, painful, confused. Mary was only vaguely aware that she was flailing at Tom with her fists. And even less cognizant of slipping down his legs to the floor, babbling in a little girl's voice:

"Oh, please, Sister. Please don't. Please. I'll be good. Please. Please. Please."

Sixteen

THE WORLD CAME BACK TO MARY—OR SHE TO IT—
slowly. She sensed the sounds, the odors, the presence
of people, and though aware of these things, she was
unprepared to deal with them. When she finally opened
her eyes and took in her surroundings, she found
herself lying in bed in an unfamiliar beige room. The
odors she'd only vaguely sensed earlier were now
clearly medicinal smells and disinfectants. Near the bed
was a tall stand for holding IV bottles. She was
obviously in a hospital.

And then she began to recall what had happened.
She'd had a middle-of-the-night blank spell during
which she might have burned down a church. She
remembered being with Tom and feeling . . . feeling
what? Calm. The calm you felt before throwing yourself off the bridge or putting the gun to your head. Had
she really been suicidal? She shuddered. The notion
was unspeakable, abhorrent.

And then she'd desperately tried to tell him, knowing
she'd never be able to get the words out. She recalled

the nausea, her inability to breathe . . . and some-where in there, the memories became confused and stopped. Though uncertain how much she had been able to tell Tom, she suspected it had been too little to make him aware of her problem and yet more than enough to mess up her life. Tom was probably con-vinced he'd married a sicko. She vaguely recalled saying she had lied to him, which, she supposed, made her a dishonest sicko.

She lay there in the hospital bed, miserable, some-thing wet trickling around her ear. It took her a moment to figure out the wetness was tears.

She had stopped crying when a nurse stepped into the room, asked her how she was feeling, then disap-peared. A few moments later, a doctor entered, asked her the same question, and then he, too, disappeared. The next time the door opened, it was Tom.

"Hi," he said, sitting down beside her bed. "How are you feeling?"

"Okay, I guess." Which was exactly how she had answered the nurse and doctor when they'd asked. "What happened? How did I get here?"

"Well, you . . ." He hesitated, and for the first time, Mary noticed the bags under his eyes. He looked exhausted. "You had a sort of nervous breakdown, I guess."

"Tell me everything that happened."

"Do you remember going for a walk in the middle of the night?"

Mary nodded. "You caught up to me, and we saw a fire, a church."

"Well, when we got home, you said you wanted to put your car in the garage. After you drove it in, you just sat there behind the wheel, and I went to see what was wrong."

"I remember all that."

"Okay, well, that's when things started happening. You looked like you were going to be sick, and then you couldn't seem to breathe." He stared at her, and there was so much concern, so much love in his eyes that Mary wanted to start crying again.

"What did I say, Tom?"

He dismissed the matter with a wave of his hand. "You really weren't making too much sense."

"Please, Tom," she said earnestly. "Tell me what I said."

He studied her a moment, then said, "Well, you said something about hurting me, that you might hurt me."

"That's all?"

"No. You also said you had lied to me." The look on his face made it plain he didn't believe she would ever do either. Oh, but I would, she thought. If only I could make you understand. She had the urge to try again, but she knew the attempt would only succeed in bringing on another "nervous breakdown."

"What else did I say?"

Tom frowned. "Well, you mumbled something about your sister. It sounded like you were asking her not to do something." He shrugged.

To Mary, this made no sense. "I don't even have a sister."

"I know."

The word hung there, menacingly. Sister. Not her sister, not a sibling, but someone addressed that way, like a nun. A figure in black, standing before a fire. Inwardly, Mary shuddered.

"Is that everything?" she asked.

Tom nodded.

"How long have I been here? And where am I?"

"You're in Eastview Heights Hospital. You've been here since last night—or I should say early this morning. The sun was nearly up when I brought you here."

She knew the hospital. It was about half a mile from the house. "What time is it now?"

"About four in the afternoon."

"When can I leave?"

"Not until you've had a chat with the staff psychiatrist."

"And then?"

"And then you go home, I guess. Let's wait and see what he says."

Mary had watched his face closely, trying to determine whether he was hiding anything from her. As far as she could tell, he wasn't.

"What was I like when you brought me here?" she asked. "Was I unconscious or what?"

"You just sort of went rigid." He frowned. "It was as if every fiber in your body had become so taut you couldn't do anything but vibrate. Does that make any sense?" Without waiting for her to answer, he said, "I know you weren't unconscious because your eyes were open. In the emergency room, the doctor just gave you something to relax you, then had you sent up here so you could sleep and so you could be kept under observation."

Mary nodded, and they were both silent for a few moments. Then Tom gently touched her through the covers.

"I love you," he said softly.

"I love you, too," she replied as another tear trickled past her ear.

* * *

"Hi," the man said, taking the same chair Tom had occupied an hour earlier. He was middle-aged, dark-haired, thin, and wore plastic-framed glasses. He smiled. "I'm Dr. Galloway; I'm a psychiatrist."

"Hi," Mary replied, suddenly feeling nervous.

His eyes dropped to the clipboard in his lap, then returned to Mary. Again, he smiled. "I'm going to ask you some questions. I already know the answers to a lot of them, but I'd like you to answer them anyway. All right?"

"Sure."

"What's your name?"

"Mary Taylor."

"Where do you live?"

She gave her address.

"Are you married?"

"Yes."

"What's your husband's name?"

"Tom."

"And your mother's name?"

"You mean my biological mother?"

"Yes."

"I was raised by foster parents. I never knew my natural parents."

The psychiatrist flipped through the pages on his clipboard, pausing a moment to examine one of them. "Tell me the name of your foster parents," he said, his eyes returning to Mary.

Mary gave him the names, and the doctor said, "What's six times six?"

"Thirty-six."

"Seven times eight."

"Fifty-six . . . I think."

Galloway laughed. "Do you feel you've been under a

lot of pressure lately? Are there things that aren't going as they should?"

Mary nodded.

"You want to tell me about it?"

"Oh, yes. I want to tell you very much." She sighed. "But I can't."

"Why not."

"Something inside won't let me."

The next morning, Monday, Lieutenant Daniel K. Larson sat in his office at the Lewiston police station, an open file folder in front of him on the desk. In it were the three replies that had come in over the weekend in response to his regional bulletin concerning old blue Fords.

One had been the getaway car for an armed robbery at a Portland convenience store. The gunman, described as a very nervous young man with blond hair, had fled with $15.74. Another vintage blue Ford had been involved in a police chase in Rhode Island. The driver, a fourteen-year-old boy, was arrested after smashing the car into a tree. He received only cuts and scrapes in the crash.

The last report came from suburban Boston, where a young woman had been attacked by a man who drove a battered blue Ford, license number unknown. Her assailant, who'd hidden out in the building supply firm where she worked and then attacked her while she was closing up, was described as a tall, thin man in his fifties. Larson decided to ask the police department in Massachusetts to keep him posted on the case.

Flipping his desk calendar to the correct date—April 26—he leaned back in his chair and rubbed his eyes. It wasn't going to do a damn bit of good. His chances of locating the guy in the blue car were extremely slim.

And even if he found him, there was no evidence to indicate the guy was the murderer. It was entirely possible he wasn't. It was just that the man in the blue car was the only lead he had.

In fact, the only other development in the case had been the confession of Paul Mitchell, a young man so unbalanced that his confession would probably have been worthless. But then the worth of his confession was an academic question because Paul Mitchell, having used the police department as his suicide weapon, was dead.

Larson sighed. Although he hadn't given up on the John Edwards murder case, he was a realist, and he knew that the odds of his solving it—never good—were getting longer with each day that passed.

"Well, crap," he muttered, pushing the file folder away from him.

And then, on impulse, he opened a desk drawer, took out another folder, and leafed through the pages until he found the report on the hit-and-run in Vermont. Again, he studied the license number: 815–TDE. Damn, he thought, what is it about that number? Ten minutes later, he still didn't know, so he closed the folder and returned it to the drawer.

It would come to him. Sooner or later.

In suburban Boston that morning, Detective Sergeant Steven Flanagan was also at his desk, trying halfheartedly to catch up on the never-ending paperwork a cop had to deal with. Rather than filling out reports, he'd spent most of the past hour staring blankly at them while he thought about the Stephanie Flynn murder case. And about Mary Taylor.

His desk was just one in an office full of desks, most of which were vacant at the moment, the detectives who sat at them presumably out in the field. Well, maybe they were out investigating their cases. There was a coffee shop not far away where he was fairly certain he could find some of them. But then goofing-off cops weren't his problem and wouldn't be until he made lieutenant, which would not be soon.

Closing his eyes, he wished he could give all this up and spend his time with Gloria and their three kids. Well, he couldn't. He was the man, the head of household, daddy, husband; supporting the Flanagan clan was his responsibility and his alone. He was of the old school; he would never permit his wife to work.

Again, he found his thoughts drifting to Mary Taylor. Something was wrong there, but he didn't know what. Did he suspect her of murdering Stephanie Flynn? Well, maybe. She was involved in *something;* of that there was no question.

And what about the attack on her? Was there a connection between that and the Flynn murder? There was no physical evidence linking the two events. The fingerprints found on the chain saw and the other things Mary Taylor's attacker had touched matched none of those lifted from Stephanie Flynn's car. He'd sent the prints from the store to the FBI, but it would likely be a few weeks before he had a reply.

Pulling over a pad, he wrote down the possibilities:

1. Offenses unrelated, committed by different persons.
2. Offenses committed by same person.
3. Mary Taylor the murderer, the attack on her maybe, maybe not related to murder.

Some of the facts seemed to point to number two on the list. The Flynn woman had been killed with something long and pointed like an ice pick, which was what had been used to jam the lock at the building supply place. The broken point had been found still locked in the jaws of the Vise-grips Mary Taylor had used to remove it. But then this by itself hardly proved the murder and the attack on Mary Taylor had been the work of the same person.

The only connection between the two women was that both worked at the same place and both had been attacked there. They'd known each other for less than twelve hours when the Flynn woman was killed. Flanagan could come up with no reason why anyone would want them both dead. Also, Mary Taylor had not been a randomly selected or chance victim. She'd been followed, visited. There was no indication that anything of the sort had happened to Stephanie Flynn.

What Flanagan needed was the man who'd left the store just before the murder, the man who might, just might have seen the killer. The detective sighed. So far, the man hadn't come forward, which meant he was unlikely to do so. And that was the only way he'd ever be identified.

Flanagan had eliminated the Flynn woman's husband as a possible suspect. His shock and grief had been real, and he had no motive. Most important of all, he had a firm alibi.

Talking to the victim's friends, parents, and neighbors had turned up no one with a motive for killing Stephanie Flynn. In other words, he had only one suspect. Possibility number three on his list. Mary Taylor.

Flanagan tore the sheet of paper from the pad, crumpled it up, and tossed it in the wastebasket. So why the hell did he suspect a wide-eyed young woman from Maine, a former orphan with no criminal record? The answer was obvious enough, he supposed. As a cop, one learned to judge people, to tell when someone was lying, when someone was holding things back. To the trained eye, the guilty were often so apparent they might as well be holding up signs proclaiming the fact. And Mary Taylor was guilty . . . of something more than just tampering with a child's swing.

Though unable to prove it, he was certain she had done that. Working in a place that sold so much hardware and the like, she certainly had the ability to sabotage a swing. But why would she do it? He didn't figure her for a sicko, but then who but a sicko would want to hurt kids? And when it came to psychos, it was never safe to assume anything. If Mary Taylor was one, she wouldn't be the first very crazy, very deadly person to display no outward indications of what lay bubbling and churning beneath.

All in all, Mary Taylor was an enigma. He hadn't spoken to her since she was attacked Friday night, but he would see her again. It was one of the few things about Mary Taylor he could be certain about. Their dealings with each other were not over. Not yet.

Squatting, Arnie Miller moved slowly along, gently pushing onion sets into the rich, dark soil of his garden. He followed a string to keep the row straight, spacing the little bulbs about six inches apart. Soon, he'd have most of his cool-weather crops in, which on a bright, sunny day like this should make him happy. But Arnie Miller was anything but happy.

He'd read in the paper about the attack on a woman employee Friday night at Zel Home and Builders Supply. And he had information about a murder in the

Zel parking lot, information he was keeping to himself. And now he had to ask himself: What if the same person attacked both women? What if it was the guy I saw getting into the blue car? Would he be in jail right now if I'd told what I know?

Dammit, he thought, I just want to mind my own business and be left alone. Is that too much to ask? Well, is it? He continued planting.

Mary parked her car under a budding tree at one end of the paved parking area and headed toward the main entrance to the McClellan Medical Office Building. She was keeping her previously scheduled appointment with Dr. Carpenter, who was unaware of what had happened to Mary over the weekend.

Dr. Galloway, the hospital psychiatrist, had spent nearly an hour with her the day before. Afterward, apparently having decided she wasn't dangerous, he'd sent her home. Well, Doc, she thought bitterly, you've never met Edna Fenton; if you had, you might not have been so quick to turn me loose on the world. Edna Fenton would have told you that I'm very dangerous indeed; that I tried to kill her kids. Mary abruptly broke off that line of thought. Wallowing in self-pity would accomplish nothing.

Galloway had advised her to consider seeking psychiatric help. Afraid that if she told Galloway Tom would find out, she hadn't mentioned that she was already seeing a psychiatrist.

Dr. Carpenter's receptionist—who knew Mary by name now—informed the doctor that she was there, then sent her in. Taking her customary seat, Mary told the psychiatrist about the attack on her Friday night.

"My goodness," Dr. Carpenter said, clearly shocked. "I don't think I could have been so resourceful. I didn't even know there were such things as guns that shoot nails."

"Something happened Saturday night, too," Mary said, "but I'm not sure how much I'll be able to tell you."

"It might be easier if you waited and told me about it under hypnosis," Dr. Carpenter replied. She sat at her desk, her intelligent gray eyes studying Mary.

So much had happened that Mary had forgotten that the psychiatrist planned to hypnotize her today. "Yes, that's fine," she said.

"Do you feel comfortable with the idea?"

"Yes. I want you to do it."

"All right then." Leaving her desk, Dr. Carpenter rolled a small stand over in front of Mary. Attached to it at eye level was a saucer-sized plastic disk that bore a black-and-white spiral. The psychiatrist flipped a switch, and the spiral began to spin.

"Look at it," the doctor said. "Stare intently at it. Are you doing that?"

"Yes."

"Good. Now try to become part of it, as if you and the disk were one, as if its essence were your essence."

The psychiatrist droned on, urging Mary to merge with the disk, and it was beginning to feel as if she really were part of it, swirling in its lovely spiral.

"As you look into the disk, you're beginning to feel very relaxed. It's a warm, comfortable feeling. You're safe, and you feel very relaxed. You're listening to my voice, concentrating on my voice. And as you listen to my voice, you're beginning to feel drowsy. Your eyelids are becoming heavy. As you listen to my voice, you're breathing comfortably and deeply, and your eyelids are becoming still heavier. You're becoming very drowsy now, and you want to go to sleep. You're listening to my voice. You like listening to my voice, and you want to do what my voice tells you. Your eyes are closing now, and you're falling into a deep, deep sleep. . . ."

Mary felt calm, at peace with the world. Dr. Carpenter told her to open her eyes, and Mary complied. She could see the disk, Dr. Carpenter standing beside it.

"Mary, you're deeply asleep, feeling relaxed. I'm going to ask you some questions, and you'll have no difficulty answering them. You'll answer them fully and honestly, holding nothing back. All right?"

"Yes."

"Good. Now, I want you to tell me about your memory lapses. When did they begin?"

Mary hesitated. She wanted to comply, to answer whatever questions the psychiatrist asked, and yet another part of her seemed to be resisting. "The censor might not let me answer that," she said.

"When you get sick or faint, is that what you call it, the censor?"

"Yes."

"I'm going to turn the censor off, Mary. And then you can say whatever you wish without it interfering. I'm going to count to three, and when I reach three, the censor will be turned off. All right, I'm turning it off now, Mary. One . . . two . . . when I reach three, the censor will be off. Three. It's off now. It's turned off, and you can answer the question. How old were you when you had your first memory lapse?"

"When I was a little girl. Right after I moved in with the Caldwells, my foster parents."

As the session progressed, Mary found herself telling everything she remembered about her blank spells, including the incident with the woman in the swimming pool, the events of Saturday night, even her fears that she might have sabotaged the swing and burned the church.

"I think Sergeant Flanagan believes I might have killed Steph," Mary said. "But I don't think I did."

"Can you be sure?"

"No, not absolutely sure, but . . . I couldn't have. I just couldn't."

And then the session was over. Dr. Carpenter woke Mary up, telling her that she'd feel fine, that she'd sleep well tonight, that she'd remember everything that had occurred while she was under hypnosis.

"I told you about my blank spells," Mary said. "I was finally able to tell you."

Dr. Carpenter, who had returned to her desk, said, "It's a beginning, an important beginning, but we've still got a lot to do."

"Do . . . do you know what's wrong with me now?"

The psychiatrist shook her head. "Not in the way you mean, no. I know what your symptoms are now, but I still haven't found what's causing them. I can understand your being anxious for results, but as I told you when you first became my patient, these things take time, often a lot of time."

"But I don't have much time. Walpurgis Night comes on Friday."

Dr. Carpenter nodded. "Make an appointment for tomorrow or Wednesday, and we'll do another session using hypnosis. I'll see what I can learn about Walpurgis Night and what happened to you at the orphanage."

Mary felt relieved. There was still time. Maybe Dr. Carpenter could help her before Friday night, when . . . when time would run out. Though she didn't know why, she was more convinced than ever that, unless the psychiatrist could somehow intervene, her life would be permanently altered on Friday night.

Dr. Carpenter's receptionist said the psychiatrist had no openings tomorrow, so Mary made an appointment for Wednesday. As she walked to her car, she felt calm and untroubled despite her apprehension concerning Walpurgis Night. An aftereffect of the hypnosis, Mary supposed.

Digging in her purse for the keys, she noticed that her car was covered with bird droppings, one of the disadvantages of parking under a tree. She could see her reflection in the car window; she looked exhausted.

As she slipped her key into the lock, from the corner of her eye she saw something move by the tree. Someone had stepped out from behind its thick trunk. She whirled, just in time to see a man wearing sunglasses stepping around the Plymouth's front fender, coming toward her. He was tall, thin; it was the man who drove the blue car.

The door was unlocked, but there was no time to get inside her car, lock herself within. Then something, some sense of survival, told her what to do. Grabbing the door with both hands, she stepped back and yanked it open with all the strength she had, as if she wanted to rip it from its hinges. It hit the approaching man solidly. He gasped, dropping something on the asphalt.

Mary ran. She wanted to scream, to cry for help, but she needed every bit of breath she had just to drive her legs. Ahead was the entrance to the medical building. Inside, there would be help, safety. And then the man was there, between her and the door. She changed directions, running frantically, blindly. Yell, something inside her urged. Attract attention. But the only sound to pass her lips was her desperate breathing as her lungs struggled to get enough air.

She could hear his footfalls behind her, his own labored breathing. She was running on the lawn, along the front of the medical building, and then she turned the corner and was running along the structure's side. To her left was a street; she could see the traffic through the trees. Suddenly, the man was there, preventing her from heading in that direction. Abruptly, he closed in on her, reaching for her with his hands. Mary turned again, rushing into an alley that ran behind the building.

Oh, God, she thought. Oh, God no. The alley didn't go all the way through. It ended, just ahead, where garbage cans were lined up along a high brick wall.

She whirled, prepared to defend herself as best she could. The man was approaching slowly, now that she was trapped. Taking off his sunglasses, he revealed his singed eyebrows. He stared at her, his eyes wide, crazed, the only sound the gasping of the two winded adversaries.

Stopping about ten feet from her, he slipped the sunglasses into his pocket. "You won't escape this time, hellcat. The Lord's work will be done."

"Who are you?"

"A servant of the Lord who knows who you are, Mary/Mara."

If the man had a weapon, he wasn't holding it where she could see it. Perhaps that was what he dropped back at the car. But Mary drew no comfort from that thought. Though slight, he was still wider and taller than she was; he would be able to overpower her easily.

She tilted her head slightly, as if trying to see something behind him. "Help!" she yelled. "He's trying to kill me!"

The man turned to look, and Mary ran. But before

Mary could get around him, the man realized he'd been duped. Lunging, he grabbed her.

She tried to kick him in the crotch, but he was ready for her this time and kept his side to her once he had a firm grip on her jacket. Then she was against the wall, and his hands were at her throat. Again, she tried to kick him in the crotch, but her whole body was pinned to the wall.

Suddenly, she remembered the thing in her purse, the thing she'd bought Saturday after visiting the police station to look at mug shots. Her bag still hung from her shoulder. She worked her right hand out from between his body and hers and slipped it into the purse.

"Praise the Lord," he said, and began choking her.

Then he screamed, releasing her neck, his hands going to his own face. Wheezing and choking, he stumbled away from her. Mary stood there as if frozen, watching him, holding the can of Mace in a shaking hand, ready to spray him again if he came at her.

It took her a moment to bring everything into focus, and once she did so, she was at first confused, then afraid. Mary was bending over the man who'd attacked her, a heavy soft-drink bottle in her hand instead of the Mace can. Both the bottle and the man's head were bloody.

She'd had another blank spell—another *violent* blank spell.

The man's eyes were closed; he lay motionless. There was blood on her clothes—his blood. Horrified, she dropped the bottle. Oh, my God, she thought. I've killed him. I attacked him with the bottle, beat him to death with it.

Then she was turning away from the bloody scene,

running. Reaching the entrance to the building, she dashed inside and into the first office she saw. A startled doctor's receptionist jumped to her feet.

"I–I'll get the doctor," the young woman stammered. Her face was ashen.

"No," Mary said. "I'm not hurt. It's—" She gasped for breath. "It's not my blood. Call the police."

The receptionist just stood there, staring at her.

"Please," Mary said. "Please call the police."

Finally, the young woman sat down and grabbed the phone. While she placed the call, Mary looked around the waiting room. A man and two women, one with a boy about six years old, sat on various pieces of matching orange furniture, staring at her. The boy's mother held him close. His eyes were wide.

While she was waiting for the police to arrive, the doctor came out, asked her if she was all right, then conferred in low tones with the receptionist. Mary was sure she was disrupting the usually orderly routine of the office; the doctor would no doubt be glad to get her out of there.

"Is anyone injured?" the doctor asked. "Does anyone need help?" He was in his fifties, gray-haired, and had a kindly, Dr. Welby sort of face.

Mary shook her head. The man was dead; no one could help him.

About five minutes later, two uniformed policemen came into the office. Mary—who'd been sitting in exile in a corner of the waiting room, everyone staying well away from her—immediately rose.

"He's in the alley," she said. "Behind the building."

"Who's in the alley?" one of the officers asked.

Mary explained what had happened; then one of the policemen took her into the hallway while the other went to check. Both cops were young, clean-cut types.

The one who'd stayed with her was slender and had a boyish face. She was explaining what had happened in greater detail when his partner came back, frowning.

"There's no one in the alley."

"But," Mary said, stunned, "but I killed him. He's dead."

The cop shook his head. "You must not have hit him as hard as you thought. I found some smeared blood and that was all."

In her daze, Mary received the news with conflicting emotions. She was relieved that she hadn't killed him. On the other hand, if he was still alive, he'd be back. It wasn't over.

Seventeen

Mary and Sergeant Flanagan faced each other across the table in a small, mostly bare room at the police station. To her left was a mirror; one-way glass, she supposed. This room was apparently used for interrogations, and she wondered whether she was being interrogated.

Flanagan held up an ice pick. "We found this by your car. The prints on it match those we found at Zel."

"I knew he dropped something. I didn't know what." She wished Tom would get here. He'd been notified and was on his way.

"An ice pick is apparently one of his favorite weapons. That's what was used to jam the lock at Zel. It was shoved in, then broken off."

"I thought I'd killed him," she said softly. But looking down at the dried blood on her jacket, she realized there wasn't nearly as much of it as she'd thought at first.

Flanagan studied her in silence.

"Would it have been self-defense if I had?" she asked.

"Probably. Unless you obviously did a great deal more than was necessary to assure your safety. Your lawyer would maintain that you kept hitting him because you were afraid he'd get up and kill you if you stopped." He shrugged. "Of course, if it turned out there was some connection between you, that you had some reason for killing him . . ." He trailed off.

Was that what he thought, that she and the man were in cahoots, partners in some evil doing? Did he see the attempts on her life as a falling out among the bad guys? "I never saw him before in my life," Mary said. "Not until he showed up on my doorstep, claiming to be an encyclopedia salesman."

The detective nodded, his eyes dropping to the papers before him on the table.

"Look," Mary said angrily, "I'm the victim here. I'm the one being stalked by this maniac. You keep acting as though you suspect *me* of something. Well, if you do, I have a right to know. What do you think I've done?"

His eyes found hers, held them. "I haven't said anything accusatory."

"That's what you seem to be implying."

"That I suspect you?"

"Yes."

"Mrs. Taylor, even policemen have the right to the privacy of their own thoughts, and I don't plan to discuss mine with you."

"There you go again! What the hell do you think I've done?"

"Mrs. Taylor, you're accused of absolutely nothing. You're listed on all our reports in this matter as the complainant, the victim if you prefer that word. There are no charges pending against you at this time."

"I know one thing you think I did. You're convinced I sabotaged the Fentons' swing."

And so am I, Mary thought, suddenly wishing she hadn't brought up the swing. She'd also attacked a woman in a swimming pool and maybe burned down a church. And today she tried to kill a man by bashing him repeatedly with a heavy bottle. Perhaps Flanagan was right, and she and the man did have something in common. They were both crazed killers.

"Mrs. Taylor," the detective said, sounding resigned, "at this time, there are no charges against you in that or any other matter."

At this time, Mary thought. He certainly likes those words. They mean that tomorrow, next week, an hour from now, things may change.

When Mary didn't respond, he said, "If I put you together with a police artist, do you think you can come up with a good picture of your attacker?"

"Yes." She could see the man as clearly as if she were still in the alley with him. "I didn't see him following me. There was no blue car. I'm sure there wasn't."

"He probably changed cars because he knew you'd be on the lookout for the blue one."

Mary was a little embarrassed because the thought that he might be in some other car had not occurred to her. But then she was a clerk in a building supply store, not a spy.

The detective rose, as if getting ready to leave, then hesitated, fixing his eyes on Mary. "You said you were there today to see a Dr. Helen Carpenter. Is that correct?"

"Yes."

"Dr. Carpenter's a psychiatrist. I checked. Would you mind telling me what you were seeing a psychiatrist for?"

"I certainly would mind," Mary replied, offended. "It's none of your business."

"If it relates to a case I'm investigating, then it's very much my business."

Tom was on his way. Now she would have to explain why she'd been secretly seeing a psychiatrist. Suddenly, she wanted to cry, to throw herself down on her own nice soft bed and sob herself to sleep. And maybe . . . maybe never wake up.

"*Does* it relate to something I'm working on?" he persisted.

"No," Mary lied. "No, it doesn't."

Flanagan had been watching her face closely. He'd known she'd lied; she could see it in his eyes.

"Come on," he said, picking up the papers in front of him. "Let's see what you and the artist can come up with."

The artist turned out to be a plump middle-aged blond woman with one of those beehive hairdos that had long ago gone out of style. When Mary left the woman and returned, as instructed, to the small interrogation room, she found Tom and Flanagan sitting at the table, waiting for her. Apparently reacting to the dried blood on her clothes, Tom paled.

"Are you all right?" he asked, rising and taking her in his arms.

Mary could feel the tension in his body. She returned his hug, then reluctantly stepped back, out of his grasp. She was unable to look into his eyes.

"This is him," she said, holding up a photocopy of the artist's drawing.

Flanagan stood up so he could give it a closer inspection. Just looking at the thing made Mary shiver. The shape of the long, thin face was recreated flawlessly, as were the thin eyebrows and lips, the narrow nose, the weak chin. The eyes had been the only problem. Although their shape and spacing were right, they were flat, sketched eyes, lines on paper. The man's real eyes burned with an insane, frightening passion.

Still, the artist was good. She had managed to put a hint of craziness in those black-and-white eyes on the paper. And the hint was enough. It was unquestionably the man.

And then, just for an instant, she saw Sister standing before the fire, her arms raised. And someone was beside her, someone tall and thin. Was it the man whose picture she was holding? She couldn't be sure.

"The sergeant here told me what happened," Tom said. "What is this guy, some sort of religious nut?" His voice had risen as he asked the question. Throughout this whole ordeal, Tom had been calm, reassuring, the rock she could lean on. Now he seemed to be on the edge of cracking.

Not that she could blame him. He'd just discovered that his wife was secretly seeing a psychiatrist. He had probably made the connection between her middle-of-the-night stroll and Mrs. Fenton's accusation that Mary had tampered with the swing, that she'd been seen in the Fentons' yard about midnight. And some madman who thought himself a servant of the Lord seemed determined to kill her.

"Sergeant," Tom said, his face reddening, "there's a goddamn lunatic out there intent on killing my wife. I want to know what the hell you're going to do about it." Mary took his hand.

"We're working on it, Mr. Taylor. At the moment we're notifying the hotels and motels, just in case the guy's from out of town. We're asking that they report any middle-aged male customers with battered faces

And starting tomorrow, whenever Mrs. Taylor goes anywhere, we'll have an unmarked car follow her. If the guy tries to tail her, we'll get him. In fact, we'll probably have her make some trips specifically for the purpose of smoking him out. We'll work that out later."

"It's about time. Until now, you've seemed more interested in harassing my wife than in protecting her."

Flanagan smiled faintly. "Mr. Taylor, I'm only doing what I'm paid to do. I investigate what has to be investigated. I don't harass."

Tom glared at him. "Sergeant," he said slowly, "if you'd followed Mary in an unmarked car after the first attack, after she told you about this guy, then he'd be in jail right now, and Mary wouldn't have been almost killed today."

Flanagan sighed. "Look, Mr. Taylor, this police department just isn't large enough to provide personal protection for everyone in the community. We do the best we can, but we have definite limitations."

"Everyone in the community hasn't needed personal protection the past few days," Tom shot back heatedly.

Her husband, Mary realized, was trying to push the detective into a shouting match, the policeman being someone on whom he could conveniently vent his frustration. Mary wanted to go home, to get as far away as possible from Flanagan—and to enjoy Tom's love while she still had it, until she did something so terrible even he would be forced to turn his back on her, to let the burly men in white take her away. She forced the image from her mind.

"Come on," she said, pulling Tom gently toward the door. "This isn't doing any good."

His head snapped around, his eyes finding hers, and for just a moment, they were hard, bitter eyes that seemed to say: *How dare you interfere!* Then the animosity faded.

"All right," he said. "Let's go home."

A few moments later, as they stepped into the bright sunshine outside, Tom said, "I shouldn't have lost my cool with Flanagan. I'm sorry."

"Are you going back to the store now?" she asked, changing the subject. They started down the steps toward the parking lot.

He shook his head. "I'm not letting you out of my sight for the rest of the day." He smiled reassuringly. "Is your car here, or did they bring you over in a police car?"

"It's here." She pointed to the area of the lot where she'd left it.

"Okay, I'm on the other side. I'll walk you to your car, then get mine and follow you."

They walked through the lot in silence. When they reached Mary's car, Tom said, "Mary, I . . . well, never mind."

"What?" They stood beside her car, facing each other.

He looked as though he was about to speak, but then he hesitated. Finally, he said, "We can talk when we get home."

Mary unlocked her car and climbed in. Tom pushed the door shut, then, through the closed window, said, "Lock it."

Staring into the confused, worried eyes of her husband, she reached over and pushed down the button.

The first thing Mary did when she got home was strip off her bloody clothes and take a shower. Now, her hair still wet, she sat on the living room couch, her husband across the room in an easy chair, watching her in silence, waiting for her to speak. He looked worried, confused.

"I couldn't tell you," she said. "I'm sorry."

"Mary, I'm just confused. I don't know what's happening."

"I didn't tell you I'd started seeing a psychiatrist because that's all I could have told you. I can't tell you why I'm seeing one. I don't mean I'm afraid to or don't want to. I actually, physically can't tell you."

Tom looked bewildered. "Mary, that doesn't make any sense."

"It's the truth. I couldn't even tell the psychiatrist until she hypnotized me."

"I don't understand. What would happen if you tried to tell me right now?"

"I'd get sick, or I'd collapse, or I'd suddenly be unable to breathe, just like the other night in the garage. Don't ask for another demonstration. Please."

Looking helpless, he stared at her a moment; then he said, "Is there anything you can tell me?"

"I've been seeing Dr. Carpenter for a couple of weeks now. She says something's buried in my unconscious, something too horrible for me to deal with. I guess it's something that happened to me at the orphanage. I don't know."

Tom frowned. "Like what?"

"I don't know. Dr. Carpenter says it will take time to find out—maybe a long time."

Again, he frowned. "Like how long?"

"Maybe next week. Maybe years. Maybe never." Except that Walpurgis Night is Friday, she thought, and after that it probably won't matter anymore.

"Is there anything I can do, Mary—anything at all?" Tom said, his eyes growing moist.

She shook her head.

He closed his eyes, squeezing them tightly shut. When he opened them again, he said, "You're the most important thing in my life, Mary. You're in trouble, and there's absolutely nothing I can do about it. Do you realize what a horrible feeling that is?"

She realized how it felt all right; there was almost nothing she could do to help herself. "I'll be okay," she said. "I've just got this problem that needs to be treated. That's all. And Dr. Carpenter will do what's necessary."

She could tell by the look on his face that he was probably recalling her words of a few moments ago: *maybe years, maybe never.* His eyes still glistened with moisture.

"This thing that's buried in your unconscious—do you think the man who attacked you might be involved in some way?"

"As far as I know, I've never seen him before. If he's had some part in my life, then it's buried along with the rest of my memories." Or, she thought, I know him from my blank spells. But she couldn't say that.

For a moment, Tom's eyes dropped to his hands. When he raised them again, searching Mary's face, he said, "The other night, when you got out of bed and went for a walk . . . could there be a connection with what happened to the Fentons' swing?"

"There could be." Suddenly, something rancid seemed to be bubbling at the base of her throat. "To the best of my knowledge, I never left the bed on the night Mrs. Fenton claims I tampered with the swing."

Tom studied her for what seemed like a long time before he asked, "Could you have done it without being aware of it . . . you know, like sleepwalking or something like that?"

"If we talk about this any more," Mary said weakly,

"I'm going to be sick." Suddenly dizzy, she lay back on the couch.

She saw Tom bending over her, looking down at her unhappily. And then she drifted off to sleep. It was comfortable and warm encased in slumber's protective darkness, and part of her kept urging that she never wake up.

Eighteen

Sᴉᴛᴛᴉɴɢ ɪɴ ʜɪs ᴜɴᴍᴀʀᴋᴇᴅ ᴄᴀʀ, Dᴇᴛᴇᴄᴛɪᴠᴇ Sᴇᴄᴏɴᴅ
Grade Jacob Goldberg watched as the green Plymouth
backed out of the driveway, then pulled away from the
house. Everything had been arranged by Sergeant
Flanagan. Mary Taylor was going to go for a drive
along Scones Boulevard. If no one other than police
officers tailed her, she'd make the trip hourly until
someone did—or until Sergeant Flanagan called off the
operation for the day.

Goldberg waited until she was partway down the
block, then started his car and followed her, keeping at
least half a block between them. Grabbing the two-
way-radio microphone from the dash, he said: "One-
twelve to two-eighty-seven."

"Go ahead," came the reply over the speaker.

"She's rolling."

"Ten-four."

The officer to whom he'd been speaking was Detective Pamela Hodge, who was waiting a few blocks away on Scones Boulevard. The two would take turns sticking close to Mary Taylor, the idea being that alternating cars would make the tail harder to spot. Goldberg's car was an inconspicuous brown Chevy, Hodge's an equally unnoticeable white Toyota. It was an overcast Tuesday morning, cool; a light mist hung in the air.

Ahead, Mary Taylor's green Plymouth Horizon paused at a stop sign, then turned left on Scones Boulevard. A moment later, Hodge's voice came over the radio:

"Two-eighty-seven to one-twelve. I've got her. Going east on Scones."

"Ten-four," Goldberg replied.

He delayed at the stop sign and when he pulled onto the boulevard, the green Plymouth and white Toyota were about two blocks ahead of him.

"Scones and Crestline," Hodge informed him.

He began closing the gap. When he caught up with Hodge, she'd pass the Taylor woman and stay ahead of her until the two officers switched places again. That way, if the car behind the Plymouth lost it at a light, the other unit would be able to continue the tail. It was a system you could use without difficulty as long as you knew where the subject under surveillance was headed.

Goldberg wiggled his nose, trying to alleviate the persistent tingling in his left nostril. A chunky man in his late thirties, Goldberg suffered from hay fever. He could look forward to an entire summer during which his nose would run and his eyes would water. The tingling he was experiencing right now was just a hint of what was to come. If someone would offer him a job at the North Pole, where there was no vegetation, he would jump at the chance. Yeah, he thought, you ought to write Santa Claus, ask for a job making toys. The only bad guy you'd have to worry about would be the Grinch.

"I'm behind you, two-eighty-seven," he said into the microphone when he caught up with Hodge.

"Ten-four. I see you."

Hodge's white Toyota increased speed, passing the green Horizon. As they drove along the boulevard, Goldberg tried to keep about half a block between himself and Mary Taylor. His eyes constantly checking the rearview mirror, he watched the cars behind and ahead. So far, there had been nothing to indicate that anyone else was tailing Mary Taylor.

After a while, the two detectives changed places again, Goldberg passing Mary Taylor. A few minutes went by, and then:

"I've got a possible, one-twelve. Green Datsun wagon that pulled in between us in the last block. Driver's the only occupant, appears to be a white male." Without giving Goldberg a chance to reply, she continued, "Two-eighty-seven to Control."

"Go ahead, two-eighty-seven," a woman answered from the radio room at headquarters.

"Need a check on a green Datsun wagon." She gave the license number, Massachusetts plate.

Goldberg stared into his rearview mirror, but a van behind him was blocking his view.

"Green wagon's still with us," Hodge said. "It looks good."

"Ten-four," Goldberg replied.

The radio went silent. Behind him, the van still cut off his view. He passed gas stations, small shops, a house being used as an office by a real estate firm.

"Control to two-eighty-seven," the female voice from the radio room said over the speaker.

"Go ahead," Hodge responded.

"Datsun wagon is listed as stolen."

"Ten-four, control. One-twelve, you ten-four on that?"

"Ten-four," Goldberg replied. "Freeway's coming up. What do you want to do?"

Hodge was the ranking detective; she was in charge. After crossing the freeway, Mary Taylor was to turn around and go back the way she had come. The two detectives would stay with the stolen station wagon, which might or might not turn around when Mary Taylor did.

"One-twelve," Hodge said urgently, "I just caught a red light. Heavy cross traffic. There's no way I can run it."

"Ten-four. I'm on the freeway overpass now. As soon as I'm across, I'll wait and see what he does." If he takes the expressway, Goldberg thought, we're screwed.

As soon as he was off the overpass, he pulled into a gas station, drove past the pumps, and stopped at the exit. Looking back the way he had come, Goldberg anxiously watched the cars coming off the overpass. An eighteen-wheeler, an orange Volkswagen, a bus . . . and then the green Plymouth, which slowed and pulled into the left-turn lane. It stopped, waited for a break in the oncoming traffic, then made an illegal U-turn, and headed back toward the overpass. Goldberg waited.

Come on, he thought. Come on, come on.

And there it was, the green station wagon. It slowed, the driver watching Mary Taylor's car as he passed it going the opposite direction. Stepping on the gas, he continued straight ahead.

Goldberg followed. Grabbing the microphone, he said: "Okay, I've got him, two-eighty-seven. He's still heading east on Scones. He didn't follow her when she turned around."

"Ten-four. The light just changed. I'm on my way. Any chance he's not our man?"

"When he passed her, going the other way, he slowed down and gave her a long hard look. I'd say it's him all right."

"As soon as I get there, we'll take him."

"Yeah, ten-four."

The station wagon continued on its way, the driver apparently unaware he was being followed by an unmarked police car.

Although a number of Goldberg's fellow officers were unhappy about working with a woman—not to mention taking orders from one—Goldberg had no difficulties with the situation. As far as he was concerned, Hodge had proven herself intelligent, competent, a worthy officer. She was levelheaded, always used common sense, and she was an expert in several different forms of self-defense. He'd seen her subdue some fairly large fellows quite handily. Her biggest stumbling block had to be Sergeant Flanagan, who thought a woman's place was in the home, taking care of the kids and washing dishes. He would always think so; people like Flanagan never changed.

Goldberg kept as close to the station wagon as he dared, never letting more than two cars get between him and the Datsun. Because no one was ahead of the subject, a red light could be disastrous. Though in a police car, he would be unable to use his lights and siren as that would immediately inform the man in the station wagon that there was a cop behind him. Ahead, the Datsun signaled and swung into the left-turn lane.

"Two-eighty-seven, he's turning. . . . Stand by." Goldberg waited until he was certain where the Datsun was going, then pressed the transmit button on his microphone. "He just pulled into the Suburban Manor Motel. I'm still behind him."

"Wait for me," Hodge warned.

"Yeah, ten-four." You're damn right I'll wait, he thought. Hero stuff's what gets cops killed.

The motel was a one-story U-shaped structure. The station wagon had pulled up to a room in the center of the U. Goldberg stopped at the edge of the paved parking area, near the street. He had a clear view of the Datsun. The man was still sitting in it; he'd made no move to get out.

Goldberg picked up the mike, intending to inform Hodge of the circumstances—and then he noticed the car next to the station wagon. A battered Ford that fit the description of the blue sedan that had followed Mary Taylor. Unable to make out the license number, he took a pair of field glasses from the glove compartment and found the Ford's plate. Maine license, number 815–TDE. Putting down the binoculars, he took out a notebook and wrote down the number. And then he heard the sound of an engine, screaming.

Looking up quickly, he saw the green station wagon, rushing at him backward, coming full tilt. He blinked, and that was all the time he had before he was thrown across the seat by the crash, slammed against the passenger door. Then he was floating, sailing along on the blackness that surrounded him and was a part of him.

"Two-eighty-seven to one-twelve," Hodge said over the radio.

After a moment, she said it again. But Goldberg didn't hear it that time either.

When Goldberg regained consciousness, he was lying on a collapsible gurney, staring up at two ambulance attendants.

"Well, welcome back," one of them said. He was young, maybe twenty, and had a face full of pimples. The other one motioned to someone. Goldberg expected to see Pamela Hodge, but instead of a round face framed by dark curls, he found himself staring up at Flanagan.

"Where's Hodge?" Goldberg asked. He felt a pain in his shoulder, another in his head. As far as he could tell nothing was broken.

"Sent her to keep an eye on the Taylor woman."

Bastard, Goldberg thought. Keeping an eye on Mary Taylor was probably a good idea, but Goldberg knew Flanagan had given the job to Hodge simply to get rid of her.

"I take it the man got away," Goldberg said.

Flanagan nodded. Looking to his right, Goldberg saw the two cars, his and the Datsun. Both were crumpled, and they looked stuck together, as if the impact had fused the Datsun's rear end to the side of his Chevy. The front part of the station wagon, where the driver had been sitting, was undamaged.

Focusing on the motel itself, Goldberg noticed that the decrepit blue car was gone. "Did he leave in the old Ford?" he asked.

"It was the only thing he *did* take. He left his suitcase in the room."

"Anything in it that will help us?"

Flanagan shook his head. "No tags on the case, and

the stuff inside could have been bought at the nearest discount store."

And then Goldberg remembered. "I got his license number. It's in my notebook . . . in the car."

"I've got it," Flanagan said, holding up the small brown notebook. "The number you wrote down agrees with the one he used on the registration card. He was registered as Ray Gunn of Whitehouse, Maine. The clerk didn't get it even after I explained it to him."

Nor did Goldberg. And then it hit him. Ray Gunn. Reagan. White House. The name was a phony.

"License number's being checked out with Maine now. Lab's in the motel room."

"I thought we'd asked all the motels to let us know if a guy with a battered face showed up. How come we weren't notified?"

"Probably," Flanagan said, "because the bulletins weren't mailed out until this morning."

Goldberg decided that he would have known that if his mind had been working properly. It was only yesterday afternoon that Mary Taylor and the police artist had worked up the sketch that accompanied the bulletins. The ambulance attendants picked up the gurney.

"I don't know if that's really necessary," Goldberg said.

"It's necessary," the sergeant declared, and Goldberg was carried to the ambulance.

"The officer's okay," Sergeant Flanagan's voice said over the phone. "He should be back on the job in a day or two. That's about it, Mrs. Taylor."

She sat on the living room floor, holding the phone in her lap. "And you have no clues as to who he is?" she asked.

"No. Like I told you, the license number is apparently a phony. His name's obviously not Ray Gunn, but we found nothing to indicate who he might be. He might not even be from Maine."

"So, what happens now?"

"I can't give you twenty-four-hour protection. But I can have you tailed whenever you go anywhere, if you'll just give us a warning so we'll know you're going. Also, I can arrange for a patrol unit to escort you home from work for the next week or so. When are you going back, by the way?"

"I have sick leave through Wednesday. Thursday's my day off, so Friday I'll go back to work."

"All right. I'll be in touch with you before then. Uh, don't forget to notify us—as far in advance as possible—whenever you're going out."

"I won't."

"Okay, Mrs. Taylor. Remember to keep all your doors and windows locked and to look before you open the door to anyone."

"I will, Sergeant."

After ending the conversation, Mara reached up and returned the phone to its position on the small table. Although Mary had lain down on the couch to take a nap, it was Mara who'd awakened, Mara who'd taken the call from Sergeant Flanagan.

She chuckled. Before returning the body to Mary, she would resume her nap. Mary would awaken, unaware of having had one of her blank spells, unaware of the conversation with Flanagan. The knowledge that she'd suffered another blank spell would only further upset her, and she was already on the edge. Although Mara despised Mary, she didn't want to see her in an institution, because wherever Mary went, Mara went.

Besides, Mary's time was nearly at an end. In just

three days, the body would be entirely Mara's—and Mary would cease to exist.

Standing, she stretched and yawned, then lazily moved to the couch and lay down. Only three more days until Walpurgis Night, she thought as she dropped off to sleep. Only three more days.

Nineteen

On Wednesday morning in Lewiston, Maine, Lieutenant Daniel K. Larson received more information from the police in the Boston suburb where a young woman had been attacked by a tall, thin man who drove an old blue Ford. Sitting at his desk, he studied the new material, discovering that the man had attacked the woman again, once more failing to kill her. He'd eluded a detective by smashing into the officer's car with a stolen station wagon. An artist's drawing of the suspect was enclosed. The license number of his blue Ford was 815–TDE, Maine, but it hadn't checked out and was probably a phony.

His pulse quickening, Larson pulled open a desk drawer, took out a file folder, and flipped it open. The license number of the old blue Ford that had run down a young woman in Vermont had been reported as 815–TDE, Maine, a number that belonged to a retired couple in Bangor. When he'd received the report from

Vermont, he'd assumed the number had simply been misread. Not so. The plate was a fake. As it had so many times before, something in the back of his mind clicked when he looked at that number. This time he knew what it was.

Picking up the phone, he dialed an in-house number.

"Detectives—Grant."

"I've got a job for you," Larson said. "One that needs to be done right away."

A moment later, Grant stepped into the lieutenant's small office. Larson handed him the sketch of the suspect in Massachusetts.

"Show this to the people who spotted the guy in the blue car near Edwards's place the day he was killed."

"You think it's the guy?" Grant asked.

"Who knows? All I can tell you is that our friend there in the drawing has attacked a woman in Massachusetts and apparently killed another in Vermont, and that he drives an old blue Ford with a phony Maine license number. It's worth checking out."

"Yeah, it sure as hell is," Grant said, and then he was gone.

Larson slid a pad over in front of him and wrote down 815–TDE at the top of the sheet. The thing that had struck him about the number was that two of its letters and one of its numbers could easily be made by altering others. The eight could have been made from a three, the *T* from an *I*, the *E* from an *F* or an L. If all three alterations had been made, then the original number could have been 315–IDF, or 315–IDL. He wrote the numbers on his pad. Of course, it was possible that only two or even just a single character had been changed. He began putting down the possible combinations: 315–TDE, 315–IDE, 315–TDF. . . .

When he'd finished, he called Augusta, read off the list of numbers, then hung up and waited. Twenty minutes later, Augusta called back.

"I've got the information you wanted, Lieutenant," the young woman said. "Only one of those numbers belongs to a blue Ford. It's 815–IDL, which was issued to a Reverend Seymour Bruce in Bethany."

He quickly jotted down all the information the Department of Motor Vehicles had on Seymour Bruce and thanked the woman. According to his driver's license data, the minister was fifty-two years old, six feet two inches tall, and weighed 155 pounds. Larson dialed information, then placed a call to Bethany.

"Constable Davidson." The voice revealed that, like a lot of small-town lawmen, this one was getting along in years.

"This is Lieutenant Daniel Larson in Lewiston. I need to ask a favor of you."

"So ask it." The constable wasn't being rude, Larson realized; he was just a typical small-town Yankee.

"Do you know a Reverend Seymour Bruce there?"

"I know who he is."

"Can you tell me whether he was out of town on April—"

"Don't bother with the date, because I can't tell you about dates. He's been gone quite a lot lately, though. I can tell you that. If he doesn't get back soon and tend to his business, he's going to have a hayfield where the lawn should be." He chuckled at his joke.

"Do you know where he's been?"

"Nope. Haven't spoken to him."

"What's he like?"

"Don't know him that well."

In a town the size of Bethany, everyone knew

everything about everyone. Larson tried a different tack. "What do folks say about him? How's he regarded up there?"

"Why you asking?"

Larson realized what was happening. He was the outsider poking his nose in, and the constable's instincts as a small-town New Englander probably outweighed his desire to assist a fellow officer. He was loyal to a way of life first, the profession second.

"It's in connection with a murder investigation," Larson said, and he wondered how long it would be before that bit of news was known by just about everyone in Bethany.

"Who'd he murder?"

"He's a possible suspect in the killing of a young man here. What can you tell me about him?"

"Not much. He's one of those hellfire-and-brimstone preachers. The folks that like that sort of thing go to his church; those that don't, don't. Most don't. Those that do, don't talk about him much. Most of them have the cable so they can watch those TV preachers. They talk more about them than they do about Bruce."

Larson gave up. After thanking the constable for his help, the lieutenant hung up and waited impatiently to hear from Grant. The detective phoned about forty-five minutes later.

"Bingo, Lieutenant. I've talked to two of the three people who saw the guy sitting in the blue car. One says he can't be sure one way or the other. But the other one says it's him, no question."

After ending the conversation with Grant, Larson leafed through the papers in front of him until he spotted the name of the investigating officer in Massachusetts, a Sergeant Steve Flanagan. He picked up the phone.

That Wednesday morning Flanagan was at his desk in the large room that served as the office for the department's detectives. Around him, officers were talking on the phone, finishing up reports, doing all the routine things detectives did. His phone rang and he grabbed it.

"Uh, I'm calling about that, uh, murder in the parking lot of Zel Home and Builders Supply." The voice was that of an older man. Flanagan snatched his pen from his pocket and pulled over a pad.

"Can I get your name, please, sir," the detective said.

"Yes. I'm Arnold Miller." He gave his address.

"All right, Mr. Miller, what about the murder?"

"Well, I was there that night—at the store, and I left just as it closed." When Flanagan heard that, he sat up straighter. This could be the break he'd been hoping for but hadn't expected to get.

"I don't know whether this will help you," the man continued, "but when I started my truck to pull out of the lot, I saw a young woman. It might have been the victim, I don't know. Anyway, right after that I saw a man watching her. He was in a blue car."

"Describe the car."

"It was a Ford. Old, very beat up."

"Describe the man."

"I'd say he was middle-aged and thin. I only saw him for a moment. That's about all I can say about him."

"We'd like you to come in and talk to us about this some more, Mr. Miller. We can have someone pick you up if transportation's a problem."

"No, no, I've got my own transportation. Did that help you any? I mean, did it really?"

"Yes, it did, Mr. Miller. It helped a lot."

As soon as Flanagan hung up, Goldberg, back on the job after only a partial day's absence, spun around in his desk chair and said, "Line two, Sergeant—long distance."

Picking up the receiver, the sergeant pressed the appropriate button on his phone. "Flanagan."

"This is Lieutenant Daniel Larson at the Lewiston, Maine, police department. I'm calling about a case you're working on, the Mary Taylor thing."

"How'd you know about that?"

"I've got a request out for any incidents involving beat-up blue Fords."

Captain Prince, the initial recipient of the detective division's daily reports, must have forwarded the information, Flanagan decided. "How can I help you, Lieutenant?"

"First, have you apprehended the subject yet?"

Flanagan sighed. "No. How much do you know of what's happened here?"

"I know about the ramming of the detective's car. That's the latest information I have."

"You're almost up to date then." Flanagan decided to hold off telling the lieutenant about the call he'd just received until he'd heard what the Maine cop had to say.

"Okay, good. Now, the first thing I want to tell you is that I think I know who this man is."

"Oh, Jesus," Flanagan said, grabbing his pen. "Who?"

"A minister from a small town up here called Bethany."

241

"A minister? What makes you think he's—"

"I'll explain all that in a moment. First, let me tell you that this minister may have killed a young man here in Lewiston and a young woman in Vermont."

The Maine policeman gave the details of the two murders and explained how he'd identified Reverend Seymour Bruce through his fake license number. The artist's sketch had been identified by one Lewiston resident as the man parked in a blue car near the scene of the John Edwards murder.

"Whew," Flanagan said. "It all fits, even the ice pick." He told Larson about the Flynn murder and the phone call he'd just received.

"These murders aren't random," Larson said. "They're planned. I think the first thing we need to consider is what these four people have in common."

"As far as I can tell, Mary Taylor and the Flynn woman had only one thing in common. They were both females in their early twenties."

"John Edwards eliminates the female angle, but all four of them were in their twenties." He hesitated, then added, "Doesn't tell us much all by itself, does it?"

"Let me give you what I've got on Mary Taylor and Stephanie Flynn," Flanagan said, taking out two folders and opening them side-by-side in front of him. "Okay . . . uh, Taylor's maiden name was Kensington, and Flynn's was Saggart. Flynn was from Boston originally, Taylor from Maine."

"Where in Maine?"

"Uh, Evans Ridge. No, wait a minute. Uh, that's where her foster parents live. I don't know what part of the state she came from. All I know is that she was an orphan."

"An orphan! Wait a minute." Flanagan could hear

papers being shuffled in Maine; then Larson came back on the line. "John Edwards was an orphan, too."

"What about the woman in Vermont?"

Again, the sound of papers being moved around was transmitted long distance. "I don't have anything at all on her background," Larson said finally.

"Even if the Vermont victim was an orphan, Stephanie Flynn won't fit. I know for certain she wasn't an orphan. I've talked to her parents. Also, it doesn't seem this guy stalked her the way he did Taylor. As far as I can determine, he never followed her or watched her."

"Hmmm," Larson said and fell silent.

Then, as Flanagan stared at the papers in the two files, his eyes fixed on the description of Mary Taylor. He then realized it wasn't Taylor's description at all, but Flynn's, and for the first time, it dawned on him just how much alike the two women had looked. He had only seen Flynn dead. Alive, she would have resembled Taylor. It had been dark in the parking lot, the two women leaving together. . . .

"It's possible," Flanagan said, "that Flynn was killed by mistake, that the killer thought she was Taylor." He explained why it could have happened that way.

"I'm coming down," Larson said. "It'll take me around three hours to get there. When I arrive, I'd like to talk to Mary Taylor. Can you let her know I'm coming?"

"Sure."

"You can do me one other favor, if you would. Check with Vermont about the background of the other victim."

"No problem. What's the name of the investigating officer?"

Larson gave it to him, then said, "Okay, I'll see you in a few hours."

Flanagan hung up, trying to empty his mind for a moment or two before attempting to assimilate all he'd just learned. He had not told Larson about the incident involving the children's swing at the house next door to Mary Taylor's, nor had he told the lieutenant about his suspicions concerning Mary Taylor. Although he no longer had any reason to think she had had a part in Stephanie Flynn's death, none of his other misgivings about her had been resolved. Something there was not as it should be.

Flanagan picked up the phone. He had to let her know a policeman was coming from Maine to talk to her. He was surprised when no one answered at the Taylor house. If she went anywhere, she was supposed to let him know so he could arrange a tail in an unmarked car. She hadn't called once since agreeing to the arrangement.

He dialed the radio room. "Control—Davis," a woman answered.

"This is Sergeant Flanagan in detectives. Do you have any units in the vicinity of West Scones Boulevard right now?"

"It's six-adam's district. He's logged as ten-eight." The officer was in his car, available for call.

"Ask him to check a house for me, see if everything's ten-four there." He gave the Taylor's address.

About twenty minutes later, Davis in control called him back. "Six-adam reports that no one answers the door, but everything there seems ten-four."

"Thanks." He replaced the receiver, frowning.

Mary moved slowly along, her eyes lingering on one stone face, then shifting to the next. Having decided to spend the day in Boston, she had started with a visit to the city's Back Bay section. At the moment, she was in the Museum of Fine Arts, admiring the extensive collection of ancient Egyptian sculpture.

She was here in Boston because she'd decided that she wasn't going to let some lunatic force her to stay home with the door barred. To do so would be to let a madman control her life, and that was simply unacceptable.

In addition to visiting the museum, she planned to do some other touristy things, such as visiting Faneuil Hall and The Old Corner Bookstore. If she had time, she'd do some shopping. She had most of the day; her appointment with Dr. Carpenter wasn't until four.

Driving into the city earlier, she'd spotted no one following her, which either meant that the police were too clever for her to detect or that they weren't tailing her anymore. She should call Flanagan and find out, she supposed, although she had no desire to talk to him. In any case, she could worry about that later. For now, she had the whole day in Boston to enjoy herself.

Sitting at his desk, Flanagan doodled on a piece of paper while he waited for Tom Taylor to come to the phone at the sporting goods store where he was assistant manager. The detective heard the familiar click that meant he was no longer on hold.

"This is Tom Taylor. Can I help you?"

"Mr. Taylor, this is Sergeant Flanagan. I've been trying to reach your wife at home, but I don't get any answer. Do you have any idea where she might be?"

"Of course. She's in Boston. Didn't you follow her there?"

"She didn't notify us." Not that he would have had an officer follow her around Boston. Had she called, he'd have told her to change her plans or take her chances.

"What do you mean she didn't notify you?" Taylor asked anxiously.

"If she went anywhere, she was supposed to let us know so we could tail her. She didn't call."

"Well, no one told me about any of this. I just assumed . . ."

"That we'd be watching your house, ready to tail Mrs. Taylor anytime she left?"

"Well, isn't that what you do when a citizen's clearly in danger? Isn't that your job?"

"No, Mr. Taylor, that isn't my job. And I explained the arrangement to your wife. She agreed to it. If she's gone somewhere without notifying me, then I have to assume she didn't want us tagging along."

"Sergeant . . ." Taylor trailed off.

"When will she be back?"

"Uh, by four. That's when she has an appointment with Dr. Carpenter. Whether she'll go home before going to the doctor's office I don't know. Is something wrong? Is something going on?"

"No, no, nothing's wrong that I know of, Mr. Taylor. There's a police officer coming down from Maine to see her. I just wanted to let her know."

"Why would a policeman from Maine want to talk to Mary?"

"We think we know who her attacker is. He's from Maine, and he may have killed someone there and someone else in Vermont." Flanagan started to tell him the Maine minister had apparently murdered Stephanie Flynn as well, but he stopped himself. He'd told Taylor more than enough for the moment.

"Who is he?"

"I'm not prepared to discuss that just now, Mr. Taylor. Could you have your wife call me as soon as she gets home, please."

"Yes, of course." He paused, then said, "Sergeant, I want you to know that I'm not happy about the way this has been handled at all. My wife's gone to Boston, there's a killer hunting her, and she has no protection whatsoever. She could be in great danger."

"Mr. Taylor, she's supposed to call *us*. She said she would, but she didn't. Besides, I would think our man's experience the other day would have cured him of following your wife. It very nearly got him caught."

"I suppose you're right, Sergeant." Which was nothing more than a polite way of dropping the subject for the moment. Flanagan had convinced him of nothing.

"Oh, one more thing, Mr. Taylor. Your wife was an orphan, as I recall. Is that right?"

"Yes."

"What can you tell me about that part of her life?"

"Very little, I'm afraid, Sergeant. She has very few memories of those years, and what she does recall must be unpleasant, because she avoids talking about it."

"Was she in an orphanage?"

"Yes."

"What was the name of it?"

"I don't know, Sergeant. It was somewhere near Evans Ridge, where she was raised. If you really want to know, you can contact her foster parents. They'd know."

"I may do that, Mr. Taylor. Thank you."

It was midafternoon when Larson stepped into the detectives' office. It was a large room with numerous modern desks seemingly placed at random. He stepped up to the first one that was occupied and found himself looking down at a middle-aged woman with curly dark hair.

"Excuse me," he said. "Could you tell me where I'd find Sergeant Flanagan."

The smile she'd given him as he stepped up to her desk abruptly faded when he mentioned Flanagan. "Over there," she said, pointing at a well-dressed man of about forty.

"Thanks."

Starting toward him, Larson tried to assess Flanagan. He had thick brown hair, and Larson's first impression was of someone who liked the flashy, macho part of the job but lacked the ability, so necessary in a detective, to plod along, finding a fact here, a clue there.

"Hi," the Maine policeman said, extending his hand. "I'm Lieutenant Larson."

"Steve Flanagan," the other man replied, rising and accepting the proffered hand. "Have a seat."

Once the two men were seated, Flanagan said, "I checked with Vermont, and the hit-and-run victim was an orphan from Maine."

Larson nodded. "Three orphans from Maine. Now all we have to do is figure out why a minister who's also from Maine wants those orphans dead."

"The only thing I could think of was that maybe they were all together at one time—the same orphanage or maybe the same foster parents. I called Mary Taylor's foster parents this afternoon, and they said Mary was the only foster child they had ever raised. They've never heard of the other victims. I even asked them about Stephanie Flynn, just in case my theory is wrong. The only thing they could tell me was that Mary came from an orphanage called the Christian Home for Children. They say it burned down years ago."

"Where in Maine is it—or was it?"

"I don't know exactly. I gather it's not too far from where Taylor's foster parents live, a place called Evans Ridge. You'd know more about where that is than I would."

"It's out in the middle of nowhere. Lots of woods and lakes and streams. Beautiful country with excellent fishing. Someday I'll retire to a cabin out there. To hell with this Sunbelt crap."

Flanagan didn't reply. Larson decided the Massachusetts detective was probably not the outdoors type. For him, it would be a condo in Florida.

"Did you get in touch with this Mary Taylor?" Larson asked.

"She's in Boston for the day and may not get back until four, when she has an appointment with her psychiatrist. Her husband will let her know we want to talk to her."

"Well," Larson said, "if you'll let me use your phone, I'll make a couple of calls and see if I can find out whether John Edwards and the woman in Vermont also happened to be residents of the Christian Home for Children."

As the lieutenant started to get up, Flanagan said, "I almost forgot to tell you. Arnold Miller—the guy who saw the man in the blue car just before Stephanie Flynn was killed—he says he's pretty sure the artist's picture is the man he saw. And his description of the blue car is right on the money."

Larson nodded.

"Why don't you use that desk over there," Flanagan

said, pointing to one that was vacant. "After you've made the calls, come back and I'll tell you what I know about Mary Taylor—or maybe what I don't know about Mary Taylor."

Larson moved to an unoccupied desk. The first call he placed was to Grant in Lewiston.

Twenty

DR. HELEN CARPENTER SAT AT HER DESK, REVIEWING her notes on Mary Taylor. The psychiatrist glanced at her watch. It was 3:55; Taylor should be arriving any moment for her four o'clock appointment.

She'd phoned to tell the doctor what had happened as she was leaving the building Monday. The psychiatrist wondered whether the man who kept attacking Taylor was someone the young woman had met during one or more of her memory lapses. Dr. Carpenter also wondered whether her patient could be a multiple personality.

It would account for Taylor's memory lapses, during which she would have shifted into another personality. The disorder, psychotherapists were discovering, was much more common than once thought. Precisely how common, no one knew, since doctors frequently failed to recognize it.

Dr. Carpenter leaned back in her chair. Multiples, it was being discovered, had usually been abused as

children. Was that what had happened to Mary Taylor
at the orphanage? Were the things done to her there so
horrible that she'd blocked them from her conscious
memory?

And was that why the man had called her Mary/
Mara? Had he met her as one of her other selves, one
that called herself Mara? If so, how many alternate
personalities did Mary Taylor have? Multiples could
have almost any number of them. Dr. Carpenter
sighed. She had no answers for these questions. Nor did
she know why Taylor's behavior during her blank
periods was so violent.

Dr. Carpenter's phone rang, and her receptionist
announced the arrival of Mary Taylor. "Send her in,"
the psychiatrist said.

Studying Mary as she stepped into the office, Dr.
Carpenter saw an attractive, determined-looking young
woman who showed no outward signs of the turmoil
within.

"The police almost caught him yesterday," Mary said
as she sat down. She told how the man had smashed
into a detective's car and escaped.

"My goodness," Dr. Carpenter said. "No one can
ever accuse you of having an uneventful life."

"No," Mary said, a hint of sadness appearing in her
eyes.

"I want to hypnotize you again today, Mary. This
time, I'm going to take you back to the orphanage and
see if we can find out what happened to you there."

"I hope it works," the young woman said solemnly.
"Walpurgis Night is the day after tomorrow."

Dr. Carpenter considered reminding Taylor that she
could hardly expect to be cured merely because she was
going to be hypnotized for the second time, but the
psychotherapist remained silent. The significance of

Walpurgis Night was a complete puzzle. Dr. Carpenter decided to question her about it while she was under hypnosis.

After using the revolving spiral to put Mary under, the psychiatrist stood before the young woman and said, "In a moment, I'm going to tell you to open your eyes. You'll still be in a deep sleep, fully relaxed, but you'll be able to see everything around you. All right, Mary, now open your eyes."

"My name's not Mary."

Taken aback, Dr. Carpenter stared at her patient's face. Gone was the determined-looking young woman who had come into the office a few minutes ago. The person sitting here now looked hostile, the eyes cruel, the mouth contemptuous. It was still Mary Taylor, and yet somehow it wasn't.

"What's your name?" Dr. Carpenter asked.

"Mara."

"Why do you prefer that name to Mary?"

"It's not what I prefer," she replied. "Mary's the person you've met previously, and I'm Mara. We're two different people." Her voice was no longer Mary's. Now she spoke deliberately, quietly, and yet her tone seemed full of malice.

"In what ways are you different from Mary?"

"For one thing, I know everything she does."

"And she's unaware of what you do?"

"She refers to the times when I'm in control as blank spells."

Well, there it was. Mary Taylor was indeed a multiple personality. Dr. Carpenter was a little surprised that Mara had taken that moment to come out, but everything Mary had said so far seemed to fit. As in most such cases, the patient had a primary self, Mary in this case, who was unaware of any other selves. Mara, on the other hand, knew everything that went on, as one of the alternate selves usually did. Though there were different methods for treating multiples, the goal was always the same. The personalities had to be integrated.

"Is there anyone else," the psychiatrist asked, "besides Mary and Mara?"

"No, Doctor, there are no others."

Dr. Carpenter hesitated, choosing her next question carefully. "Why is Mary unable to tell anyone about her blank spells?"

Her patient smirked knowingly. "Because that's the way Sister arranged things."

"Who is Sister?"

"She's the one who put me in Mary's body."

"Why did she do that?"

"Why should I tell you?"

"Why shouldn't you? You're not afraid to tell me, are you?"

"Afraid?" Mara laughed. "The information will be quite useless to you, so I'll tell you. The others and I, we'll take over the bodies on Walpurgis Night of this year. That's when the new struggle for our master's reign on earth will begin. That's what Sister taught us."

"When were you taught these things?"

"We were taught as children."

"At the orphanage."

"Yes, at the orphanage."

"And who is your master?"

"My master is Satan."

Perplexed, Dr. Carpenter considered what her patient had just said. If one took her words at face value, then her dual personality had been deliberately arranged. Was such a thing possible? Although she had no answer for that, the psychiatrist knew that some dramatic personality changes had been brought about through what was commonly referred to as brainwashing. Had such techniques been used on children—on helpless orphans? The doctor shuddered at the thought. Very few brainwashing techniques were pleasant.

Had the orphanage been in the hands of Satanists who tried to manipulate the minds of the youngsters in their charge? Or was all this nothing more than an invention of a very disturbed young woman's mind? Using hypnosis, the psychiatrist had tapped something, but not necessarily truth. Mary—or Mara—believed it to be true; of that Dr. Carpenter was fairly certain. But then another patient of hers was convinced he communicated with beings from space. To him, it was real.

"Tell me about the orphanage, Mara. Tell me what—"

"You want to destroy me, don't you?" she said, interrupting. "You're on Mary's side, against me."

"Destroying you would be impossible, because you *are* Mary. A part of her anyway."

"No!" she said fiercely. "I'm not part of her. I'm separate and different. When the body becomes mine, I'll destroy her forever."

"You'd be destroying yourself as well."

"No. It's not like that. It's more like cutting away bad tissue to preserve the good."

"If you're not part of Mary, what are you? How did you come to be?"

Mara smiled. "Sister created me. I already told you that."

"Who is Sister?"

"You can't hurt me, you know."

"Why would I want to?"

"To save Mary. But you can't save her," Mara said smugly. "No one can."

"Tell me about Sister."

"She was at the orphanage."

"What did she do there?"

"She was in charge."

"What did you mean when you said Sister created you?"

"I can't tell you any more. You want to use the information against us."

"What do you mean by us?"

"Sister and me . . . and the others."

"What others?"

"I won't tell you that."

"Mary doesn't remember anything about the orphanage. Do you?"

She shrugged.

"Do you remember what happened at the orphanage?"

"I'm not supposed to remember."

"Why not?"

"Sister doesn't want us to."

"Do you do everything Sister tells you?"

"Of course."

"Why?"

"I have no choice. I am what Sister created me to be. Mary has no choice either, because Sister's will is always with her. Sister's will is Mary's censor."

Dr. Carpenter took a moment to sort out her thoughts. One thing she found particularly puzzling was Mara's insistence that she would take over the body permanently on Walpurgis Night. The psychiatrist was unable to recall a case in which one personality stated the precise time at which it would destroy the other. Was such a thing possible? Could the different personalities turn the body into a battleground on which one would slay the other? Could the primary self be slain?

It was also possible, Dr. Carpenter supposed, that if one personality was somehow done away with, then another might arise to replace it—possibly a Maria or a Marion in Mary Taylor's case. The fifty-minute hour was almost up. Before seeing this patient again, she needed to do some reading on multiple personality and consult with someone who'd dealt extensively with the disorder. She wondered, too, whether she knew anyone who'd worked with patients who'd been brainwashed.

"Mara, are you still here?"

"Yes, Doctor, I'm here."

"Let me speak to Mary."

Instantly, the hard look faded from Taylor's face, replaced by Mary's softer one.

"Mary, is that you?"

"Yes, of course it's me," she said, eyeing the doctor curiously. "Who else would it be?" Mary's businesslike but gentle voice had replaced Mara's harsher, crueler one.

Glancing at her watch, Dr. Carpenter realized that she didn't have time right now to explain to Mary what had happened during the session. Also, she needed a chance to think things through and determine how to handle this.

"Mary, I'm going to wake you up now. When you awake, you will remember nothing that happened during the session and you won't be curious about it. You won't want to ask me any questions."

When she had awakened Mary, she told her to make an appointment for the next day. Then Dr. Carpenter leaned back in her chair, lost in thought.

After making the appointment, Mary slid behind the wheel of her car and headed for home. Having been reluctant to end her day in Boston, she had left the city with just enough time to make her four o'clock appointment with the psychiatrist. In the trunk were two new outfits she'd bought on impulse while shopping in the city.

It would be nice if she and Tom went out for dinner, she decided. There was a new restaurant she wanted to try. It was called— The thought was never completed because Mary was no longer driving the car.

She reached Scones Boulevard and headed west, irritated that she had so long been denied control of the body. Unable to impose herself on the body at will, she had no option but to wait until it happened of its own accord. But, then, Mara had found herself in control more and more often lately—and in only two days, the body would be all hers; Mary, the hated Mary, would be gone forever.

Yes, Mara thought, Mary will be no more. Gone will be her drab clothes, her boring life, perhaps even her dull husband. Good-bye sweet, uninteresting Mary. And good riddance.

It would happen on Walpurgis Night, a day of religious celebration equalled only by Halloween. Sister had explained that on that night the grand climax of the spring equinox was celebrated. Witches held sabbats, and demons and banshees came forth throughout the land.

Though comforting, these thoughts improved Mara's mood only slightly. The session with Dr. Carpenter had been disquieting because Mara had no idea what had transpired while she was under hypnosis. She distrusted the psychiatrist, and she especially disliked being under the doctor's control during hypnosis. Mary, damn her, had made an appointment with the psychiatrist for the next morning at eleven. Though unaware of what was on the tape, Mara was certain she didn't want Mary to hear it. But what could she do? How could she keep Mary from hearing the tape?

And then she knew. Ahead was the freeway. Instead of crossing it and continuing on toward the little yellow house on the quiet tree-lined street, she took the expressway and headed north.

Larson glanced at his watch; it was 6:55. He was eating alone in a booth at a small Oriental restaurant near the police station. To be different, he'd ordered a Korean dish, which had turned out to be beef and broccoli in a sauce with cellophane noodles. It had a unique flavor that he liked.

Flanagan had gone home for dinner. He'd invited Larson to come along, but the lieutenant had declined, feeling that a last-minute dinner guest would be an imposition on Mrs. Flanagan.

When they'd left for dinner, there was still no one answering the phone at the Taylor house. The store where the husband worked probably didn't close until six, and an assistant manager might not be able to leave right at closing. Mary Taylor had probably stopped at the grocery store or maybe a friend's house after her visit with the psychiatrist. It would be very late when Larson got home to Lewiston.

From Flanagan, he'd learned that something was amiss with Mary Taylor, and like the Massachusetts detective, he was interested in knowing what transpired between her and the psychiatrist. Such communications were privileged, of course; he'd find out what was said in the privacy of the doctor's office only if Mary Taylor elected to tell him.

He'd phoned Grant and had him check on John Edwards and Margaret Donovan, the Vermont hit-and-run victim. Both had been in the Christian Home for Children. Grant had been trying to learn about the place, but he'd found information about an orphanage that burned down fifteen years before hard to come by. State officials said they had no records regarding the place, and county officials said there had been records, but nobody knew where they were.

Again, he thought of Mary Taylor, and he found himself wondering if she wasn't home because something had happened to her. He dismissed the notion. There was nothing to indicate anything was wrong. Still, alone and unprotected, she was out there somewhere, and so was a killer intent on making her his next victim.

He and Flanagan had puzzled over the why of it, coming to no conclusions. There *was* an explanation, a reason why a small-town hellfire-and-brimstone preacher was killing former orphans, but chances were it only made sense to Seymour Bruce.

Temporarily pushing all this from his mind, Larson took a sip of Oriental tea, then concentrated on finishing his meal.

Confused and sick with worry, Tom Taylor paced the length of his living room. His whole life seemed to be falling apart lately. With that thought, he realized he'd just summed up how important Mary was to him. It was actually Mary who was falling apart, but Mary *was* his whole life. After his divorce, his existence had become a huge emptiness. But then Mary had come along, filling the seemingly unfillable void and making him whole again.

And now their lives were spinning out of control. Someone was trying to kill her. She disappeared from bed in the middle of the night; she said there were things she couldn't tell him and dangers she couldn't explain. And now she was missing.

He'd last seen Mary at breakfast that morning, and he'd understood that she was going into Boston, that she'd return in time for her psychiatrist's appointment at four. He hadn't seen her go. He really didn't know that she'd gone to Boston. Unable to reach the psychiatrist, he didn't know if Mary had shown up for the four o'clock appointment.

He'd called the police. Sergeant Flanagan wasn't there, so he'd explained things to the woman who'd taken his call, left a message for Flanagan. Nothing was being done, he was sure; the police would call him tomorrow, during normal working hours: *Your wife? Nope, haven't seen her. I'll check the morgue if you'd like. Hold on.* He shuddered.

Feeling overwhelmed by events he was powerless to influence, Tom Taylor went into the kitchen, got a beer from the refrigerator, and sat down at the breakfast table. So far, he'd hidden his emotions from Mary, not wanting to let her see how close he was to becoming unhinged. Whenever possible, he'd responded to her needs while keeping his tightly locked away.

When Mary returned—and she would be back; he

refused to allow for any other possibility—he would again try to be the emotional rock she'd need. But for the moment, there was no need to try to fool himself. Pushing the bottle of beer aside, he folded his arms on the table, rested his head on them, and wept.

Twenty-One

IT WAS AS IF THE SUNNY SUBURBAN AFTERNOON SHE'D been looking at through the windshield had abruptly changed to a new scene, a dark rural one—as if she were sitting in a theater rather than an automobile, the windshield a movie screen. But Mary wasn't sitting passively, watching the scenes change; she was controlling the car, her car, driving along a dark country road. Time had elapsed, enough time for the sun to have set and for her to have driven here—wherever here was. And she knew, though she didn't want to think about it, that a great deal of time might have passed, that the sunny afternoon hadn't necessarily been a few hours ago, that it could conceivably have been days, weeks, even months ago.

Feeling the urge to panic, she controlled it. Allowing terror to dictate her actions would only make things worse. All right, she told herself, take stock of the situation. You've had another blank spell. You need to find out what day this is and where you are. Then, unable to prevent herself from doing so, she started trembling. Come on, she thought bitterly, so you've had another blank spell. You've had them before. Big deal. Who cares? A tear trickled down her cheek.

No amount of bitter self-pity would convince her to resign herself to this. She hated being like this. She despised being at the mercy of her sickness—or her abnormality or whatever it should be called. Her curse, she decided. It was her curse.

The country through which she was passing was densely wooded. A tree with a gnarled trunk suddenly appeared in her headlights, an ancient, enormous tree that could have been here before the Pilgrims had landed. Mary found herself wanting to find another big tree, press the accelerator, aim the headlights at the center of the huge trunk. . . .

But she wouldn't do that. She'd think about it, toy with the idea, but she'd never do it. No matter how miserable and beaten she felt, no matter how little control she had over her life, some part of her, some small and very stubborn part, would never give up.

And then she did see another large gnarled tree. Partway up the trunk, just below the first branches, was a hole in which squirrels or some other small animals had probably made a home. There was something very familiar about that tree . . . and the first one, too, now that she thought about it. She was near Evans Ridge, on the road that led to the home of her foster parents. *Her* home for most of her life.

Glancing at the dashboard clock, she saw that it was about nine, which she found reassuring. It was the time she would be arriving here if she'd left Boston at five, so she'd probably only lost a few hours, not days or weeks. How am I going to explain my showing up like this to my foster parents? she wondered. And then a new thought struck her: Tom! He had no idea where she was. He'd be going crazy.

She'd call him as soon as she got to the house. But how would she explain her behavior? What could she possibly tell him that he'd accept? If only I could tell him the truth, she thought, if only I could. Well, that was the one thing she couldn't do. She'd tell Tom and the Caldwells something. She'd open her mouth, and lies would come out. She hated herself for having to deceive the people who loved and trusted her. At times, she felt the lies were the worst part of her curse.

Ahead was the familiar mailbox, CALDWELL on the side in red letters. Glancing into the rearview mirror, she signaled and began to slow. There was one pair of headlights behind her, maybe an eighth of a mile away.

Opening the door, Tom Taylor found Sergeant Flanagan on his doorstep, accompanied by another man. He searched Flanagan's face, looking for a hint of what news the policeman had brought, his emotions a mixture of desperate hope and terrible fear. Oh, please, he thought, let it be good news.

"This is Lieutenant Larson from Lewiston, Maine," Flanagan said.

Tom vaguely recalled that a policeman from Maine was here to see Mary. "Have you heard anything—anything at all?"

"We got in touch with the psychiatrist through her answering service," Flanagan said. "We know that your wife kept her four o'clock appointment, but that's all we know so far."

Tom led the two policemen into the living room. The officers sat down on the couch, Tom in the easy chair.

"Does the name Seymour Bruce mean anything to you?" the cop from Maine asked.

Tom shook his head. "Is he the one who's been trying to kill Mary?"

"It's not certain, but we think so."

Looking at Flanagan, Tom felt a small surge of anger, something inside insisting that all this was the detective's fault. But then the emotion faded. Getting mad was not only pointless, but he lacked the strength for it.

"We've got a locate out on both her and the car," Flanagan said. "It's throughout the Boston area right now. If there's no word by morning, I'll expand it to a regional locate."

Would there be word by morning? Tom wondered. When would he know what had happened to Mary? Tomorrow? The next day? Next week? Next month? Never? No, not never; he would hear. And the more time that elapsed until he did, the more likely it would be that the news would be terrible. On the verge of thinking the unthinkable, he forced all such notions from his mind.

The two policemen, looking efficient yet suitably somber, sat on his couch, watching him. He stared back at them miserably, just a little resentful because their loved ones were most likely home, safe. He knew it was a childish feeling. He didn't care.

"Mary!" Maxine Caldwell exclaimed as soon as she'd opened the door. "What on earth are you doing here?" Instantly, the surprise on her face changed to concern. "Is everything all right? Is anything wrong?"

"Give me a chance to catch my breath, and I'll fill you in."

"Nick," Maxine Caldwell called, leading her foster daughter toward the living room. She was the quintessential country woman: big-boned, ruddy-complexioned, wearing a blue denim dress. In her fifties, she had sandy-colored hair streaked with gray.

"Well, I'll be darned," Nick Caldwell said, standing up as Mary entered the living room. He looked very much Maxine's mate. Dressed in khaki work clothes, he had big hands and, like his wife, that reddish complexion that seemed to go with country living. These were bighearted down-to-earth people, and Mary loved them dearly.

Obviously pleased to see her, Mary's foster father stepped forward and took her in a gentle embrace. Releasing her, he stepped back and said, "Max, you didn't tell me Mary was coming."

"I didn't know she was," Maxine Caldwell replied. She stood beside Mary, looking perplexed.

Nick Caldwell turned his eyes on his foster daughter.

"It was a spur-of-the-moment thing," Mary said lightly. "I thought I'd surprise you."

She quickly seated herself on the couch. After a moment's hesitation, her foster mother joined her, and Nick Caldwell returned to his favorite recliner. Across the room, a car chase was in progress on the color TV set. No one paid any attention to it.

The house very much expressed the Caldwells' lifestyle. Big rough-hewn beams supported the stained-wood ceiling. Sturdy, functional furniture; a big stone fireplace in the living room. In the enormous kitchen, a wealth of pots, pans, and other utensils hung from the walls and ceiling.

"Your things still in the car?" Maxine Caldwell asked.

"Things?" Mary replied, caught off-guard.

"Your bags. You know, clothes, toothbrush, and all that."

Mary shrugged. "Well, I said it was a spur-of-the-moment decision."

Her foster mother frowned. "Now, don't be flip with me," she said sternly.

"I'm sorry," Mary said, her thoughts swirling. How much to tell? She had to give some sort of an explanation, and the truth—at least some of it—was all she had to offer.

"I . . . well, I had to get away," Mary explained. "You see, things have been happening. A woman who came to work at Zel was stabbed to death her first day on the job, and I was the one who found the body." She closed her eyes, as if doing so might keep her from seeing Stephanie's bloody corpse in the front seat of the car.

"Oh my goodness!" Maxine Caldwell exclaimed, gently squeezing Mary's arm. "I'm not surprised you wanted to get away."

Mary went on. Having revealed that much, she wanted to let it all out now—all that her internal censors would allow. "And there's a man who's been following me. He's tried to kill me twice. Once at the store. Another time when I was leaving after a doctor's appointment."

The Caldwells exchanged shocked looks. "Oh, Mary," her foster mother said.

Mary went on, relating the details of Steph's murder and the attacks on her, omitting that the doctor she'd seen was a psychiatrist.

"So that's why that policeman called this afternoon," Maxine Caldwell said almost absently.

"What policeman?" Mary asked.

"Flaherty or Flannery or something like that."

"Flanagan?"

"Yes, that's it—Flanagan."

"What did he ask you?"

"Just about you, about your background."

"I guess he's got to check me out because I'm the one who discovered the body," Mary said cautiously.

Her foster mother nodded. Apparently, she found nothing particularly unusual about a policeman's calling her under such circumstances.

"Do the police think it was the same man," Nick Caldwell asked, "the same one who attacked you?"

"You mean, was the guy after me the same one who killed . . ." She trailed off. That her attacker might also be Steph's killer was obvious, completely obvious, but it had never occurred to her. And then, horrified, she realized why he might have killed Steph.

"My God," she said. "He killed her by mistake. Steph and I looked a lot alike; it was very dark. . . ."

"Hey, come on," Maxine Caldwell said. "Don't try to make it out to be your fault. You don't even know if that's what happened. And even if it was, you weren't in any way responsible for what happened to Steph."

Oh, God, Mary thought, how do you know what you're responsible for when you don't even know what you've done?

Letting her foster mother slip her arm around her, Mary rested her head on the woman's shoulder. Although she made no effort to hold back her tears, none came. Concern that these wonderful people might be hurt because of her was the only thing that kept her from feeling totally flat, lifeless. It was as if life had squeezed out every last tear, wrung from her all the emotion she had to give, leaving her with nothing inside except a vast emptiness.

Nick Caldwell shook his head. "The city's become a

terrible place. Even the suburbs, where you are. Anytime you'd like to come back here to the country to
live, you're always welcome, you and your husband."

"When you first showed up on our doorstep," his
wife said, "I figured you'd had a fight, you and Tom."

"Oh, my God," Mary said. "Tom."

Her foster mother stared at her. "You mean . . . you
mean he doesn't know you're here?"

"I've got to call him," Mary said, getting up. "He'll
be worried sick." The phone was on a big desk at one
end of the living room.

After dialing, she stood there, the receiver to her
ear, listening to the telephone company's long-distance
equipment making connections, reaching out along the
wire to suburban Boston, to Tom. Across the room, her
foster parents were watching her intently.

"Hello," Tom said after only two rings.

Mary opened her mouth to speak but couldn't seem
to find any words. Finally, she said, "Hi, it's me."

"Mary, is that you?" he asked urgently.

She realized she had spoken so softly her words must
have been nearly inaudible. "Yes," she said louder,
"it's me."

"Mary, are you okay? Where are you?"

"I'm fine. I'm in Maine, in Evans Ridge."

"What are you doing there?"

"I . . . I just had to get away, Tom. I'm sorry I didn't
call you. I am—really. It was just an impulsive thing. I
decided I absolutely had to get away. I'm sorry if I
worried you, but I'm okay. Honest."

"Mary, the police are here. They've got a bulletin
out on you. We didn't know what might have happened
to you. I . . . well, I thought maybe you were lying
dead somewhere, that maybe that man had gotten

you." His voice conveyed both relief that she was safe and anger at her unfeeling behavior.

I didn't do it, Mary thought, not consciously. If only I could tell you that. She said, "I'm sorry, Tom. I . . . I couldn't help myself. I just couldn't." She sucked in her breath as a pain shot through her abdomen. That was more than she was allowed to say.

"Mary, what are you talking about?"

"I'm sorry," she said as a tear trickled down her cheek. "I'm sorry, Tom. I'm just so sorry." And then she found a well of tears she hadn't known was there. "I'm so sorry," she sobbed. "Oh, God, Tom, I'm so sorry."

Her foster mother joined her, gently taking her arm to steady her.

"Listen, Mary, I'm coming up there," Tom said. "I'll call Ben at home and tell him I won't be in tomorrow; then I'll—"

"No," Mary said, interrupting him. "Please don't come up."

"But . . . why?" He sounded hurt.

"I just need to be alone for a few days. It's . . . it's the strain, I think. You know, Steph's murder, the attacks. I just need to be alone for a little while. It's not that I don't love you or want to see you. It's . . ." She trailed off.

He was silent a moment, then said, "You're right. You have been through a lot. I'm sorry I gave you a hard time."

"No, you were right to point out how unfeeling I'd been. I don't know exactly why I didn't call you. I just didn't. Maybe it shows how desperately I need some time to get myself together."

"When will you be back?"

"Friday night. I'll call from here and square it with Mr. Adkins. That's just one more day of sick leave, and he already said I could have more time if I needed it. Also, I was supposed to see Dr. Carpenter tomorrow morning. Will you call her for me?"

"Sure."

"I'm sorry I'm . . . I'm so much trouble to you. I love you more than I can say."

"Don't apologize. After what you've been through, you've got a right to behave a little strangely. And I love you, too. And I'll miss you."

Mary sniffed, holding back yet another round of tears. "It'll be the first time we've been apart since we got married."

In the background, she heard a muffled conversation; then Tom said, "There's a policeman here from Maine. He wants to talk to you."

The phone was silent for a moment; then a man said: "Mrs. Taylor?"

"Yes."

"I'm Lieutenant Daniel Larson of the Lewiston Police Department. I guess it figures that if I came down here, you'd go up there. Anyway, I gather you'll be there a couple of days, so I'm going to drop by to see you. Will that be all right?"

"You mean you went to Massachusetts just to see me?"

"I'm afraid so."

"What is it you want to talk to me about?"

"Does the name Seymour Bruce mean anything to you?"

"No."

"We believe he's the man who's trying to kill you. It also appears that he killed a young man in Lewiston

272

and a young woman in Vermont. Both of them were orphans; and both were at the Christian Home for Children."

Mary considered what the policeman had just said. It meant her attacker wasn't someone from one of her blank spells; his connection to her came from the past, from that time she was unable to remember, from a time during which things had happened that were profoundly affecting her life now. Unbidden, an image of two people standing before a fire popped into her head. One was a woman, the other a tall, thin man; both were dressed in black.

"Who is he?" she asked. "Where does he come from?"

"He's a minister from a small town in Maine."

"But why would a minister want to kill me, or those other people?"

"I don't know. I'm hoping you can tell me. That's why I want to talk to you."

Mary's stomach began to churn. "You mean that you want me to tell you about the . . . the orphanage?"

"Yes, I—"

"I can't help you. I can't remember anything about it."

"It can't be a total blank. Surely, there must be some memories."

"I'm sorry, but there aren't."

After a pause, the policeman said, "I'd still like to stop by and talk to you. I'm sure you want to do everything you can to help get this man out of circulation. Would tomorrow morning be all right?"

No, no, no, Mary thought. You'd ask about the orphanage, and I'd be unable to tell you, and if I tried I'd get sick or have pains or faint. "I'm sorry, but I'm sure it would be a waste of your time. I've been through quite a lot lately, and I really don't feel like talking to any more policemen."

"It's your decision, Mrs. Taylor. I certainly can't force you to talk to me."

"I'm sorry. Please, can I speak to my husband again now?"

When Tom came back on the line, they said their good-byes and hung up. Mary's foster mother, who was still standing beside her, said, "Have you had anything to eat?"

Mary shook her head.

"Come along, then. I've got some leftover stew I can warm up for you."

Mary followed, grateful that her conversation with Tom and refusal to talk to the police hadn't triggered a barrage of questions from her worried foster parents. But then, that was their way. They would let her work things out as she saw fit. Meanwhile, they'd be here, ready to lend their support, whether it be moral or financial or just a sympathetic ear. Thank God for the Caldwells and Tom, Mary thought. Even if I don't deserve them.

Later that night, Mary lay awake in the bed in which she'd spent so many nights as she grew from a child to a teenager to a young adult. Here there were no city lights to shine in through the bedroom windows, only the dim glow of the moon. Invisible in its faint illumination were the knotty-pine walls and the small holes where she'd tacked up pictures of actors and rock stars, none of whom seemed to matter anymore. Life had been so simple then, so carefree—except for the blank spells.

The man who wanted to kill her was apparently a

minister. It fit in with what he'd said as she'd faced him in the alley behind the medical building.

Who are you? she'd asked.

A servant of the Lord, he'd replied.

But why would a small-town minister want to kill her and other former residents of an orphanage in rural Maine? What could mere children have done that would result in a series of killings so many years later? Had they witnessed something that could seriously hurt someone? Was the clergyman there, at the Christian Home for Children?

She bit her lip to keep from crying out as a pain shot through her stomach. She wasn't supposed to think about that place.

Forcing her thoughts away from forbidden areas, she recalled her attempt to confront the man at the shopping mall. Why had he called her Mara? Was there some significance in its being a variant of Mary?

The Lord's work will be done, he'd said after trapping her in the alley. Was that the Lord's work, killing her and other former orphans? It made no sense.

Although not all the links were clear, everything seemed connected to that time she was unable to remember, and to her blank spells. She knew what she had to do. Even before the Lewiston policeman had told her about the orphanage connection, the idea had been in the back of her mind. That was one reason she'd told Tom not to come up. If it was to be done, it had to be done alone.

It might be a waste of time, she told herself. You might learn nothing that will help you. After all, there's nothing there now but ruins. If that's true, another part of her said, if there's nothing there at all, then why are you so afraid?

Because, the first part answered, there *is* something there. *Ghosts.*

Mary shuddered. Then, feeling woozy, she tried to push the orphanage from her thoughts. She rolled over and closed her eyes.

As the night wore on, time and time again she began to doze, only to be awakened by the frightening, misshapen things that raced through her mind. She vaguely sensed that they were thoughts, the monsters from her unconscious, and she knew that whatever horrors dwelled there had a name. They were called Mary.

And Mara.

Twenty-Two

LIEUTENANT LARSON HAD COME TO WORK IN A BAD
mood. Sitting at his desk, he glowered at the paperwork that had accumulated while he was in Massachusetts. Frustrated by Mary Taylor's refusal to talk to
him, he'd arrived back in Lewiston about one A.M. This
morning, he suffered from the aches that afflicted him
whenever he failed to get enough sleep, the worst being
a dull pain that seemed to hang just behind his eyes.
Once, four hours of sleep had been enough; now he
needed at least eight.

Again, he found himself thinking of a retirement
cabin in rural Maine. Turning the page on his desk
calendar, he noted that today was Thursday, April 29.
Tomorrow would be the last day of the month.

"What the hell's wrong with her?" he muttered to
himself. "Doesn't she realize it's her ass that's on the
line?"

Then he decided it was a dumb question. Of course

she realized she was in danger. Seymour Bruce was hardly pursuing her because he needed a fourth for bridge. Mary Taylor had her reasons, reasons that made sense to her.

But what made sense to her might not be too terribly logical to anyone else. As Flanagan had pointed out, she was a strange one. He'd tried not to let the sergeant's words prejudice him toward Mary Taylor; he liked to make up his own mind about people. But then her unexplained sudden departure for Maine and her refusal to talk to him had convinced him that Flanagan was right: All was not well with Mary Taylor.

As far as understanding any of this went, she was his only lead. Despite Grant's best efforts, they'd been able to trace no one else—no one alive—who'd been an orphan at the Christian Home for Children. Nor had they learned the name of a single person who'd worked there.

None of this information would help him to apprehend Seymour Bruce, but then catching him was not the problem. The constable in Bethany would tell him when the minister returned; it was just a matter of waiting. The rub was that there wasn't enough to convict him. Because no one had actually seen Bruce murder Edwards, the case would have to be circumstantial, which meant the prosecution would have to establish the clergyman's motive, and right now, Larson didn't even have a wild guess as to what that motive might be.

Of course, Vermont authorities did have a witness, but here, too, there was a snag. Even if the witness was a reliable one—a sober pillar-of-the-community type—a good defense attorney could tear his testimony apart: two vehicles speeding past each other, a split-second glance at the driver, the witness in a state of shock because of what he'd just seen.

Besides, what the minister had done in Vermont or Massachusetts or anywhere else was the problem of Larson's counterparts in those places. He was concerned with what Seymour Bruce had done in Lewiston, Maine; and here was where he intended to see Seymour Bruce tried and convicted of murder, the murder of John Edwards.

Scowling once more at the paperwork on his desk, he stood up. He was going to Evans Ridge. First, he would knock on doors near the spot where the Christian Home for Children had stood, hoping that someone would remember something—a name, anything. Then, he would visit Mary Taylor at the home of her foster parents. It would be more difficult for her to refuse to talk to him when he was there, face-to-face with her.

The man sat on a cushion of old leaves he'd piled up, his back against a tree. Afraid to show his bruised and singed face at any of the motels near the home of Mary/Mara's foster parents, he'd slept in his car. From his position in the woods, he could see the Caldwells' house through the trees. Weighing his next move, he watched, waited.

It was midmorning when Mary finally worked up the courage to do it. She was sitting at the big wooden table in the kitchen. Her foster mother was removing glasses from the dishwasher.

"Don't know why I bother with this thing," Maxine Caldwell said, holding a glass up to the light. "It's supposed to save you the trouble of washing dishes, but you've got to pretty much wash them before you put them in the machine. So, what's the point in having one, I ask you?"

"I've never wanted one," Mary said.

Her foster mother grunted. "Well, at least we had enough sense not to buy one of those trash mashers." She chuckled. "All that money for something that turns ten pounds of garbage into ten pounds of garbage."

"You sure there isn't something I can do to help?"

Having finished with the glasses, Maxine Caldwell started putting the silverware away. "I want you to relax while you're here, kiddo," she said, giving Mary a stern look. "Besides, houseguests, even daughters, are no trouble at all until they start trying to help. Then they're constantly underfoot."

Neither the Caldwells nor Mary had ever used the term 'foster' in the other's company. Mary had always addressed them as Momma and Daddy; they'd always considered her their daughter.

"Well," Mary said, "if you don't need me, I think I'll take a nice relaxing drive through the woods. You know, commune with nature and all that."

Closing the silverware drawer, Maxine Caldwell studied her a moment, then said, "Will you be back for lunch?"

"I'll try."

"That's the same answer I got from Dad. I think lunch had better be sandwiches—the make-your-own-when-you-get-here kind."

Nick Caldwell, after thirty-five years with the state highway department, had taken early retirement the year before. Among other things, he'd been the one who drove the snowplow each winter. He'd retired simply because their land was paid for, their expenses minimal, and he was tired of working. At the moment, he was off helping a neighbor rebuild some piece of machinery—a pump, Mary thought. Out here in the country, people still helped one another when the need arose.

For a moment, Mary wondered whether she had been foolish to exchange this blissful rural existence for life in the city. No, she decided, I wasn't. You can't have any secrets out here in the neighborly country. And if there's one thing I've got, it's secrets.

Hell, she thought bitterly, I even keep secrets from myself.

She rose, trying not to let her anxiety show. "You don't mind, do you?"

"No, of course not," Maxine Caldwell said, again studying her foster daughter's face. "You just get your mind off things and do whatever seems right."

"I won't be too long."

"Take your time and enjoy yourself," Maxine Caldwell said.

The man approached the house from the rear. It was a fairly large place with walls of stained wood. Ahead was a garden, the rich-looking soil newly turned. Staying among the trees, he moved around the garden, getting closer to the house. He could feel the ice pick through the material of his jacket.

Then he heard a car door slam at the front of the house. Quickly, he headed toward the sound, keeping far enough from the house so he wouldn't be spotted. A car started, and still he had not moved close enough to see which car—or who was driving. Branches scratched his face and hands, grabbed at his clothing. He plunged ahead, trying to get to a position where he could see the front of the house. Then, through the trees, he caught a glimpse of a car pulling away. A green car. Mary/Mara's car.

Dammit! he thought. Dammit, dammit, dammit! His first inclination was to run for his own car, but then he realized how foolish that would be. He had to find out which way she turned at the highway. She'd be out of sight by the time he got there with his car; he wouldn't know which way to go, not unless he found out now. He ran, fighting his way frantically through the trees and bushes.

Hurry, he kept telling himself, hurry. The driveway was only two-hundred-feet long; she'd already be at the highway. Something unseen caught him by the ankles, and he fell, his face coming to rest in old leaves and soft, moist earth. He heard the car pulling onto the highway, accelerating. Looking toward the road, he could see only tree trunks and bushes, so he listened. The sound was moving to his right. She'd turned right; he was sure of it.

Scrambling to his feet, he ran for his own car.

A large black dog barked menacingly but kept its distance as Lieutenant Larson walked to the door of the neat white house. When he stepped onto the porch, the door opened, the woman who'd opened it staying on her side of the screen. She was middle-aged, chunky, her light brown hair in curlers.

Showing his ID, the detective introduced himself. "I'd like to talk to you about the orphanage, the Christian Home for Children. Were you—"

Her eyes had narrowed at the mention of the orphanage. "You're about fifteen years too late. It burned down. It's not there anymore." She looked beyond him at the still-barking dog. "Missie, hush!" The animal instantly fell silent.

"Were you here when it was in operation?"

"Not here in this house, but I lived in the area. Nobody thought much of the place, I can tell you that."

"Why was that?"

"Well, it's hard to say exactly. The people out there kept to themselves, didn't associate with the rest of us. It was just a feeling you had about the place, but everybody had it." She shrugged. "Maybe we're just too mistrustful of outsiders."

"Who ran the place, some religious group?"

"What makes you think it was a religious group?"

"Well, it was called the Christian Home for Children."

"Oh, yeah. I forgot about that. To tell you the truth, mister, I don't know whether that name meant anything or not. I never heard of any church being involved or anything. Of course, that doesn't mean one wasn't." She frowned. "As I recall, the place was run by some woman who called herself Sister. Not like Catholics do—you know, Sister Anne or Sister Grace or whatever. She was just plain Sister."

"Do you know her last name?"

The woman shook her head. "That's all I ever heard her called, just Sister. I remember what she looked like though. Tall and thin, with dark eyes and long black hair. You could tell by looking at her that she didn't take any guff from the kids. Hell, I doubt she took any guff from anybody, to tell you the truth."

"Do you know where she is now?"

"Sister? She died in the fire. As I recall, no one else was even hurt. She was the only victim."

"Do you recall the name of anyone else connected with the place?"

"Sorry."

"Who still lives around here that might?"

She wrinkled her brow, then said: "Oh, I know. Maybel Javes. Keep on this same road, about a quarter of a mile." She pointed as she spoke. "She lives in a log house. It'll be on your right."

"Thanks."

As he turned to go, she said, "Why is a policeman from Lewiston interested in the old orphanage?"

Stopping at the edge of the porch, he turned to face her. "Because someone's killing off the orphans now that they've grown up."

"I'll be damned," she said, thoroughly surprised. Larson saw an image of her rushing to the phone to spread this intriguing bit of news.

"By the way," he said, "have you ever heard of a minister named Seymour Bruce?"

She shook her head; then her eyes widened. "Is he the murderer?"

"No one's been charged yet," he replied, stepping off the porch before she could ask any more questions.

Mary drove slowly, looking for the turnoff. She'd come about twenty miles and had another five or ten to go. There were few homes out here; the Christian Home for Children had been fairly well isolated.

Unlike Boston, where spring was well under way, here the trees were still leafless and would be until mid or late May. The grass was greening though, and some of the trees were evergreens. She saw a sign indicating an intersection, a road to the right, and a moment later she turned off the two-lane highway, onto a narrower two-lane road that twisted its way through the trees. In the fall, with the leaves changing colors, this would be a beautiful drive.

None of the things she had feared as she set out had occurred so far. She'd neither thrown up nor fainted nor been hit with the chills. She had a vague sense of foreboding, and that was all. Glancing in the rearview mirror, she saw no one behind her. A yellow car had been there earlier, but it had disappeared five or ten minutes ago.

Maybel Javes turned out to be a plump gray-haired woman of about eighty. She and Lieutenant Larson sat in the antique-filled living room of her log house.

"I'll tell you what they were," she said, taking a sip of coffee from an ornate and very old-looking cup. "They were Devil worshipers."

"How do you know that?" Larson asked. He and the woman faced each other across a coffee table, both of them sitting in small upholstered chairs.

"I saw them," Maybel Javes replied, looking the detective squarely in the eye. "I heard things about the place and I decided to find out for myself, so one night I sneaked up there. It was during the summer, and they were all out there—adults, kids, everyone in the place. Dancing and prancing around a big fire, mumbling some kind of mumbo jumbo, all of them dressed in black robes. All of them except Sister, that is. Ohhhh, that one! She didn't wear just any ordinary black robe, no sir. Hers was emblazoned with red. She stood there by the fire, her arms raised, egging the rest of them on."

"Did you ever ask anyone at the orphanage what it was all about?"

"Sure, I asked—or rather my husband Bill did, bless him. He's been dead nine years now. Anyhow, he went up there and confronted Sister face-to-face. And you know what she told him? That it was just a big outdoor get-together, like they were having nothing more than a wienie roast."

"Was that possible?"

"Of course not. She was chanting in Latin, young man. I've been a Catholic all my life, and I know Latin when I hear it. I also know what *Satanas* means."

Larson took a swig of coffee from the fragile-looking china cup. He hated drinking from anything that had to be handled so gently for fear of breaking it. A mug would have suited him much better.

"A little while after that," she continued, "I got warned to mind my own business. I found a wooden cross hanging upside down on the front door. It had blood smeared on it." She made a face. "I burned the filthy thing."

"Can you recall Sister's name or the name of anyone connected with the place?"

She thought for a moment, then said, "Nope, I can't. As far as I know, that Sister woman who ran the place didn't have any other name besides Sister. And if I ever heard the name of anyone else out there, I've long since forgotten it."

"Have you ever heard of a man called Seymour Bruce, a minister?"

"Nope."

"I understand the orphanage burned down."

She nodded.

"Did you ever hear what caused the fire?"

"Nope. But I'll tell you what I think happened." She fixed her intense blue eyes on his face. "Sister died in that fire. The only casualty. I think God did it. I think He burned that evil place to the ground and Sister along with it."

Twenty-Three

Stopping her car, Mary studied the small road that angled off to the left and up a hill. It had deteriorated badly from neglect. The asphalt was crumbling, the dry stalks of weeds showing that nature had been busy reclaiming this strip of earth man had taken from her. Although Mary had never returned to the orphanage, she had passed this spot a time or two with her foster parents. She knew this was the right turnoff.

Her heart pounding, Mary pulled slowly onto the road, steering around the potholes as best she could. Her vague feeling of foreboding had been replaced by a growing fear, although fear of what, she did not know.

In places, the trees were so close on each side that the road seemed to be a tunnel enclosed by their leafless branches. In one spot, she had to maneuver around a tree that had fallen, blocking three-quarters of the narrow roadway. She'd driven less than half a mile when she came to a chain across the road, a sign hanging from it saying KEEP OUT. There was no way around it.

Switching off the engine, she got out. Nothing here looked familiar to her, but then any recollections she had of this place would be those of a young girl, memories dulled by time and the inability of a child's mind to retain them. Stepping over the chain, she continued on foot. The road continued to climb. Ahead on her right was a meadow, its grass green.

She shivered. Uncertain what was pushing her on, yet unable to resist it, she put one foot ahead of the other, moving closer to something more than just the remains of an orphanage.

Her thoughts swirled. Why had her internal censors allowed her to come here? Perhaps only remembering was prohibited; returning to this place was all right . . . as long as she didn't remember. So many answers she didn't have. Would she find them here? Would she *allow* herself to find them?

A few moments later, Mary reached what had been the parking area for the Christian Home for Children. Grass and saplings grew from the disintegrating asphalt. Of the two-story frame building that had been the orphanage, only a small portion remained. The rest was reduced to a heap of charred wood. The portion that still stood was a brownish gray, its former color unrecognizable.

No wonder she had been able to come here. Seeing this told her nothing. And yet, she was still shaking, still afraid of this place, for it was unquestionably evil. Even now.

It looked as though the fire had started at one end and burned toward the other, the blaze extinguished just moments before it consumed the entire structure.

What remained of the building had been worked over by time and vandals. Windows, their glass shattered, overlooked the parking area. Above, the roof was missing half of its shingles. Directly in front of Mary was a doorway, the door itself missing, leaving a shadowy rectangle through which darkness seemed to ooze out into the sunlight.

Some force she didn't understand propelled her forward. No, she thought. No, no, no. I don't want to go in there. But she continued toward the doorway, cautiously stepping over the charred chunks of wood that lay in her path. And then she stood inside, staring at a bare, dusty room with graffiti on its walls. In spray paint: ALICE, 555-3814, LOVES TO FUCK. Below that in felt tip: EVEN SHE WOULDN'T SCREW BILLY K. Carved into the faded, peeling wallpaper: EDDIE CLIPP WAS HERE.

Nothing was familiar. This barren room could have been in any derelict structure anywhere. She moved slowly into the room, causing particles of dust to swirl lazily in the sunbeam coming through a shattered window. The floorboards creaked under her weight. Suddenly, a new bit of graffiti caught her eye, this message apparently left here years ago because it was nearly as faded as the wallpaper it was scrawled upon: *Sister is dead, and now the Devil doesn't live here anymore.*

Mary felt something tug at her memory, and then a stomach cramp nearly doubled her over. The pain was gone as quickly as it had come, along with whatever memory she'd been reaching for. She shivered.

In front of her was a hole in the floor, probably the work of a vandal with an axe. She peered into the opening. Below was only blackness, a cellar of some sort. From somewhere in the depths of her mind, she heard a little girl crying out pitifully: *Please, Sister. Oh, please, please. I'll be good. Please don't. Please.*

And then the cramp came again, causing her such agony that she sank to the floor with tears in her eyes. But the memory didn't stop; it poured out, sweeping her away like a flood, overpowering the pain in her stomach, making it seem insignificant. She saw a little girl in a dark place and she knew it was the place she'd peered into through the hole in the floor. The child was in a cage suspended from the ceiling. Sitting naked on the floor in the midst of her own excrement, the girl cried, knowing that soon she would have to go again and make her already-disgusting environment even more sickening. It was totally black, the only sounds the child's whimpering, and the occasional creak of the cage as her movements caused it to sway. The girl had been there for days, although how many she didn't know. When her feces hardened, she would kick them out of the cage, and she'd been there long enough for many of them to have landed below.

Sister had put her here, but it wasn't Sister's fault; it was hers. If she would be good and do what Sister wanted, Sister would be kind. After all, Sister was their leader; Sister was good. All Sister wanted was for her and the others to serve the true master. And I will, the little girl thought, I will. Eventually Sister would come for her, and she would be happy to see Sister. She would love her, respect her, obey her. And worship the true master.

The child could hardly wait for Sister to come, to see her and love her and worship the master with her. It was everything she wanted. Maybe this time, when the door opened and the candle appeared, it would be Sister coming to let her love her and be with her.

And then, a few minutes or maybe a few hours later, the door opened and the candle appeared. But it wasn't Sister; it was the little red-haired girl, Margaret, who'd come with the daily meal.

"Is Sister with you?" the imprisoned girl asked. "Is she going to let me out?"

But the red-haired girl said nothing, for when one of them was in the punishment place, the one who brought the food wasn't allowed to speak to the one being punished. Why am I being punished? the girl wondered. But the answer eluded her. Or maybe there was no answer, except that she hadn't been good enough, tried hard enough.

Setting the candle on the floor, the little red-haired girl stepped through the doorway and disappeared. The room was barren, filled with cobwebs, the door made of old, splintery wood. The child returned, carrying a tray of food, the one meal the imprisoned girl received each day. Stepping over the feces that had been shoved from the cage, the red-haired girl reached up and pushed the tray through the slot at the bottom of the bars.

"Don't go," the imprisoned child pleaded. "Please don't take away the light."

The other girl looked at her sadly for a second, then picked up the candle and left, closing the door behind her. And the light was gone. The blackness was back. The girl suppressed the scream that she felt in her throat. It would be bad to scream, just as it had been bad to ask the other girl to stay. Would she ever learn? Would she ever behave properly, think properly, so she could earn Sister's love and respect? Fumbling in the darkness, she reached for the tray, her fingers finding something soft and warm. Taking some on a finger and putting it in her mouth, she discovered it was mashed potatoes.

Thank you, Sister, she thought. And thank you, master of everything and everyone.

The image swirled away. Mary was on the floor beside the hole, staring into it. She braced herself, but the pain in her abdomen did not return. Slowly, she got to her feet, swaying slightly as she rose. The little girl she'd seen cruelly imprisoned in the cage had been she. What kind of a place was this? she wondered, appalled. In what kind of a place would children be treated like that? It seemed like something from a horror movie, a lurid creation of some scriptwriter's imagination. But the scene of the girl in the cage had not been imagined; it had been remembered.

Mara. The name jumped into her head. The little girl had been her, and yet it had been Mara as well. That name again. Mara, Mara, Mara. Who are you? What are you?

Having crossed the room, Mary found herself standing at the bottom of a stairway. Until that moment, she hadn't even realized it was there. Still pushed on by something she was unable to explain, Mary started up the stairs, the rotted green carpet seeming to crumble beneath her feet. On the walls, more graffiti: NEED A GOOD BLOW JOB? CALL ANNE, 555-2892.

Upstairs, she found another barren room with peeling wallpaper, paneless windows, and more graffiti on the walls. It was off a hallway that ended after about fifteen feet, where it reached that part of the building that no longer existed. There were a few feet of charred flooring, then a drop-off to the blackened debris below. She entered the room cautiously, uncertain of the condition of the floor.

Instantly, she was overwhelmed by another vision. The room was no longer empty; now it had candles, black curtains, and an altar behind which was a large symbol, a star inscribed within two concentric circles. A woman stood before her, a mysterious figure with long dark hair, wearing a black robe trimmed with red.

"Who are you?" the figure asked.

"I'm Mara, Sister."

The image vanished. Why had she said her name was Mara? Oh, God, she thought, what was done to me in this place?

Suddenly, her eyes, which had been fixed on the spot where Sister had stood, were drawn to the window. Someone was out there; she'd heard gravel crunching under a shoe, a twig snapping. Still not trusting the floor, she moved gingerly to the window. Directly below her, staring up at her was the man with the blue car. As their eyes met, she gasped.

"Praise the Lord!" he shouted, removing an ice pick from his pocket and holding it up, as if offering it to Mary. "Praise the Lord, for today His enemy will be slain." And with that, he headed for the doorway through which Mary had entered. She heard his footsteps on the floor below . . . then on the stairs.

How, she wondered, how did he find me? She pushed the question aside because only one question mattered right now: How would she survive? There was only one way down: the way the man was coming up. She scanned the room, desperately searching for a weapon. There was nothing.

Rushing to the window through which she'd spotted her assailant, she looked out, finding no way down. She hurried to the other window. Oh, God, she pleaded, let there be a downspout, anything I can use to get out of here. There was a downspout, a good ten feet away, well out of reach, and an old rickety-looking wooden trellis that ran right next to the window. Having no time to consider the wisdom of what she was doing, Mary slipped her legs over the sill, grabbed the wooden latticework, and swung onto it. It swayed under her weight. Bits of rotted wood showered down from above.

For a moment, she clung there, not daring to move, but when she heard the man rush into the room, she started down. The wood was old and weathered, gray and paintless, the nails rusty. Whatever vines the trellis might have supported were gone; not even a single withered stalk remained. Hold together, she thought. Just a few more minutes; then you can collapse if you want to. She glanced up, expecting to see the man staring down at her, but there was no sign of him. And then the piece of wood under her foot gave way.

For a moment, the next crosspiece held her; then it, too, gave and the next three snapped the instant her foot touched them. The part of the trellis she'd been clinging to came off in her hands, and she was on the ground, her fall cushioned by the soft earth. Slowly sitting up, she checked herself for damage, finding none. Her eyes located the window through which she'd escaped. The man wasn't there. And then she heard his footfalls on the stairs.

Trying to stand, she nearly fell on her face. A weapon. She needed a weapon. She was sitting in the midst of broken pieces of wood from the trellis, all of which looked too fragile to do her any good. And then she saw the brick. She grabbed it, pulled it close. The man rushed out the door, slowing when he saw her, apparently realizing that she could not get away.

"It's over, hellcat," he said. "I am the Lord's instrument, and through me He will destroy you, as He has destroyed all the other monsters created in this place."

She held the brick tightly against her hip. Having

approached her from the side, he was unaware that she had it.

"You're the monster," she said, surprised to hear her own voice. "God would never be on the side of someone like you. You're a killer. You're crazy."

The man stared at her, his eyes wide, a bizarre picture with his singed eyebrows and bruised face.

"You killed Steph," she said. "Don't tell me God made you do that."

"In war," he said softly, "the innocent sometimes suffer."

Uncertain what effect her words would have—or even what effect she wanted them to have—Mary said: "Anyone who kills innocent people is working for the Devil, not for God."

His bruised face flushed. "Lies! Lies! Lies!" he shouted, raising the ice pick. Then he grinned. "But you serve the Father of Lies. What else could I expect?" And then he charged.

She gripped the brick, waiting, knowing that she had only one shot at it, yet uncertain whether her muscles would respond. Still holding the ice pick high, he was only two strides away when, in a single movement, she raised the brick and hurled it at his face. Though unable to see where it hit him, she knew she had because she heard the smack when it struck. The man's feet came out from under him, and he was down, gasping.

Shakily, Mary rose, her heart pounding. Her attacker lay on his back, a bloody gash on his cheek where the brick had hit. It lay about three feet from him; there was no sign of the ice pick. Her thoughts a jumble, she looked around, spotting a two-by-four in the grass about fifteen feet from where she stood. Walking unsteadily, she got the board, one end of which was charred, and returned to the unconscious man.

She raised the board, a part of her saying: *Hit him! Hit him! Hit him until he can't hurt you—ever!* Still shaky, she stared at the man, uncertain what to do. *Now!* that part of her urged. *Do it now, while you still can.*

She stood there over the man, gripping the two-by-four with both hands, swaying slightly while two parts of her mind seemed to battle for control of the muscles in her arms. The man's eyes fluttered open, at first registering only bewilderment; then they found Mary and instantly widened in fear.

"Oh, Lord, I've failed you," he said. Then to Mary he said, "You can take my life, but my soul is God's."

Still holding the two-by-four ready, Mary began to back away. "Don't get up," she warned.

Fool! a part of her seemed to say. *You had your chance and you blew it.* But I couldn't, Mary thought. I just couldn't. Not like that.

She turned and ran toward her car. When she reached it, out of breath, she found a small yellow car behind hers. It would be a tight squeeze, but she wasn't blocked in; she could maneuver around it. The keys were in her pants pocket and she hurriedly pulled them out and slipped behind the wheel, her eyes scanning the vicinity for any sign of the man. She locked the door, shoved the key into the ignition, and hit the starter. The engine cranked over but wouldn't start. She tried again. And again. It still refused to start.

Oh, no, she thought. Oh, no, no, no. It's got to start. Please start. But the engine refused.

Seeing nothing to indicate the man had pursued her, she reluctantly left the safety of the car and opened the hood. She spotted the problem instantly. The wire that connected the coil to the distributor was missing.

Uncertain what to do, Mary stood there, staring at

the Horizon's engine. And then she realized that there was still a way to make the car run. She could steal a replacement wire or even one of the spark plug wires from the car behind hers. Rushing to the yellow compact, she hunted for the hood release mechanism. Unable to find it, she looked into the car's interior, seeing a knob marked HOOD to the left of the steering wheel. She tried the door; it was locked.

Again, she looked around her; the man was nowhere to be seen. Spotting a hefty-looking rock near the edge of the road, she quickly fetched it, intending to smash the window. But then she saw the man. Having circled around her, he was approaching from the direction of the road, cutting off her most obvious escape route.

He was a hundred feet away, and he would be on her before she could even finish breaking into the yellow car, much less raise the hood and steal anything. He was coming slowly, as if he weren't human at all but a machine programmed to plod after her for however long it took to catch and kill her. Again, some part of her cursed her stupidity for not clobbering him with the two-by-four when she had the chance. Dropping the rock, she turned and ran into the woods.

Twenty-Four

Her hands and face scratched from her run through the woods, Mary sat on the cool, moist earth, her back against a tree. She'd stayed ahead of her pursuer without too much difficulty, in part because she was younger, in part because of the blow she'd dealt him with the brick. But temporarily eluding the man had not solved all her problems. She was lost. One spot in the woods looked just like another, and she had no idea where she was in relation to the highway or her car. There were vast areas of wilderness up here; a wrong turn could take her smack into one of them.

Well, here I am, she thought, lost in the woods and pursued by a crazed killer. Her mind accepted the summation of her status matter-of-factly. She was too exhausted, too drained to respond emotionally to the terrifying aspects of her situation.

She chuckled quietly but bitterly. A person who had her problems hardly had the right to call anyone else crazed. It was just a case of one lunatic fleeing another.

Instead of running from the man, she should join forces with him. They were both psychos; they belonged together.

Oh, God, she thought, stop it. Stop thinking like that. Pulling up her knees, she rested her forehead on them and quietly cried.

Suddenly, she saw herself as a young girl in a room illuminated by candles, a figure with long dark hair standing before her, a group of children watching silently, intently.

"Your parents didn't want you," Sister said. "Even your name, Kensington, is made-up. They wouldn't let you have their name. They thought you were awful, disgusting."

Mary stood there, trembling, tears running down her cheeks.

"You have no family. Absolutely nobody loves you or wants you. No one cares what happens to you."

Mary just cried.

And then the image vanished. She was back in the woods, listening, her eyes scanning her surroundings, looking for any movement. She'd heard a sound. Close. Very close.

Slowly, silently, she rose, ready to spring into the trees and run for her life. And then she heard it again, off to her left, something moving. It had to be the man. As quietly as she could, Mary began moving away from the sound.

Made up of decomposed forest materials that had accumulated over the centuries, the earth was spongy underfoot. The layer of leaves on its surface was moist, making her footfalls almost noiseless, as were those of her adversary. She stopped and listened, hearing nothing.

Suddenly, appearing from behind a tree to her left,

the man lunged at her. Startled, Mary froze for a second; then she was running as hard as she could. Feeling his hand on her back and knowing his fingers were about to close on her jacket, she cut sharply to the right just as she passed a big tree. For a moment, the man's hand was no longer on her back, but in the next instant, she plunged into a thicket of saplings, their flexible trunks whipping her savagely, and the man had a grip on her jacket. Dropping her arms, Mary struggled out of the garment, and then she was running again, her heart thudding, her legs driven by terror. From behind her, she heard a crash and a groan. He had fallen.

A few moments later, her strength gone, Mary collapsed on the forest floor, gasping for breath. Looking around, she saw nothing but leafless trees, the immensity of the woods making her feel small and insignificant, lost and helpless. Oh, God, she thought, how am I going to get out of here?

Think, some part of her commanded, think. The highway is east of you; all you have to do is head east. And which way is that—right, left, forward, backward? She shook her head. The sun, she thought, use the sun. It rises in the east and sets in the west. But when she looked up, it was directly overhead. It was almost noon. She'd have to wait.

What else can I use? she wondered. What can I use besides the sun? She'd read somewhere that, if you're lost, you should follow a brook or river downstream until you found civilization. The trouble with that idea was that, so far, she hadn't encountered any streams to follow.

Then a new idea struck her—moss. You could tell directions by the moss on trees. It always grew on the north side. Scrambling to the nearest tree, she checked its trunk, finding no moss. She tried another tree, then another. None had any moss on their trunks.

Suddenly feeling the pain in her body from being whipped, scratched, and stabbed by branches and trunks, she sank to the soft earth, pulled up her legs, and rested her head on her knees. Just be patient, she told herself. Wait until you can tell which way the sun's going in the sky; then keep it to your back and you'll be heading east. But then somewhere—she couldn't be sure where—a twig snapped, and she knew she wouldn't be able to simply sit there and wait for the sun to direct her. She had to keep moving, or her attacker would catch up to her.

Rising, she stood shakily on legs that suddenly felt too weak to carry her more than a few feet. Again, Mary heard a noise, closer this time, and she started walking, forcing her tired muscles to move. Just stay ahead of him, she thought. Don't let yourself get into a situation where you have to run, because you probably can't.

Through the trees she thought she saw something. A moment later she saw it again. A building. An old two-story house. Rushing toward it, she stepped from the woods and abruptly stopped. What she'd seen through the trees had been only a portion of a building, the part left standing after most of the structure had burned. She was back at the orphanage.

From behind her came a noise, reminding her that she couldn't stand here forever.

All at once, she realized that she'd found the way out. From here, she knew the way to the highway and to her car. With time, a minute or two would be plenty, she could steal the coil wire from the other car and get away in her own.

Then something, some sense, made her duck. An

object swished past her head, barely missing it, and Mary turned to find herself face-to-face with her attacker, who was holding a large chunk of wood in his hands. He raised it, obviously preparing to swing it at her again. She turned and ran, discovering strength she hadn't known was there, the pain in her muscles overridden by the need to survive.

The ruins of the orphanage were ahead of her. She glanced over her shoulder; the man was coming after her, still clutching the chunk of a tree limb he'd found in the woods. Then Mary's foot hit something, and she fell.

As she scrambled to her feet, she felt the pain in her ankle, nearly falling again when she tried to put her weight on it. The man was forty feet away, rapidly closing the gap. She limped forward, every step agony.

Knowing she was now unable to outrun her pursuer, Mary hobbled to the charred debris, desperately searching for a weapon. Finding none, she did the only thing she could do: she began climbing the huge mound of blackened debris, the man right behind her. The pain, though nearly unbearable, was better than what would happen if he got hold of her. And then he did have her, by the leg.

Clinging to a charred piece of wood, she tried to pull herself free from his grip but couldn't. He had her good leg; she tried to kick him with the other one, ignoring the pain. Suddenly, the two-by-four she was gripping broke off in her hands, leaving her with a piece of wood four feet long. She swung it at him. He released her, backing out of her range, and Mary scrambled up the mountain of debris, taking her weapon with her.

As soon as she was sure that she was well out of his reach, Mary braced herself and, using both hands, raised the two-by-four over her head. The man crouched below her, staring up at her, his eyes almost glowing with the intensity of whatever was driving him.

"Why," she asked, surprised at the squeak that was her voice, "why do you want to kill me?"

"Innocence?" he said breathlessly and grinned. "I'm wise to you, Satan. Don't try to trick me. Innocent you are not."

In spite of her desperate situation, Mary laughed. "You think I'm the Devil? You're crazy. Do you really think you could chase the Devil up here like this—and make him fend you off with a board?"

"Mock me if you wish," he replied, his eyes boring into hers, "for I shall not be fooled. I know you, hellcat, and nothing you say can change what you are or what must be done."

Suddenly, the image of two black-robed figures standing before a fire popped into her head—Sister and her helper. For the first time she saw the helper's face clearly. It was the same man who crouched below her, looking up at her, wanting to kill her.

"Brother Seymour," she said. "The other children and I called you that. You were one of them. You were Sister's accomplice in all this."

"Yes," he said slowly, "I was one of the evil ones. But I saw the error of my ways. I renounced Sister and all her evil followers. I begged God's forgiveness, and I repented, and I dedicated my life to the service of the Lord. I burnt this place down and Sister along with it." He laughed.

"But," he went on, "there was still more to be done. Sister had infested four children with her evil. Four children who were programmed to become servants of Satan in the future. I should have destroyed you while you were children. It took me years to find out what had happened to the four of you."

"How did you find us?" Mary asked, trying to keep him talking.

"I found out where the records relating to the old orphanage were kept and I stole them. You are the last, Mary/Mara. One of the monsters committed suicide, and I've dealt with the other two. As soon as I've destroyed you, I will have undone all the evil I helped to create. Only you remain, hellcat. Only you."

Glancing around, he rose, then moved to his left, bent down, and picked up another charred two-by-four. He studied her a moment, then began advancing.

Her heart beating madly, Mary waited. Unable to escape because of her sprained ankle, she had but one choice: to stand and fight. That physically she was no match for him was unimportant. She had defeated him before and she could do it again. She would use every last bit of strength she had in her effort to survive. The man lunged at her. Mary swung her two-by-four.

The man used his own board to block the blow, chips of charred wood flying. Pain momentarily clouded Mary's vision as her weight shifted onto her bad ankle. Then she realized what had happened. Her board had broken, leaving her with a piece only a foot long. She flung it at him and missed. Then, before she could try to escape, he had her, the two-by-four gone now, his hand clutching the ice pick.

Mary fell backward with the man on top of her. Before he could raise the ice pick, she used one of the few weapons she had left and clawed at his eyes with her nails. When he used his hands to fend her off, she grabbed the one holding the ice pick, and sank her teeth into it. He screamed, dropping the ice pick, which disappeared into the debris. He reached for it, shifting his weight just enough for Mary to wriggle out from under him.

As she tried to scramble away, the debris beneath her shifted; then, to her left, a large portion of it caved in, crashing down into what had been the basement. In her hands was an object she'd grabbed for support, a heavy piece of pipe about three feet long. His attention diverted from Mary, the man was staring into the pit that had appeared only five feet from where he stood. Trying to be silent, Mary moved toward him, raising the pipe. He looked up, and she hurled herself at him.

Seymour avoided the pipe, which swished harmlessly through the air, and then flew out of Mary's grasp. But he couldn't avoid Mary; she crashed into him, knocking him backward, waves of pain rising up from her ankle as it gave out under her weight. She fell, feeling the splinters sink into her hands and arms, but not caring because that pain was so much smaller than the one in her ankle. She rolled over, trying to make one last feeble effort to defend herself, but Seymour didn't attack.

Mary sat up, looking around. The man was gone. Quickly, she glanced behind her, cringing in anticipation of what she'd find, but he wasn't there, either. Then she saw him, clinging to the edge of the hole that had opened up, swallowing part of the ruins. It was ten feet across. Dust rose from the opening. From where she sat, Mary could see nothing below except blackness.

The man's entire body was in the hole, dangling above whatever lay below, but he had a firm grip on the edge. And then Mary realized he was slowly pulling himself out. Crawling to avoid the unbearable pain that would come from any attempt to put weight on her damaged ankle, she moved toward him, grabbing a loose piece of wood as she went. Seeing her, Seymour struggled all the harder to pull himself out of the hole. She reached him while he was still helpless.

He shook his head, his eyes saying, *No, don't.* Mary rose up on her knees, staying just out of his reach. Again, he shook his head, his eyes pleading. Mary lifted the board, a jagged piece of wood.

The man turned his eyes skyward. "Oh, Lord, how could I have failed You? How could I?"

Abruptly, he pulled his body up and forward, grabbing Mary's upper legs and shouting, "We'll go together, hellcat! Together!"

Mary struck him on the head with the board. When he didn't let go, she hit him again. And again. Releasing her, he slid back to where he'd been before his lunge. Once more, his eyes locked onto hers, pleading, yet at the same time defiant. There was no question about what she had to do.

"This is for Steph," she said, bringing the board down on the man's head. He slipped a few inches but maintained his grip on the edge of the hole, and she hit him again.

Once more, his eyes found hers. *I'm a human being,* they seemed to say. *Can you murder a human being?* You did, she thought, and hit him again. He slipped another few inches, then dropped, disappearing into the blackness. Mary didn't hear him hit bottom. He's in the punishment place, some inner voice informed her. No one should ever have to go there.

Suddenly, the world was whirling before her eyes, and then she was a little girl again, standing in a room illuminated only by candles, their flickering light revealing the face of Sister, who towered over her.

"What do you always do, Mara?" Sister asked. The two of them were standing before an altar, behind which was the star inscribed within two concentric circles. It was the symbol of Satan.

"Whatever you tell me to do," the child answered.

"What else do you always do?"

"I always serve the master."

"Does Mary serve the master?"

"No, she's stupid."

The woman smiled. "She's weak. When will you destroy her?"

"Walpurgis Night." And then Mary heard herself say a year, this year.

"Good, good. And what will happen after you destroy her?"

"She will be gone forever, for I will never let her return, and I will serve the master in all the ways I've been taught."

"And does Mary know about you?"

"No, but I know all about her. I hate her. I hate sharing this body with her."

"It's best that way. Let Mary go into the world, make friends, get married, get a job, have children, whatev-- er. Then, if it pleases you, you can destroy everything she's done. But in the meantime, you'll be safe. No adults will try to reshape you, because they won't know about you. You'll be a secret until it's your time."

"Yes, Sister. I love you, Sister. And I love the master."

Then a series of images began popping into Mary's head. She saw herself as a participant in many elabo- rate ceremonies, always with Sister standing before the circle-and-star symbol, her arms raised. Mary saw herself as a teenager, alone in the home of her foster parents, trying to lure a salesman into the living room so she could seduce him—an incident unrecalled until now. She saw herself swearing at the man when he refused. And then she saw other things done but not remembered, things done during blank spells. She saw herself in the swimming pool, attacking the woman who had accidentally gotten in her way, trying to . . . to what? Mary shuddered. She had wanted to drown the woman. But there was no time to dwell on that because the images were still racing through her mind. She was in the Fentons' yard, a Crescent wrench in her hand, carefully unloosening the bolts that held the swing together. Then she was at the church, splashing gasoline on the side of the building, striking a match. . . .

"No," she cried, "it's not true."

But it *was* true. She was two personalities, one good, one evil. The woman calling herself Sister had made her that way by doing things to her here in this place. She and some others were a select group, a handful of orphans chosen by Sister to do the work of her master —the Devil.

Although the man who'd wanted so badly to kill her had been driven by his madness, he hadn't been entirely irrational, thought Mary. *I know you, Mary/Mara,* he had said. *I know what you are.* He'd been here and he had known about her, known how evil she was. I'm vile, Mary thought. I'm a . . . a monster.

No, another part of her seemed to say. Only part of you is evil, and that part isn't the real you. It was entirely the creation of Sister, who manipulated the mind of an innocent child.

But it's still there, still evil.

You can defeat it.

How?

With your will.

There's no time. Tomorrow, I'll be Mara. *I'll* be gone.

Not if you fight.

"Are you hurt? Can you sit up?"

The last voice had come from without, and for a moment, she was too confused to sort out the internal and the external.

"Can you hear me?"

Suddenly, she was looking into the concerned face of a strange man. She blinked, somehow expecting the heavyset man bending over her to fade away and become the lunatic who wanted to kill her. But the image before her eyes remained unchanged.

"Who . . . who are you?" Mary asked. She was on her back, lying atop debris from the burned-down orphanage.

"Lieutenant Daniel Larson, Lewiston police."

"The man . . . I . . . he's in the hole."

The policeman nodded. "You're Mary Taylor, aren't you?"

"Yes."

"Are you hurt? Are you in pain anywhere?"

"My ankle."

He disappeared from her view, and suddenly she cried out in agony as he moved her leg.

When he reappeared in front of her, he said, "Sorry, I didn't mean to hurt you. It looks like you've got a bad sprain, but I don't think it's broken." Again he disappeared.

Mary closed her eyes, and the world went away. For a time—she was unsure how long—she floated peacefully; then she heard a siren and voices. She had the sense of being moved, picked up, carried. And she heard someone say something about a man in a hole, a man who'd fallen and broken his neck.

The last thing she heard before returning to that place where she floated so comfortably was the name Tom. Someone was going to notify Tom Taylor. Hearing that name left her with a warm, cozy feeling. Tom would help her, and everything would be all right.

Epilogue

Mary and Dr. Carpenter sat in the two comfortable upholstered chairs that occupied one corner of the psychiatrist's office. It was here, away from the formality of the desk and the cliché of the couch, that most of Mary's therapy was conducted these days. Nearly a year had passed since the minister had fallen to his death at the ruins of the orphanage.

"The month of April makes me a little nervous," Mary said. "What if . . ." She let the words trail off.

"We've discussed this before, Mary. There's nothing to worry about. The thirtieth will come and go, and nothing will happen, except that you'll be a little older than you were on the twenty-ninth."

"But that date's so important. I can almost feel it approach. And . . . and I can't help but wonder if Mara . . ." Again, she trailed off.

"That's impossible," the doctor said firmly. "Mara's gone forever. In fact, she never really existed. You were the victim of some very sophisticated brainwashing, most of which we've undone over the past year. You're doing so well, in fact, that I'm going to cut your visits down to one a month. Within a year or so, you can probably stop seeing me altogether."

"You've done a fantastic job," Mary said, meaning it. "I don't know what I would have done without you."

"Nonsense. You did most of it. All I did was guide you."

"Another thing that still worries me is that I did all those things, that I was capable of such acts." She grimaced.

"You were very thoroughly brainwashed. You weren't responsible."

"But . . . but I didn't resist; that's what really bothers me."

"But you did. It's all come out during hypnosis. Why do you think you spent so much time in the punishment place? You were resisting—at least to the extent a small girl is capable of it. You almost had to succumb, considering what you were up against. Spies, people who are trained to resist, are successfully brainwashed. You were only a child."

Mary nodded. Although the psychiatrist's words helped a little, they didn't offer complete exculpation. She had attacked a woman, harmed innocent children, burned down a church. She hadn't confessed to any of these things, Tom having convinced her that doing so would serve no purpose.

All in all, the bits and pieces of Mary's life were coming together nicely. She'd had no further blank spells since the one during which she'd driven to Maine a year ago. She remembered it now, as she remembered them all.

The church she'd burned down was being rebuilt, and sometimes she'd drive past it, just to check on the progress. Mary was donating as much as she could afford—anonymously—to the rebuilding fund.

One thing that seemed unlikely to ever be mended was her relationship with the Fentons. The family next door continued to avoid her and probably always would. Not that she blamed them. She had, after all, done what Mrs. Fenton had accused her of.

Surprisingly, the thing she had the least trouble dealing with was the death of Seymour Bruce. That she'd killed him intentionally was undeniable, but she accepted no guilt for the act. Injured and unable to run, she had done the only thing she could do. On that basis, she could live with the act.

The why of the whole thing eluded her. She knew that a group of Satanists had been running the orphanage, but she didn't know how or why they'd got themselves into that position; or why they put so much effort into brainwashing a handful of children. Perhaps the brainwashing was a project undertaken for no reason at all, just for kicks. The one thing of which she was certain was that they were deranged, sick. Just as Seymour Bruce had been.

"How's the new position?" Dr. Carpenter asked.

"So far, so good. Of course, I've only been doing it for a week. Give me time; I may learn to hate it."

Mary was now an assistant manager at Zel Home and Builders Supply. Mr. Adkins as well as other supervisors had gone to the new store at Worcester, opening up a number of managerial positions at the local operation. Lynn, too, had been offered a supervisory job, but she'd turned it down. After doing so, she'd explained to Mary that, having always hated bosses, she didn't want to be put into a position in which she'd have to hate herself. Lynn would always be Lynn.

Mary had never told Lynn the whole truth of what

had happened, fearing her friend wouldn't understand. In time, Mary supposed, she would. Lynn, who'd been as supportive and helpful as she could be, hadn't pressed her for more information, although she had to realize there was much she hadn't been told.

Tom, of course, knew everything. Mary had needed him a lot over the past year, and he'd always been there, ready to listen when she'd wanted to talk things out, to be a rock when she'd needed his strength, to give his love whenever she'd required affection and tenderness. His first wife was such a fool to divorce him, she thought for the ten-thousandth time.

"You're smiling," Dr. Carpenter observed.

Mary laughed. "Oh, I'm just thinking how glad I am that someone was a fool."

The psychiatrist didn't ask for an explanation.